High Low In-between

IMRAAN COOVADIA was born in Durban and educated at Yale. He is the author of two previous novels, *The Wedding* and *Green-eyed Thieves*, as well as a study of V.S. Naipaul. He has written for *n+1*, *Threepenny Review*, *The Sunday Independent*, *The Hindu*, *Bombay Gin*, *Baobab*, *Boston Herald* and *Politikon*. He works at the University of Cape Town.

High Low In-between

IMRAAN COOVADIA

HarperCollins *Publishers* India

First published in India by
HarperCollins *Publishers* in 2010

Building 10, Tower A, 4th Floor, DLF Cyber City, Phase II,
Gurugram Haryana – 122002, India
www.harpercollins.co.in

2 4 6 8 10 9 7 5 3

P-ISBN: 978-817-223-970-1
E-ISBN: 978-93-5029-449-9

Printed and bound at
MicroPrints India, New Delhi

Britta

Acknowledgements

Tony Morphet, Rajesh Gopie, Isobel Dixon, Gus and Nicky Ferguson, Rebecca Servadio Kenan, Ingrid de Kok, Annari van der Merwe, Frederik de Jager, William Dicey, Vikas Swarup, Maureen Isaacson, Philip Oxenstein, Luba Ostashevsky, P H Mtshali's *The Power of the Ancestors* (for the account on pages 213–216), and Townes van Zandt.

tu se' ombra e ombra vedi
(you, a shadow, see a shadow)

— DANTE

The Broken Window

~

IN PREPARATION FOR THE VISITORS THE HOUSE WAS BEING cleaned from top to bottom. Everybody was miserable.

The professor was miserable because it was impossible to concentrate as mattresses were carted onto the patio, beaten with sticks, and abandoned in the sunshine. Since the operation his attention had not fully returned.

After scanning *The Lancet* in preparation for court his gaze wandered to the front of the house. There was glass on the tiled section of the driveway. Estella had managed to break a window while moving the mattresses onto the veranda.

Estella, the maid, was miserable because of Nafisa, her employer. If one was unhappy then so was the other. In this one way Estella and Nafisa were, people said, like mother and daughter.

Nafisa was miserable because her son Shakeer was about to arrive from San Francisco. He was taking the photographs at his father's retirement party. It seemed that an entire generation was stepping down.

Nafisa was sensitive to her son's opinion. He was her only child. She didn't want him to arrive when the house was in disorder even if Shakeer did not know the difference. There was only this one morning to straighten up. But neither Estella nor her husband were disposed to cooperate. They were obstacles!

The situation was bad within the four walls of the house. Beyond them it was worse. For some reason her authority had never extended across the property to the garage. Nafisa didn't understand what happened in the garage. People without names had dumped things in there since they moved to the Westville house. Nor could Estella be persuaded to clean it from top to bottom.

Nafisa was panicky. Her hands shook. It seemed that her hold on circumstances, which had been unsteady in recent years, had been revealed as such. She thought she would fall down.

Normally the state of the garage made no difference. The dog slept in a basket between the cars. Nobody much else went in. But Arif's retirement party was going to be large, as raucous as such an evening could be. Some of the guests, in search of privacy, were sure to find their way up.

The contrast between the bright morning and the cool inside the door blinded Nafisa at first. She tripped on something. It was the toolbench cluttered with wrenches and spanners. She needed glasses. Shakeer, with his father's concordance, had been telling her so for five years.

From beneath the bench Nafisa picked up a bicycle chain. It belonged to a bicycle of which she had no recollection. The oil coating the links came off black on her hands. She dropped the chain as if it had scalded her.

But it was hopeless! Nafisa retreated to the door. Things had been allowed to ride for too long. They were out of her control. The house was hopeless!

From the steps she spied further disorder on the veranda. After breaking the window Estella had brought out the beds to air. Something in the spectacle of the four Posturepedic mattresses, piled on the wall to reveal their discoloured undersides, made Nafisa's eyes fill with tears.

The odd thing was that she could not recall crying as a young woman. Other people had a different impression. On her wedding day her husband's friend Jadwat, Dr Jadwat, had mentioned her particular expression of sunshine and rain.

Jadwat was unreliable. It hadn't been true then. There had been no rain at her wedding.

Today there was no sunshine. The reservoir of these tears had accumulated in the course of a difficult year. If she was distracted while driving, or couldn't add two numbers together, or misplaced the key to her surgery, they found their way to the surface. They embarrassed her.

Nafisa believed that her ready tears were pre-emptive, the prediction of some circumstance of which she had no knowledge. Since her husband's operation she had sensed some catastrophe waiting to show itself. Of course it was such thinking, magical thinking, which Arif criticised in the country. He made judgements. So she had been unable to confess this sensation to him.

She put a hand across her forehead to conceal her condition from nobody in particular. Just as she did this Estella emerged from the house. Nafisa closed the door to the garage and hurried down the steps.

"Just where are you off to?"

Estella said, "As you can see I have put out the last mattress. They need some time to air. I will be back in the house just now, Nafisa, and sweep up the glass. I am going to collect my telephone from the room."

"And why is that? Explain it to me."

"I know you don't like me to use the house telephone for personal use." Estella paused and saw that she needed to give a better reason. It was a tricky matter, to use her employer's own words against her. "I must ask my neighbour, Peter Dlamini, to keep a check on my daughter this afternoon. As I told you, Nafisa, she had another fit in the night. Somebody has to be there."

Nafisa wasn't sympathetic. She had trained herself to be suspicious where Estella was concerned, especially when a long explanation was provided. Estella borrowed her words and her way of speaking. It angered her to be studied in this way. Yet the problem was real. She had Estella's daughter under observation. The epilepsy was serious.

"Do you want to know what I think? I think it's got nothing to do with your daughter. I believe it's some new boyfriend you need to call on the dot every hour. And at a time like this! People will be here soon. Shakeer, for one, will be here this afternoon. So please don't make a fool of me, Estella. I know precisely how you act when a new man appears. You've been wearing perfume."

"I haven't ..."

"Look, your private life is your own business. All I ask is that you do the job. Since we are on the subject ... you cannot be too careful as an African woman. You have to be tested and have your boyfriends tested before you sleep together. This is the one thing which will lead to your comeuppance. You're crazy for men."

"Not at all, Nafisa. From the time I had my daughter men don't interest me. I have learned my lesson."

Nafisa searched in the other woman's face for a measure of self-consciousness regarding this untruth. She didn't find it.

There wasn't a lot to trust in this face. Its faults were on the surface. One couldn't deny that Estella was gorgeous. Her complexion was copper, almost like a copper pot. Her nose and cheekbones were so cleanly pressed that to look at them Nafisa was reminded of origami.

Beauty changed with the times. Unlike the African women of the previous generation, products of farms and villages, Estella had grown up in a nearby township. She took care of her looks. They were her capital. Her hair was firmly braided, beaded, and scolded into a bun.

Nafisa could guess at the effort channelled into this enterprise. It was a chore to be beautiful. She knew about the pair of high-heeled Cuthberts shoes, rolled in a sheet of rose-pattern gift wrap, and stored on the concrete shelf beside Estella's bed. She had seen them transported onto the bus in Estella's handbag. They represented a fortnight's wages.

For some reason these red shoes stayed in Nafisa's mind. They summarised some fact about Estella.

Driving back from work Nafisa found her worker waiting at the municipal bus stop on Forester Avenue. She sometimes stopped to ask Estella something about the house. She could swear that, through the window, she detected the scent of her Lacoste perfume which should have been locked in the bathroom cabinet. She couldn't imagine how Estella had found the key, if that was indeed how she had found her way into the perfume.

Nafisa had informed her husband of her discovery of the theft. He laughed about it. Arif's reactions were unpredictable. He refused to take her side. He claimed to be objective. Yet there was an element of mockery in Arif's attitude and it was directed against her. She smelled its presence as surely as the diluted Lacoste.

Remembering this incident Nafisa was irritated and dismissed Estella to her room. She sensed that the girl had eluded her. Once upon a time the shoe – that red-throated Cuthberts shoe – would have been on the other foot.

The first of the guests to arrive was her husband's oldest friend in the world. Jadwat was a day early for the celebration but he was a divorcee and had time to burn. He planned to sleep over at their house in Durban as he generally did on a long weekend or public holiday.

This Jadwat was universally known by his surname. He seemed to have lost his first name in the course of the years. He was the former deputy mayor of the town of Richmond, one hour's drive inland from the suburbs of Durban.

Recently Jadwat had made known he was done with day-to-day politics. Liberation had been unkind to his ideals. His fellow councillors in Richmond had been taking money from the agricultural companies in exchange for favourable treatment. They were bankrolled by the big industries in the province: sugar, maize, factory chickens. It was difficult to ignore the Jaguars and Land Rovers hovering like dragonflies at the council offices. The men who got into them were former socialists and communists. Indeed, as often as not, they remained due-paying members of the Party.

Jadwat consoled himself by studying volumes of Trotsky printed in Golders Green – "The Zimmerwald Manifesto", "Platform of the Joint Opposition", and *The Revolution Betrayed*. Several such books lay on the passenger seat of his car, a Mercedes. If somebody was riding with him he moved his books to the back.

Perhaps the companionship of his books recalled Jadwat's student years in Bombay when he moonlighted as an extra on a movie with Nargis and read Leon Trotsky on set. He had tried to enrol Nafisa in his socialist philosophy but with next to no success. She made it three paragraphs into the cyclostyled text of "Platform of the Joint Opposition" before giving up. She had never enjoyed reading.

Jadwat's other consolation was his affairs. It provoked laughter in Nafisa to think that stocky, short-legged Jadwat, captaining the helm of his orange Mercedes, fancied himself a Casanova. He was entirely bald, bespectacled, ridiculous. She compared the purple of his thin and wormy lips to an eggplant.

Nafisa's laughter had a cause deeper than the absurdity of her husband's oldest friend. She was furious because he behaved so badly. She was complicit in his bad behaviour. Over the years Jadwat had painstakingly courted a series of women to whom she had introduced him.

It seemed that a proposal was about to be made. Fever broke out in Jadwat's camp. He dieted, didn't sleep, bought new suits from Rex Trueform. He flirted, paid compliments, talked up the target of his affections to Nafisa over the unsteady telephone line from Richmond.

Yet Jadwat never in fact proposed. It embarrassed Nafisa in so far as she considered herself his sponsor. She had vouched for his good intentions to the unlucky lady. She continued to help Jadwat long after she knew what was going on. Had she learned nothing from the failure of her good offices? In future she would act differently.

There was a macabre dimension to Jadwat's romances. When he heard of a husband passing away he started visiting the unlucky household. He went far afield to meet the widow, driving as far as Athlone in Cape Town and even to Nafisa's place of birth, Botswana's capital Gaborone, when he had the report of a man's death. He brought flowers, videos, *qawali* tapes, earrings, yellow roses. He left behind cash in an electricity company envelope.

If flowers and money were well received, he pestered the widow into seashore dinners and Bombay-style musicals at the Durban Playhouse. He went to every length. Then, nothing. It was as if his short legs froze in mid-stride. Six weeks, six months into the adventure, and Jadwat severed contact with his intended.

Afterwards he never apologised, accounted for his actions, or referred to any of his discarded women sympathetically.

Nafisa tried to understand his thinking. It seemed that Jadwat took pride in having a past, a past with women, and in enlarging that past one widow at a time. The idea that she had helped him make a conquest, and might help him in the future, filled her with horror.

To make it worse, the man didn't learn. In the absence of shame, Nafisa thought, experience had nothing to teach. So Jadwat would listen closely whenever the report of a man's death came up in conversation, parking his big musky brown head at an angle, plucking the skin on his neck as he waited for mention of a surviving wife.

Today it was happening again. As he drove her to town Nafisa recognised the schoolboy disposition of his features.

Jadwat stretched out his short legs under the steering wheel. He turned easily in her direction while stopping for the light on the corner of Brickfield Road. Nafisa knew what was coming. This time she wasn't going to yield.

"So, Nafisa. Nafisa, my dear, I heard the bad news about your cousin Goolam ..."

He opened the car window and stowed his elbow on the door to relieve the pressure on his shoulder. It was already hot.

"About two weeks ago, I must have heard. I was distressed by the news. I distinctly remember meeting him and his wife at Shakeer's wedding reception. Goolam was your second cousin, wasn't he? And a man approaching the prime of his life. Ah, it seems we have had more than our share of bad news recently." He ran his hand along his crook shoulder. Nafisa had been giving him injections to suppress the inflammation. "Goolam's family must be devastated."

"That's a safe assumption."

"Of course. My heart goes out to them. But perhaps I might convey my regards."

The suggestion hung in the air. The robot turned green. Eventually Nafisa said, "Jadwat, could you concentrate on the road, if you don't mind?"

The catering for her husband's retirement party was being done by a restaurant near the old city centre where Greenacres used to be. Pakistanis ran the place, Karachi Delights, as well as a great number of cafés and fast-food joints. They had taken over many of these nearby shops because they were willing to work in parts of town where Durban's better-off Indians, not to say the whites, didn't set foot.

The Pakistanis were tough new characters, recent arrivals from the subcontinent. Nafisa knew they were usually in the country without papers. She had only really registered their presence in the past year.

Since the advent of the new government nobody enforced the rules on immigration. Unending blocks of Johannesburg were dominated by the Nigerians who moved heroin and morphine from Lagos to Los Angeles. The Senegalese and Congolese were established in Cape Town. Then there were groups of Zimbabweans, Mozambicans, others from the Horn of Africa who had served in infantry battalions in Eritrea. But the Pathan Pakistanis were reputedly the toughest.

Nafisa admired them for their severity. They were quite unlike local Indians, having earned a reputation as fierce fighters. They carried short knives under their jackets which she had seen them take out when they felt threatened.

The Pakistanis went everywhere, did everything they wished, and in this way were the freest inhabitants of the country.

It astonished Nafisa, driving by on Marine Parade, to see them playing cricket late on the grounds behind the youth hostel. The water lay black in the harbour and amongst the docks. The roads were otherwise deserted. Anyone who could afford it was locked behind bars and gates. The players in threadbare white jerseys were like gnats in the evening. Cricket, of course, was a Pakistani religion.

Besides cricket the Pakistanis were superb cooks. Arif was devoted to them for their preservation of the old ways. Indian cooking, in its supreme incarnation, according to her husband, was very much a masculine affair. The Pakistanis used sumptuous quantities of *ghee* in their *degchi*, capacious iron pots smouldering on coals in the alley behind Karachi Delights.

"Stay inside, Jadwat," she told him. "Keep the air conditioner on. Otherwise this will be cooked twice over by the time we arrive. There may be not enough time to unpack before I take off for the airport. I can't leave Estella to do the unpacking because she is keeping me company. I cannot ask her to do two things at once."

"Arif's not planning to greet Shakeer at the airport?"

"He wants to, you know, but he has an important call with the Americans, some legal centre in Baltimore, to prepare for the case. I can hardly get him out of the house anyway. To tell the truth, Jadwat, his spirits have been down recently, more so than at any time since the operation. He feels that his work isolating the virus has been completely squandered by the government. You can imagine how he feels about being forced out of the university. He doesn't show you the whole truth."

Jadwat said, "You must push him out of the house, Nafisa. Push him out. Otherwise depression is bound to settle in. How many times have we dealt with this from the other side, as doctors? After such a serious surgery ..."

"What can I do, Jadwat? I am at my wit's end. I am at my wit's end. At least we got Karachi Delights to cater for the party, on your recommendation. It's the one thing which truly lifts his spirit. Sometimes I believe that you are the only one of us who understands Arif."

Nafisa sensed the sweetness of coal smoke while standing by the car and supervising the loading of the food. From the *degchis* the waiters scooped rice and lentils, fried potatoes, and mutton into light green tupperware which they brought out to the car. Jadwat had cleaned out the boot.

Nafisa noticed that he hadn't mentioned her cousin Goolam

again. Maybe, on that particular topic, he would keep his mouth shut. Maybe he would see that other people had other problems and these other problems were deeper and more profound than his own. Even human beings could change.

Even as Nafisa considered the possibility she saw she would be disappointed if he didn't repeat his question about Goolam's widow. For years she had been looking forward to having it out with Jadwat. She wasn't ready for him to change his stripes. She wasn't ready for anything.

Nafisa knew that change discomforted her, whether it was for better or worse. Noticing some alteration, even in so indifferent a thing as the tiles missing in the roof of a house on the route she took to work, caused her stomach to contract. She was in poor shape. She was unable to be kind.

Her fears had multiplied. Just this morning she had been unable to get out of bed for ten minutes. Only the need to set the house to rights got her up and moving while Arif continued to sleep. But he slept lightly, so that if the door creaked when she went out he would sit bolt upright and call her back. He didn't like to be alone in the bed.

After everything was packed in the trunk Nafisa went inside to pay the bill. Karachi Delights was dark. One bulb burned at the end of a string. They must be economising on electricity. Trust the Pakistanis to economise on electrons. No wonder they did well in Africa.

Above the counter the owner had posted a calendar covered in what she recognised, by its flourishes, as Urdu script. A bin stood open in the corner showing piles of onion skins. It was so dark she could hardly make out the manager seated behind the massive iron register. A thrill ran up her spine.

"Tell me. It's okay to pay in cash?"

The manager, Mohammed, looked sadly at her out of black eyes. He didn't stand up.

He was young, she saw, not much older than his teenage staff, and his skull was prominent in his forehead. He had come to her once for treatment. She hadn't charged him because, like most people in his situation, he didn't belong to a medical aid scheme. It wasn't unusual. Her rates weren't high compared with the younger doctors. Yet, depending on the economy, one in ten of her patients didn't have the means to pay.

Her secretary worried about the stacks of accounts in default. But she and Arif lived well; they had money. There was no need to get blood from a stone.

Before he answered the question Mohammed wrote his calculations in the margins of a Karachi newspaper, writing quickly with his pencil. He let her read them.

"Yes, cash is king. We prefer not to declare, isn't it?"

Nafisa took the newspaper and checked the sums. "You won't give me a better discount on the total? My husband, who's at the university, or used to be until today, is a great admirer of your cooking, he and Dr Jadwat. There will be a lot of business now that we have discovered Karachi Delights. I mentioned your place to the Indian Consul."

"Very sorry. Twelve and a half percent is the best I can do."

They soon agreed on the round figure of twenty, which involved Mohammed redoing the sums in the margins of another newspaper page.

Nafisa counted out the notes from a Barclays Bank packet. As she did so she noticed the bank logo, an eagle stencilled in blue beneath the seal, had been almost rubbed away. Barclays had left South Africa during the period of sanctions and had never returned under their own name.

Seeing the speed at which that world receded brought Nafisa's heart to a halt. So much of their lives, so much life and energy, had gone into opposing the old government. Nafisa experienced the strangest tug of fellowship when she saw ministers from the defunct National Party mentioned in the newspapers. After a while old enemies were almost like old friends.

She was struck by their obituaries. It was odd that you could regret the passing of an old enemy. In retrospect, compared with what had followed, the old government had been too obvious, too inexpert, to disguise its malignity. There were more subtle enemies ...

Whatever the character of the government, certain economic facts remained in place. The Barclays packet she brought to Karachi Delights was one of several in the upstairs bathroom, besides the cartons of perfume and unopened stockings. Altogether there were tens of thousands of rand in there, perhaps a hundred thousand. She didn't keep good track. It was off-the-books money, what Indians from Cape Town to Calcutta called *ooplung*, black money.

There was a more substantial sum in an undeclared account in London which Nafisa had set up twenty-five years before. Everybody did it, who could afford it, although it was not legal. If the same thing happened here as in a dozen countries to the north then the money in London would secure them a start, a precious few months of breathing room in Vancouver, or Sydney. Unlike the Indians of Uganda, or the farmers driven out of Zimbabwe, they would have a roof over their heads.

Nafisa tried to keep her husband out of these matters. Yet a few months ago, after he had come home from the operation, Arif had opened a statement from overseas and found out about the London account. He had been furious with her. His temper wasn't good. He didn't like to take risks.

But there was more to it than a difference in temperament. Nafisa suspected that the difference in their attitudes was determined by origin. Unlike her husband she had been born into a poor family in Botswana. They had almost nothing when they were growing up. Schoolbooks and uniforms for her brother Nawaz and herself had been hand-me-downs from their cousins around Gaborone. Her father had begged his relatives for school fees. When she had an appendectomy in Standard Four the hospital had sent a bill collector to the door.

In consequence Nafisa had fears she couldn't convey to Arif. To communicate something properly, she had decided, the other person had to know what you meant before you began to speak.

She put Arif's anger out of mind. He had not entirely recovered to this day. Govin Mackey, who had operated on Arif, had warned her that post-operative depression could persist for six months. What Govin said made sense. He was a good doctor and he knew Arif well, having once been his student. She was patient for this reason.

Jadwat was arranging the tubs and pots in the boot, dutifully separating them with newspaper so they wouldn't knock against each other. Then he tipped the workers with change from the ashtray in his Mercedes.

The sight, as she was coming out of the restaurant, softened Nafisa's grievances against Jadwat. Shame!

The man wasn't as black as she had painted him. Unlike her husband, Jadwat was good at practicalities. Yes, he was an operator. But he was also a fixer and a Jack of all trades. He knew as much as a trained advocate about bank fees, estate duties, conveyance charges.

So what if he was stingy? It just meant he was afraid to die. When a plug had to be rewired, when the tuner in her Sanyo television was on the blink and showed only a bar of electronic colour, Jadwat was happy to take on the problem. And he kept at it until the thing was fixed even if he had to get a part from the dealer in Johannesburg.

It was nothing out of the ordinary to find tiny Jadwat in the hall of the house, balancing on one chair which was itself balanced on another, replacing a dead bulb on Estella's request. If he was in town he accompanied her to the Old Fort Road Hypermarket or, as today, to Karachi Delights.

Nor did Jadwat complain about the demands on his time. He had a single man's surplus of time and energy. Maybe he hung around with widows and divorcees because they needed him the most.

Nafisa knew, about herself, that it was difficult to be happy without being needed. The men in her family were disconcertingly independent. She had never quite adjusted to her son's independence. She had brought him up incorrectly.

And her husband was almost as bad. Her brother, Nawaz, was in his own world of religion. They were absorbed in themselves; they were men. To be unnecessary to all three of them disappointed Nafisa. So she couldn't blame somebody like Jadwat for wishing to be wanted.

Jadwat's motivation could be as guiltless as all that. What sentence did he like to quote from Trotsky? Was it Lenin? From each according to his ability, to each according to his need.

Jadwat finished packing the trunk and tied string across the top to secure the contents. He rubbed his hands together.

"So, you fixed it up with the Pakistanis?"

"We can go. *Chaalo.* I paid up."

"With *ooplung*, I suppose, from an old Barclays packet?" He observed her expression. "People never change."

"No, they don't."

Jadwat opened the door for Nafisa and closed it behind her. He came around and got in himself, smiling.

"You still keep it under Sharky's old mattress? I made a mental note to talk to you on that subject." They clattered off the pavement onto the road. Jadwat rolled up his window. "The order has come through from Pretoria for the Receiver of Revenue really to crack down. I have it on good authority from my contact on the Richmond council. The days when we could rely on our friends in the movement are long gone. Today it's every man for himself. The worst part is they don't have to catch you red-handed."

She was irritated again. "Nobody's going to catch me red-handed, Jadwat."

"No, but by the new code they don't have to catch you. They simply have to show a discrepancy between the level of income you report and your standard of living. They send people out to take photographs of your house, your car, anything to show that something is happening under the table. They've already caught many of the doctors in Richmond, Greytown, Newcastle, all over the country. And big fines. You wouldn't believe the fines. Where they catch you, Nafisa, is on the compound interest on the tax you owe. They're brilliant men, and women, I suppose."

"Oh, I am sure they are the most brilliant of the lot."

"Nafisa, I will never steer you wrong. I made you put money overseas in the first place, you remember. Since he found out about my role in it Arif has never forgiven me. But I am telling you that we have to tread carefully. In the past, when it comes down to it, this was not our country. It belonged to the Europeans and the multinationals. In the future it is not likely to be our country either."

Nafisa made no answer. During the drive back to Westville she was lost in her thoughts. She couldn't calculate how much to admit. Jadwat didn't know that a demand from the Receiver for information had been forwarded to her accountant. It was a carbon copy of the original and she was carrying it around in the bottom of her handbag.

On the way home Jadwat took the road to Tollgate where, stopped in traffic at the top of the hill, she observed the sunshine slanting over the slope of red-roofed houses and flats, the platforms of container ships out on the ocean, and the high-wire sides of the tennis courts at Westridge Stadium.

Some of the apartment buildings along the motorway were in a state of disrepair. She saw the many unpainted walls and doors and wondered what the city was coming to.

Yet the smudged format of the form, safe in her handbag, was more vivid to Nafisa than anything around them. She had read it the first time with trouble, with tears, because, like her son Shakeer, she suffered from a mild form of dyslexia. When she was emotional it was twice as hard to read.

The investigator included photographs of her car, her husband's car, their overseas travels and other expenditures, details of the latest round of renovations to the Westville house alongside a local builder's estimate of the cost.

It was the letter she had feared for twenty years. Only complications could ensue. Kader, her accountant, had given the name of a reliable tax lawyer. Yet to dial the man's number cost a fortune.

How to proceed? Nafisa couldn't bring herself to tell her husband. He would be appalled at the idea of a court proceeding. They had both given the better part of their lives to the movement.

Jadwat was correct. This new country they had helped to create was more treacherous than one might have anticipated. That was why it was important to have something overseas. Yet Arif had been angry enough when he found out about the London account. Admitting the situation to Jadwat, after their conversation, was out of the question.

For two weeks this letter had lain at the bottom of her consciousness from morning until night, even in her dreams, glittering into her mind like a coin in a wishing well. Was this letter, with its barcoded permit stamped in the corner, the news she had been fearing? She didn't believe so. There was something else. She couldn't yet admit this unidentified piece into her thoughts.

Jadwat revived the conversation as he and Estella emptied the trunk of the car, ferrying the pots to the top of the stairs.

Jadwat talked in front of Estella without reservation although Nafisa often asked him not to. There were some subjects servants didn't need to know about. But once he was started Jadwat would not keep quiet.

"Keep my words in mind, Nafisa. They say this new direction comes from the very top. I don't have to tell you how the big chiefs feel about your family. The last straw for them was when, on CNN, Arif criticised the Premier, the one who claimed he could cure people by the touch of his hand. The way this country works, they don't fear losing an election. They don't mind three hundred thousand deaths per year. Their one sensitivity is to how they are portrayed in the international press. That's Africa. They will go a long way to punish their former friends. That's Africa too."

Estella went down with the pots. Jadwat parked his car in the driveway so that others could enter and leave without difficulty. The dog ran up the stairs and followed them down to the door. He was not a beautiful animal but his big shoulders made you feel as if you had a bodyguard trotting beside you.

It wasn't clear if Arif was awake. Since the last round of surgery, especially with the regimen of immunosuppressive drugs, he was likely to fall asleep in the afternoon.

Jadwat added, "With the new dispensation they're even putting people in jail ... Doctors!"

"Okay, Jadwat. That's enough. You've convinced me to go straight." Nafisa forced herself to smile. "I would have thought, as a socialist, you fully supported the government to lock up the entire productive class in this country. As you have told me a hundred times, aren't we the exploiters? Shouldn't all of us be locked in prison, including yourself?"

Jadwat stood outside the door and seemed to ponder the issue as if for the first time. "I can't side with them against my own people, certainly not against my oldest friends in the world. I have known Arif since day one of medical school. While I am an admirer of Trotsky, I owe too much to you also. Think of the trouble you've gone through, over the years, to find me someone to share my happiness and unhappiness with."

It must have been his roundabout way of apologising. Jadwat waited for Estella to unlock the security gate. He put his battered corduroy suitcase inside the house.

He went on. "Apart from all that, since they choose to perpetuate a system based on individual selfishness, since they have decided to forget everything we learned about socialism in the old days, then what do they expect?" He patted his suitcase, which had brown masking tape run along the handle. "Tell me, my dear, where I should put my things. It just struck me that, for once tonight, Sharky will actually be occupying his own room. That's how you always call it, you know."

Jadwat was correct. Nafisa smiled to be reminded of the discrepancy. She had no mysteries. Even Jadwat, Jadwat the fool, knew who she was. The large room on the ground floor had belonged to her son almost twenty years earlier, a span of time so great that surely it could not apply to her own existence.

Nafisa felt she must have slept through these twenty years. Her understanding had not caught up with them. Her son's long absence, his experiences in San Francisco and around the world, were facts she hadn't accommodated. She was slow, she knew, to work out what happened around her. Others were rapid.

We will put you down in Shakeer's room, Nafisa frequently said to a guest. It was all she could do not to add: He won't mind. He wasn't around to mind. Her son travelled a good deal, to take photographs for *National Geographic* and other photo magazines.

Shakeer had aspirations to be a photographer in his own right, but his choice of subjects was curious, and even outdated. When she visited him in California he had an exhibition in a Santa Monica gallery comprised of portraits of holy men in Benares, Varanasi. She had seen something similar in a gallery in Knightsbridge when Harold Wilson was still in office.

But you really could never tell with Shakeer. Nafisa sometimes identified something irrelevant in his character. It caused her pain to see it, to see anything imperfect in her son or husband or brother. Shakeer had been talking about writing a novel for years. Yet, like her, he couldn't read more than a few pages at a time without developing a headache. To the best of her knowledge he had never actually set down a word of his proposed novel on an actual piece of paper ...

Nafisa's mind contained several casements. One looked out on her husband, another upon her brother Nawaz, one on Shakeer. Whatever else was occupying her attention on the outside she continued to watch them in her imagination. Indeed it was a defining fact of her consciousness. This glow, this subtle stony light from magic windows, pervaded her experience.

On certain nights Nafisa woke to recall that, in her dream, she had been gazing at her son. It wasn't necessary to speak a word to him. Nor was it necessary, in the dream, that he acknowledge her presence.

Weeks went by without her chatting to Sharky, particularly when he was on assignment in places like Papua New Guinea and Antananarivo, but she was as close to him as if he were sleeping downstairs in his room.

So it didn't make that great a difference if Sharky was physically present in the house. He had never really been gone. Nothing was lost. Nothing had changed.

As Nafisa was preparing to leave for the airport, the professor came up from the house and through the garage.

He was still in his dressing gown although his hair was perfectly combed. He opened the passenger door and leaned across Estella.

Without saying anything Arif rootled around in the cubby hole of the car. He was smiling, as he always did when he interrupted someone. It produced a thrill in Nafisa – some odd kind of a thrill – to see that she was married to an old man. How had it happened? His hair had turned completely white.

"You don't want Jadwat to come along to the airport? He offered to accompany you if you want Estella to keep working. If you don't take him he will insist that I play cards with him until he pushes off to see one or another of his women. When it comes to playing tunny he is insatiable. You know he has devised a two-handed version. Oh, he won't let me sleep a wink if he's in the house. On top of it I have the court case to deal with. Take him, Nafisa."

"You keep him. It's good for you to talk, to share your feelings. Estella is more than enough company for me. And the highway is safe at this time of day, so long as we don't have to stop at that bad ..." She started. "Arif, what on earth are you doing?"

"This. As Jadwat was dealing the cards I remembered that the last time I drove to the university I used your car. Mine was in for a service on Monday. And you know, since the operation, I haven't wanted to go back to a manual if there is the alternative. Afterwards I left this behind. I would have left it until tomorrow except I know you can't stand to have it around."

With care Arif lifted the pistol out of the cubby hole. It was a heavy Smith & Wesson, ridged along the handle, and coal black rather than metal black, as if the colour would rub off when you touched it. Everybody in Durban, except Nafisa, carried something.

People were stupid. They didn't know how to use them. The

same people tried to talk you into the feeling that you needed one as well. However Nafisa had a horror of guns. She made a gesture of displeasure.

Her husband didn't show that he noticed her reaction.

He went on, "Jadwat, apparently, has some mysterious appointment he doesn't want to specify. I assume it's with a lady friend."

Arif and Jadwat talked about each other sarcastically although they were never directly critical. It was a habit left over from their student days. They were still students. They were still trying to understand the universe and had gotten nowhere.

Still leaning in the window, the revolver lodged incongruously in his striped red dressing gown, Arif said, "Our friend is up to his old tricks. He just asked me about that cousin of yours, Goolam, who passed away. I didn't give anything away. I agree with you wholeheartedly that Jadwat cannot tool around and victimise widows all his life. So what do you suggest I tell him?"

"Tell him I lost the number."

"So he'll look it up in the directory."

Nafisa said, "Then it won't be my fault and my responsibility." She clapped. "I have washed my hands of Jadwat, Arif. He is your friend from medical school and that famous first-year anatomy class. I have my own friends, my own set. You make sure he conducts himself with dignity. Now, if you please, allow Estella and me to set off."

Past the Esplanade the road to the airport ran between hills that were terraced with baked brick buildings descending almost to the tarmac. The city was succeeded by poorer suburbs, schools and workers' hostels, then grey pairs of grain silos and sugar warehouses behind high cement fences.

Nafisa drove slowly in the far left lane. Overloaded trucks and vans skidded past the car, presenting their rusted bumpers until they too vanished around a bend. They were as distant, she imagined, as if they were visitors from a different time. They were spectral trucks. She couldn't hold onto their reality.

Instead, while Nafisa tried to focus on the road, she began to see her reflection in the windshield. She noted her smile, a fixed expression, which covered her entire countenance. It reminded her of an alligator. She had learned the habit, which she disliked, from her husband. She couldn't help smiling when it was necessary to bring up an embarrassing subject. There was no way around it. She had to have a word with Estella.

"Do me a favour?"

"Whatever you ask."

"Do you mind that while Shakeer is here …" Nafisa ran out of words and restarted her sentence. "Estella, I will let you into something. In the past year Shakeer has not had an easy time of it. You remember that he separated from Ginger? That could have been predicted. Now, I grant you, it is one thing or another with Shakeer. That is my son. In some ways, he is a ridiculous person." Nafisa wasn't sure why she was explaining at such length. She said, "He has never learned to be serious about life. But that is beside the point. Could you try not to complain to him about me?"

"I don't know what you mean, Nafisa."

Nafisa sharpened her tone. "I mean, Estella, don't go to him behind my back because he's a soft touch. If something worries you, have a word with me, as you would do ordinarily. I beg you, don't take money from Shakeer. At the end of the month I will give you an extra four hundred rand. I acknowledge that you've been working many more hours because of Arif's retirement. Please don't exploit my son."

Estella didn't reply. Nafisa realised she had finally provoked her to anger, after trying all day to do it. That clean copper face tightened at the edges as if someone had sharpened the folds.

Nafisa didn't mind angering Estella. In fact she was relieved by having done so. She wasn't a saint.

Indeed Nafisa didn't want to be perfect. Her benevolence was erratic at best and, if only because of her job and family, it seemed that she was spread out in too many directions. She often forgot, or seemed to forget, a promise, whether it was to visit a friend in hospital, pay school fees for her nephew, or the like, only to remember after a fortnight and deal with the issue. She shelved things in her mind until it was convenient to dispose of them. But in the long run she was unable to let people down or to leave a thing unfinished.

The two women parked without saying another word and walked down to the terminal building. The airport was dull, comparatively busy, hazy in smoke from the power plant, untidy and surrounded by untidy hills on the opposite side of the apron.

Inside, the smaller coffee shop did brisk business. The waitress, in a green bib, had opened a packet of Choc-kits and was arranging them two on a saucer. Next to the shop Nafisa found two spaces on a bench, where she and Estella sat uncomfortably together, facing an advertisement for a cellphone company.

Again, and for the fourth time in so many hours, Nafisa's state of mind turned upside down. Her feelings were so unsteady. She didn't like to quarrel with her worker. It was her own fault. Nor was it a product of her volatility. Her feelings about Estella were irrationally intense, as if the two of them were unhappily married.

There were mornings Nafisa couldn't stand to hear the younger woman's voice outside the garage. She would leave for work early in order not to look at the girl and risk revealing her emotion.

Simultaneously she very much wanted to reveal her feelings. She wished to fly on Estella and beat her around the head, to fling Estella with her red shoes into the street, laughing and crying, and be rid of her lorryload of troubles.

Yet there were other occasions – this minute in the airport when Estella studiously avoided her gaze – when Nafisa felt something close to love starting up ... when she overheard Estella singing unselfconsciously in the scullery, when she observed the corner of a red heel in her denim handbag, or when she got home exhausted from the clinic and was struck by the idea that on the planet Estella was the individual who needed her, Nafisa, the most. To each according to his need ...

Besides Estella, everybody else, Nafisa believed, had outgrown her. Her son had outgrown her. So had her husband. Since Arif had uncovered the existence of the London account he had been more withdrawn than usual. But he had been different with her even before that.

In general, since the transplant and the endless weeks of suffering in the checkerboard hospital room with tubes in every part of his body, her husband seemed to have acquired some piece of wisdom which was inaccessible to her. Only Estella, in all the universe, had remained on her level.

Now it was all Nafisa could do not to touch the other woman on the cheek, in the middle of the airport building, and inhale the Pears shampoo in Estella's plaited black-brown hair. Most of all Nafisa wanted to suspend her need to think. She had such a fear of what report the day was bringing to her.

Just as she was about to apologise, to try to apologise, Estella laughed.

"Madam, you're not in a good mood this afternoon. You are not. I don't blame you for it. I understand the feeling you have, as a mother, because I feel something similar with my daughter. The professor says, whenever Sharky is about to arrive, you go on a rampage."

Nafisa didn't smile. "Rampage? I really can't imagine my husband used such a term to describe me."

"No, that's the exact word. Ram-page. I remember it because I asked him the meaning."

Nafisa laughed out loud for the first time that day. "My husband ... my husband will never get tired of teaching the wrong things to the wrong people. Ah, Estella. My son, my husband, they always know better than everyone else. They read books and they think that books, and a large vocabulary, and whatever understanding you can find in a book, are a substitute for experience. But I have to say, I don't believe in books so much. They are no substitute."

Nafisa wanted to pursue this argument. She wasn't usually critical of Sharky or of Arif. Yet the more she thought about her husband and her son the more dissatisfied she discovered she was. They had no compunction about placing her in the most difficult of situations. Their views and attitudes about life were set in steel. They never imagined that she had her own point of view. She was alone in her family.

Nafisa was about to say something about this to Estella when the disembarking passengers were upon them. The flight had landed without announcement. The passengers advanced into the reception area one by one. The doors which opened to the bag carousels opened and shut as each person came out.

Nafisa got up to read the arrivals board. She noticed that the mechanical letters which chattered as flight information changed had been replaced by an electronic display.

"It looks like they're here. In fact they've been on the ground for fifteen minutes. It doesn't happen every day that a flight arrives quicker than you're expecting. With the airports in the state they're in ..."

"Yes, Nafisa. Should I go and look for Sharky?"

"No, don't worry. They will come this way."

Nafisa stood up. She unhurriedly examined the passengers. A

group of them met at the taxi stand. A girl was whisked into the back seat of a car by her mother. This went on for a while.

Estella said nothing further. They had arrived at an equilibrium. After a few minutes Nafisa saw a man who must have been in his forties. This man was far older than her son. She knew that America had taken Sharky and made him fat, thick, uncomfortable. America had swallowed up her son. Only she, as a mother, could calculate how much beauty had been lost ...

His experience in San Francisco had taken years from her son, had removed his expectation of happiness, but had it made him unrecognisable? Could Shakeer be so old? No, it was impossible. Nafisa looked away and then back again.

The man was wearing a brown track suit with piping on the shoulder, similar to something she had bought for her son at a men's shop in Musgrave. He was pushing a cart loaded with luggage. From nowhere Nafisa remembered the suitcases, and the roped-up black sleeves which protected lenses, cameras, tripods, flash batteries.

From the age of nineteen her son had been encumbered by all this equipment. Nafisa herself had grown up almost without possessions. She had moved into her husband's family's house after her wedding with a twenty-inch valise which remained at the back of her cupboard to this day.

Her son, by contrast, moved in a convoy of objects. Everything had a price and everything was disposable. Her son had become American amongst his possessions. He moved. He made a life. He tore it up and moved again. But what was this person that she had created?

Before Nafisa recognised the man, she noted again that he was older than she'd expected, with a full face and mouth, too full of feeling to be handsome. His eyes were almost black and scowling. He moved tiredly in her direction, as if he knew her.

She moved towards him before she knew that it was Sharky. Even before she reached him her heart was filled with the brightness of a Catherine wheel. On New Year's Eve, 1990, when the racial restrictions on the beaches had collapsed, she had seen thousands of Catherine wheels revolving on hidden poles held in the hands of revellers packed on the dark sand.

"So what is the matter, Nafisa?" Sharky asked. He sometimes called his mother by her first name when he wanted to make a point. "You look as if you have seen a ghost." He brushed off the shoulders of his track suit. "And how are you doing, Estella? Both of you look utterly miserable. I hope the preparations for the party are well underway. I am looking forward to seeing everybody."

The rest of the day, the afternoon which divided her life from everything afterwards, continued in a slow-motion pan from the airport and power plant and past the factories and domed sugar terminals on Malvern Hill.

This industrial side of the city was even hotter, crowded with buildings and power lines, a concrete barrier fencing in the highway. It hurt her mind to think about the concentration of people and buildings.

At the same time there was a sensation of warmth flowing in her arms and up her neck. It always started when Shakeer was physically present, when her son and husband were in the same place, and it went up into the back of her head.

Eventually they got to the Westville ramp. The suburb was situated a few hundred feet above town. Fifty years ago it had been considered beyond the city limits. It was spacious. The streets were much wider than in town. In Westville whites and Indians with some money had lived side by side since before the laws officially changed.

Nafisa asked, "How was the journey? Almost twenty hours in the plane alone."

"No, it wasn't bad. But I think, after all these years, I am finally tired of travelling. All I have been thinking of, since eight this morning over Cameroon or whichever country it was, is a hot bath."

"You can have one the moment we get home. There's no one to disturb you."

Sharky said, "First I have to unpack some of my equipment. You know it's finicky. Unless everything is working I won't be able to take the photographs of the party tomorrow."

"So we'll do that first."

Shakeer said almost nothing else, worn out by the thirty-hour journey from San Francisco, but when Nafisa thought back to the journey she imagined that her son was enclosed inside himself. So was Estella.

They were, she recalled thinking at the time, like three mourners. She could never forget the sense of some great event rushing towards them in the afternoon. However fast she drove, they seemed to be motionless.

The car glided through the still-strong sunshine into the driveway where glass from the window Estella had broken was scattered on the tiles like grains of bridal rice. The gate and the front door were unlocked.

The dog, whose name she couldn't recall at that very moment, was barking at the back of the house. He couldn't come to the front because of the gate at the corner. They walked quickly into the house. Nafisa immediately went up to the bedroom in which her husband lay on the big bed shot dead by the pistol he had taken from the cubby hole.

Arif was lying face down on the bed so that his white hair was all she saw when she went into the bedroom. The dressing gown clung wetly, the material thick and black, to his body. The gun was lying on the bed beside him.

Afterwards Nafisa recalled that at the very moment she entered the bedroom she recognised the scene just as if she was remembering it from the day before. There was nothing in the room to surprise her. She could understand exactly what had happened. She had known about this in the morning. She had known about it the day before, the month before, and in fact since the moment of her birth.

Without asking, without saying a word to Shakeer standing beside her, Nafisa knew that Arif had murdered himself, and murdered her along with him. He had picked up the gun and put an end to his own suffering. There wasn't a doubt in her mind.

Nafisa was struck, at that moment, by the thought that her life had just begun.

Nawaz

~

EVERYTHING HAPPENED WITH GREAT SUDDENNESS. THE ARrangements for the burial were being made. It was necessary to complete the ceremony before sundown. Nobody could panic because time was short.

Telephones were ringing all around the country. Friends and relations were summoned from Pietermaritzburg, Newcastle, Greytown, Dundee, as far afield as Laudium in Pretoria and Lens, the Indian township of Lenasia outside Johannesburg, where they might still catch the four o'clock flight to Durban.

Many of these people would not make it to the funeral in time. Others happened to be in town to attend the professor's retirement party.

There were a few familiar faces. Sharky had noticed his father's former student Govin Mackey at the gate as well as his long-ago friend Leila. Govin had on a blue pin-striped suit, with square shoulders, which sat uncomfortably on him. Govin, as Shakeer remembered, was rarely at his ease.

Govin Mackey and Leila were talking to each other. Sharky hadn't seen either of them in years. But he had no desire to greet them. He couldn't imagine resuming a connection with Mackey or Leila on the same day, in the same month or year, that his father had shot himself.

Shakeer followed his mother's lead. So had the Westville police officer who appeared on the scene. Though she hadn't said it out loud his mother believed his father had shot himself. She was afraid to say so out loud. Everyone was afraid to say anything about it. It was beyond possibility that the professor could have shot himself. Yet it was immediately understandable.

The shame should swallow him! Yet, in the very same instant, Shakeer knew that the situation had not begun to bite, as if a kite had been released and had not taken up the string.

Shakeer disliked the disorder around him. A Muslim funeral was invariably haphazard, given the restriction on time. It was difficult to organise. But news spread. The house was already full of strangers.

In the master bedroom the women had the task of washing the body. It was unusual but his mother had insisted that it should be the women's responsibility. Estella came downstairs to summon him.

"They are calling you to come."

"Who is?"

"Your mother asked you to come."

"I'll come upstairs just now, Estella. I have a telephone call to make so long," Sharky said.

He wanted to call Ginger, in San Francisco. He had once been married to Ginger. Sharky still talked to her first of all when something happened in his life or when he felt something was about to happen.

He couldn't explain this compulsion because, when it came down to it, he was unsure if Ginger understood a word. Moreover Shakeer couldn't think what to tell her. He couldn't explain about his father. The situation was beyond explanation.

"Let me make the call then. You go ahead."

But Estella waited. With her stern face and exact bearing she resembled the statues Sharky once visited on Easter Island. He had been sent to photograph the monoliths by a travel magazine. They were an over-used subject but the effect was still dramatic. They had been lodged on the side of a hill overlooking the Pacific: stone-skinned and impermeable.

You stood below the stonework on Ahu Akivi to wonder at the great heads above you. It was futile. Like Estella, like his father since the operation, they were impossible to scan.

It had more to do with himself than with others. Yet Sharky remembered that Estella's cold beauty called out something suspicious in others, especially in his mother.

Shakeer wanted to think about his father, not his mother. Nonetheless it struck him that Nafisa bordered on the irrational in her distrust of her maid. His mother was convinced that Estella stole from her and mocked her trust. Yet, for all her passion, Nafisa had never managed to fire her worker.

Sharky was an outsider to this conflict, and could afford to be more generous. People were clouds of possibilities. His father had taught him as much. His father was tolerant by indifference. There was no point becoming entangled in petty disputes when there were large questions in the world.

Yet the professor had shot himself. He had pierced himself in the chest! All his teachings were therefore suspect.

Sharky couldn't see where to begin; how could he unpack everything he had learned falsely from his father? Nothing prepared him. His mother seemed to understand better. Nafisa, so far as he could tell, didn't have any questions about what had happened.

Of course there had been warning signs. There were always warning signs and they were identifiable only in hindsight. You had to think backwards and live forwards. But to shoot yourself, to murder yourself, to abandon your body on a bed for the world to stumble across!

Shakeer had known that his father was not in normal spirits

after the surgery. He had avoided coming home for just this reason. It was important to believe that his family enjoyed a certain immunity from circumstances. He relied on this conviction of good luck every day of his life.

But the situation had been a serious one. His father had been in dreadful pain for many months and feared the return of his illness. If rejection occurred a second transplant was out of the question. It had been nearly impossible to find a matching kidney in the first instance.

Besides who wouldn't be depressed to discover the government dismantling the work of a lifetime? Hundreds of thousands had lost their lives, and for what?

Instead of dialling Ginger's number Sharky gave in.

"All right. I'll call later." He was talking to himself rather than to Estella. "After all, it's not as if Ginger was close to my father. The news would mean nothing to her. Ironically, apart from this government and Hansel Metzger, Ginger was about the one person who didn't get along with my father. They had that spectacular argument in Boston once. She asked him to stay in a hotel."

He went upstairs with Estella. The bedroom door was closed.

When Sharky went in he found his mother moving a stool beside the bed so that she could shave the body. Under normal circumstances it would be the job of the oldest male relative but Nafisa thought otherwise. Nobody had the authority to overrule her.

His mother, Shakeer thought, was as distant from him as those heads on Easter Island. He couldn't imagine speaking to her directly. And she didn't want to be approached. She didn't acknowledge his presence as he came in.

There were a number of women standing behind Nafisa ... ravens. They wore long dresses and black scarves beneath which Sharky could make out one of his aunts, married to his mother's brother Nawaz, as well as Zuleika Mayat, the famous philanthropist.

Zuleika was as huge as a Zeppelin. She was even bigger than he had remembered her. It was astonishing that, when his father was gone, Zuleika should still be alive and mobile. That Zuleika should live!

Zuleika! She was a former activist. She had once participated with his father in a sit-in at the British Consulate to protest the State of Emergency. They had been there a fortnight. The British had been powerless to move her from the entrance. Sharky had wondered how anything but a bulldozer could transport her against her will.

Zuleika! It was astonishing that one could begin as a single cell and grow to such a magnitude in the course of a single life.

This Zuleika motioned to him to close the door. Sharky did so, leaving Estella in the hall. Nafisa held an ivory-handled razor. He had never seen it before. She ran the razor underneath his father's chin just as naturally as if she had been doing it for years, rinsing the blade in a basin and every so often leaving it in the steaming water while she applied shaving lotion to the skin.

The liquorish smell of this lotion, which was supposed to be violets, was suddenly very piercing around Sharky, and even made him dizzy. There must have been a drop of camphor in the water, as prescribed in the religious literature. The room, the barge of women who stood in silence around his mother while she dried the razor on a small green towel, revolved about him.

Sharky staggered back, then put his hand behind him on the dressing table to steady himself. He had never experienced such a thing. He thought he would fall down.

Meanwhile Nafisa had finished shaving his father and cleaning his face. The basin was removed and she now began to comb out his hair, parting it severely on the right the way he would have done it for himself.

Since his sixtieth birthday, a decade earlier, his father had been the possessor of an utterly white head of hair. From a distance, and particularly from behind, it had been his father's most recognisable feature. It was like finding a lighthouse. You could pick out the professor a mile away by his hair and then, up close, by his partial smile.

The memory of meeting his father's gaze, of recognising his unformulated smile, was so bright in his mind that Sharky looked down to avoid it.

It was inconceivable that he should never see it again. He remembered, as a child, that before school his father would brush his hair rapidly, even harshly. Despite the harshness the combing would cause a sensation of warmth in his neck and behind the ears while it was going on. So many years later, just to think about it, he could feel the same warmth starting up behind his ears.

His head cleared. Just as suddenly as the trance had begun, it ended. The contents, and the other occupants, of the bedroom again became clear. Indeed they were supernaturally clear, as if a light were shining right out of the walls and upon the redwood dresser and the heavy red rings astride the curtain rods, upon the motley women gathered around the bed, and upon his mother's parchment hands, and above all on the body itself.

The body was wrapped in two bathroom towels and had shrunken into itself. The dead, as he knew, change their lengths and shapes, their faces.

After he left university without his degree Sharky had been a photographer in Bosnia, at first in the countryside and around Split, then in the capital when there had been artillery duels with Serb gunners in the hills. He had seen people curled up, stone dead, after an explosion in the Sarajevo market. They assumed a look of disappointment at the nature of things.

Yet he had never seen the same alteration in someone he was close to. He couldn't conceive that this man had been his father.

There was a square set to the jaws lending a hard expression never present in life. The soles of his father's feet protruded from the edge of the towel onto the bed. They were solid purple, the same shade as a man whose heart is beating right up into his face.

A new feeling now overcame Sharky. It was a most unwelcome and unexpected sensation, dangerously close to laughter at his father's predicament ... just as if he had pushed somebody over ... just as if he was exulting over the fallen man.

From where had this feeling come? His feelings were badly constructed. They reacted in the opposite direction to what was natural, then reacted against themselves. Shakeer was awkward in the presence of a beggar, a child, or invalid. In Madras, where he spent four months on assignment, he had regularly walked three blocks out of his way to avoid the legless man camped on the pavement beside the Thomas Cook office.

Today was no different. Instead of weeping, he wanted to laugh out loud. He would smile into Zuleika's face until she hobbled from the room on the trunks of her legs. For he could hardly be more scornful of his father's action. It was a contradiction of everything he had been taught to believe. For his father to point a gun at himself! This deed was, of course, directed at him, on the very afternoon of his arrival.

Sharky wanted to strut around the room, to insult his mother and the other mourners, to yank the towels and the sheets from the bed and throw the body onto the floor.

Just as this desire became overwhelming his mother beckoned him over. She took his hands in her own.

"Sharky, this will be the last time I see your father. Let's look at him together."

They sat next to each other on the bed. The other women began to leave the room. This close, Sharky could identify the wound, which had been cleaned. Apart from the bruise it was scarcely visible. How small it was! It was startling that life should escape through the eye of a needle.

Sharky put his arm around his mother who then drew him down to the body. Nafisa was stronger than he had thought. He could sense the weight of the three of them on the sturdy bed. The bed itself had been a long-ago wedding present from his father's family. As a child he had often slept along the bottom of the bed, pressed against the brass footboard, to his father's displeasure.

Women didn't come to the cemetery, or to mosque. Govin Mackey offered him a ride after the prayer at the Westville mosque but it was preferable to go with a member of the family. Govin looked worse off than he did. His suit jacket hung off his shoulders.

In the end Sharky's uncle Nawaz, Nafisa's younger brother, drove with Sharky to Brooks Road. Nawaz placed his cellphone between the seats and inspected the display at every traffic light.

Nawaz didn't speak much. As far as Sharky knew, he had spoken very little to anybody in the course of his existence, including his own children. He couldn't recall his uncle taking part in anything like a conversation. Nawaz was a man of monosyllables. He was shut up behind his salt and pepper beard.

Shakeer was not displeased by his uncle's reticence. He didn't want to utter a word to anybody, in particular Nawaz. In a large family the distance between any two points was correspondingly large. It occurred to Shakeer that he didn't have the first idea how Nawaz thought or what he thought about. There were only gaps between them. A small family was a molecule. A large family was a scale model of humanity ...

Shakeer pieced together his own thoughts. He hadn't had a minute to consider the magnitude of the situation. His family was supposed to have turned the corner. His father had been recovering from the serious illness of the previous year. The transplant, performed by Mackey and David Gerson, had given him the chance to live. A kidney had been found in the nick of time.

It was an irony, but a pleasing one, that Govin Mackey had once been his father's student and that Gerson, who was perhaps the leading surgeon in the country, was a good friend of his mother's.

Of course, in this country, there was no promise of an undisturbed life. In the months after the operation his father had been upset by the action for defamation filed by Hansel Metzger. His father had been forced to retire from the university and had watched with dismay as the government followed Metzger's lead. Metzger, Sekolo the vice chancellor, and the President derailed plans to manage the epidemic, thus costing the country hundreds of thousands of additional infections. And for what? For what?

Then, in a sense, this singular action was the endpoint of a far longer process. His father's life had escaped through an exit far greater than a bullethole.

Even as he explained the situation to himself in this way Shakeer saw that he didn't believe a word of it. But it was preferable to think than to feel.

What little his uncle did say during the ride to Brooks Road seemed to be directed to himself rather than to his passenger.

Nawaz nodded as he spoke. "It's better, yes, that we get there early. Nafisa is correct to say so. Why wait? We must be there before the body arrives. It's better that somebody from the family is present."

The cemetery was an irregular piece of ground the same size as a soccer pitch. Men in old black and brown suits stood at the gate. Others sat half inside their cars, listening to the radio. They didn't seem to be connected with the occasion.

Muslims, Indians, Africans were haphazard. None of them were remotely familiar to Sharky. He wanted to find out who they were, and determine the cause of their disrespect. They had overrun an event which didn't belong to them. Shakeer didn't want the funeral, after his father had shot himself, to be a matter of public interest.

While he was thinking this, Nawaz found a space on the verge and manoeuvred the car onto it.

He said, "I am afraid we may have a long wait ahead of us, until the body arrives. Well, that is the nature of the case. Such things don't happen at our convenience."

His uncle made no move to get out so they sat in silence in the car. Nawaz went back to his cellphone. He typed rapidly on the keyboard as if it was a calculator, dour at his task. The man was the youngest of his mother's siblings yet he was also, paradoxically, the most solemn.

They were the products of a poor provincial family about which Sharky understood less than he liked. He had heard only the rudiments from his mother who seldom referred to her childhood or to her experiences before marriage and her years as a medical intern.

His mother's family were from Botswana, originally from Porbandar in India, Memons, a designation derived from the Arabic term for the faithful. Nafisa had been the beneficiary of a scholarship to medical school in Bombay, courtesy of the richest Indian family in the capital Gaborone. Whereas her brother hadn't completed Standard Eight.

A brother and sister couldn't be more different. Nawaz supported his large family buying and selling cut-rate clothes from the boot of his Datsun. He obtained his merchandise from the factory stores on the South Coast, not far from Scottburgh, where there were barracks of young women armed with Singer sewing machines.

The goods were conveyed in smaller parcels to traders in town who serviced a principally black market. Nawaz sold shirts at thirty rand, mock cashmere jerseys at sixty-five, knockoffs of Diesel jeans at a hundred rand a pair.

The one occasion Shakeer dealt with Nawaz involved clothes. Sharky had scandalised his mother by buying a suitcase of cheap clothes from Nawaz to take back to California. Nobody, nobody respectable, in Durban would do such a thing. Yet he had worn them for years, and would have continued to do so if Ginger hadn't thrown them out.

But then Ginger had been in a state of mania at the time and had thrown out a good deal else besides, including a television set and some of his photographic equipment.

The only person, of course, who sympathised with Sharky on this issue of second-hand clothing had been his father. The professor had laughed about it.

It was impossible to imagine a world without such a sympathiser. It was impossible to imagine a life with this uncle as a replacement for his father. Sharky could hardly look at Nawaz and accept that his father had succumbed to this uncle and everything mindless he represented. It was impossible, an impossible humiliation! He had suddenly fallen in the world down to the level of this uncle.

Nawaz was a figure of the past, almost of the eighteenth century. His days as a clothing salesman were numbered. The garment business throughout Africa was going extinct because of Chinese competition. China was the future, the world's workshop.

Shakeer had firsthand experience of the transformation. He had spent January in Shanghai, on assignment for Discovery. He had never seen so many cranes as around Shanghai and inland. All the world's cranes were situated in China. Sophisticated South African businessmen went to Guangzhou and Taipei to make deals on steel and electronics, furniture, even carpets. Chinese carpets!

Sharky figured his uncle hadn't spoken to a Chinese or Hong Kong man or woman in his life. Oddly, like his own mother, his uncle could look rather Chinese. From a certain angle his face seemed nearly flat while his beard was spare and silky.

Sitting in the car Sharky saw that his mother and uncle were members of the same set. It was one of those facts he repressed unless it was there, staring directly at him. Subtract the Fu Manchu beard, then the three neat gold teeth buried at the back of his mouth, and Nawaz's similarity to his mother was uncanny.

Both were sombre human beings. They were reluctant to laugh, as if to do so was giving something away. They shared the same miniature frame and ferny black hair which turned brown in the Durban sun.

They had a gesture in common – a method of narrowing the eyes and talking to you sideways. To see Nawaz doing it produced in Sharky the electrifying sensation that here was his mother in disguise. It was as if he had uncovered an impostor. There was something in this connected to his father's death but, like a tooth, it wouldn't come loose in Shakeer's mind.

Nawaz closed his cellphone and looked across at him, almost closing his eyes as he did so, and Sharky felt this tingle of secret recognition.

"You won't believe it, Shakeer. When I was starting out, many years ago now, I would come to this very cemetery. Each Tuesday morning, I met one of the labourers right over there by the opposite gate. We would do our business and be on our way."

"I'm sorry. What do you mean?"

Nawaz pointed to the far side of the cemetery. "This is where I would buy my clothes. I mean before I had worked out an arrangement with the factory shop in Shepstone where I take on credit and pay at the end of the month. I also had a contact at St Aidan's Hospital. He may still be working there for all I know. He gave them to me for fifteen rands a kilo." He nodded. "But I am talking about the old days now, when there was some meaning to the idea of a rand."

"You mean you bought clothes belonging to the dead?"

"No. Now you are drawing a conclusion. Where they came from, that I don't know enough to say. I just thought it might interest you to know the background. There was one point when I sold some of my goods to you although afterwards Nafisa would not let me hear the end of it."

Nawaz didn't smile. Nor did he in any other way indicate an awareness of how monstrous his words were. He subsisted in an alternate reality, claws scuttling beneath a faraway ocean.

This brought Sharky to the final point of comparison between the siblings. In Nawaz's company, just as in his mother's, Sharky became convinced that every human being inhabited a separate universe. There was no means to convey a message from one to another, or if there was, it was transmitted by the logic of the broken telephone so that it was garbled on arrival.

For nothing Sharky said to his mother was ever received as intended. Nafisa misunderstood or took wrongly everything he said. The reverse must be true. This fact defined their relationship.

On the other hand there was little harm in his mother. Nor was there necessarily harm in her brother. He wasn't a bad soul. His intentions were good. His soul was as small as a peanut. No doubt Nawaz intended his claptrap about second-hand clothing as a means of cheering up his nephew.

Sharky looked out at the modest white stones in the burial ground. There must have been two hundred, grouped in irregular squares on the slope. His other uncles and his grandfather were buried here in clay. But it wasn't their tradition to visit the graves.

The cemetery's walls were covered in razor wire. The sides of the ground were populated by yellow rose bushes and bisected by hedges filled with mustard yellow flowers that seemed to acquire their colour by absorption from the clay.

The scene confirmed the intensity of his solitude. It was impossible to admit that the cemetery was about to receive his father with his hair about his shoulders, as Sharky imagined it, as bright as a lamp.

Meanwhile the hearse had appeared on the tracks leading to the gate. The vehicle was wide and dilapidated, something from the 1970s and, given the times, perhaps older than many of its occupants.

You could see that the floor in the back of the hearse had been replaced by a number of ill-fitting planks. Sharky constructed a picture of his father riding to the cemetery in the narrow rear space, unable to raise his head or change the position of his legs. One of the workers opened the gate and directed it through.

Sharky and his uncle got out of the car and walked through the entrance.

As they went into the cemetery, Nawaz began, in the voice of a man who had prepared a discourse, "I didn't always agree with your father, Sharky. That is a plain fact."

"I'm sure."

"I had my opinions and he had his opinions. Not that I made a point of it. Although he was not religious, ultimately his behaviour was religious. In spirit, rather than by the letter, is what I mean. When the previous government was out of bounds, then he stood up to it, whatever the cost. And I am proud to say that when this government also went wrong, although many of our friends were sitting in the parliament, he spoke out. He was not prepared to watch in silence as the Premier cast spells on sick people. Arif was one man who had no tolerance for rolling bones. So, on my side, I kept my disagreements to myself."

"You did what?"

Nawaz said, "I didn't wish to cause him any additional difficulty. He didn't need to hear from me. Look what has happened. We cannot afford to say anything about it otherwise the cemetery will refuse to give us a plot. Suicide is a mortal sin." His voice became higher. "It is an unforgivable sin for a Muslim. But to go back to your father ... Only now can we understand that the operations, not to say the criticism from the government, undermined his mental state more than we knew. It broke his heart. So I am pleased I didn't cause the professor any extra complications."

The idea that his father would have taken notice of the opinions of an insect like Nawaz made Sharky choke. Where did this guy get off?

Nawaz, positioned behind that Chinese beard, had developed a scheme of life in which his own small thoughts and activities were central to the operations of the universe. If the Secretary-General of the United Nations were to fly to South Africa to seek his opinion, Nawaz would be unsurprised. He would take it coolly.

Thinking of the unreality of his uncle's beliefs, the distance which separated the man from his context and his significance in the world, Shakeer became angry. He was furious to be connected to this creature. He was furious to have to talk politics to Nawaz when all the politics in the world added up meant less than a seashell.

At the same time it was a relief to be angry compared to the strange laughter which had possessed him in the bedroom. Here he wanted to weep, to dance around, to slap his uncle in the face, and bloody his mouth. For he wanted to punch the truth into the man's head. He wanted his teeth to break on the truth ...

Of course he did nothing of the sort. Instead he stood there beside Nawaz, taller than him by a foot, and watched as three men from the cemetery unloaded the hearse. The men moved the body to the far side of the ground on a stretcher which they brought back after a minute. Nawaz had a discussion with the imam which Sharky didn't follow. The two of them seemed to know each other.

One of the few traits Sharky could tell he had inherited from the paternal side was his father's reserve. Buildings could be falling inside him and, apart from his tremor and the cord which went tight in his neck, nobody would be the wiser. It wasn't practical to reveal one's emotions. They didn't translate well into the world because others were not so volatile.

In any event, as his father would remark, there was no good reason to argue with his uncle. A being like Nawaz was incapable of wisdom. About as much of the world could fit into Nawaz's intellect as into a dog's mind.

When Sharky thought about it in these terms his mother was just as bad or no better. Nafisa was out of contact with reality just as much as her brother. This yard of clay was reality.

One expected one thing of religious people and invariably discovered they were another thing altogether. The imam in charge of the ceremony was exceedingly gruff. He had a stiff white beard, hard as the bristles in a broom. This beard jutted out of his face at the person with whom he was conversing.

It seemed to Sharky that the imam was scolding him rather than asking questions. Maybe it was right that he should be scolded.

The imam barked out his questions and instructions to others as well, commanding a group of assistants who came and went from parts of the cemetery where they had been digging. They were engaged in more than one funeral at a time. Some of them were cleaning their spades. They were called over and given a number of specific directions.

So was Sharky. He was told where to stand, when to join the procession, and asked to read the Arabic text on a stained photostat page. He could pronounce the words but not understand what he was saying.

After he had explained the ceremony in detail the imam said, "Maybe it is time to get ready."

But then the imam did nothing. They continued to stand there.

It took another forty minutes to prepare the grave and assemble the members of the family.

The time passed without consciousness on Sharky's part, as if he were reading a book with an absent mind, forgetting the pages just as soon as he turned them over. Rain arrived from a clear sky, washing through the mourners at an angle. It wet the sheet around the body so that, after a few minutes, its outline was articulate.

The imam offered more instructions to the bearers. He led them to the trench which had been dug, putting his hand on Sharky's back and singing verses in Arabic. Sharky, assisted by his uncle and two of his father's cousins, picked up the body.

Between them they held the weight aloft for a full minute – astonishing how little mass there was in a lifetime – after which they allowed it to descend. The men began to ladle soil over the body. Shakeer took the spade for a minute. Then another man took it from him.

Nawaz peered into his face.

"You're okay, my boy?"

"Yes, I'm fine," Sharky said.

Nawaz touched his beard. His fingers, Sharky saw, resembled chicken bones. "Then shall we go back to the house? Nafisa will be waiting. She mustn't be alone. It is important that all the family members must be at the house at this time."

"Give me a moment, if you don't mind. My mother will survive."

Sharky imagined he was lying there, inside the sheet, in the place of his father. He was too terrified to breathe as the clay fell on him, building up and rapidly blocking the light.

His translation into the ground was so decided that, for an instant, he felt the cool pressure of the sheet on his own arms and smelled mud in his nostrils. He felt the movement of the blood in his head. It was loud as a truck.

Above him was a column of earth which supported men, animals, rocks, stones and trees. Above them, in turn, were the moon and stars. Above them were the silent cubits of space.

Suddenly this orientation reversed and it seemed that he was about to fall into the abyss above him. Then the vision passed, the sound of the blood in his ears went down, and Shakeer was left there beside his uncle.

"Let's go then."

Sharky was still reluctant to leave. There was horror at abandoning his father to the elements on such a miserable afternoon – the still damp ground, damp sheet, damp body. You wouldn't leave a dog outside on a day like this. It was inconceivable that you should drive off and leave a member of your family in a strange place. The logic was ridiculous but at that second it was compelling. He had, after all, abandoned his father for years after he left university.

Sharky was pierced by the responsibility for what transpired in his absence. There were a hundred things he could have done to change the outcome. He could have picked up a telephone. He could have reassured his father of the one thing he was certain of, that his father was inside him and at work, every minute, inside his own soul. But he had done nothing despite understanding the severity of the situation, as if paralysed. Oh, it was as if he had picked up the gun himself.

Sharky could scarcely stand up as he was brought out of the gates. He had to lean on the Datsun before he got in.

Besides, he was leaving his father to a religious establishment to which, in life, the man had refused to belong. Others married with its blessings, saw the cosmos in its image, suffered under its protection, and passed away in the surety of its promises. But not his father who had clung to unspoken unbelief throughout his life. One chose, at first, between science and superstition, only to discover that the choice came again in every minute of life.

In consequence Sharky feared he was leaving his father in the custody of a hostile army. Could one rely on its decency? The imam, whom, he saw, was tall as a building, was the prison sergeant who would never permit his charges to escape.

As they left the cemetery Nawaz gave the imam two one-hundred-rand notes which the man added to a plastic wallet that he kept on a string around his neck. Shakeer was reminded of the bargemen who collected coins from the eyes of the Roman dead.

Throughout the ceremony and afterwards his uncle seemed hardly to have been affected. Nawaz hadn't cried, nor shouted, nor appeared in any way impatient or surprised. He was perfectly untouched and self-contained inside his shell.

It was, Sharky judged, an effect of the man's narrow but powerful ego. The guy was unable to imagine that any other man's death carried certain implications for his own destiny.

Sharky still wanted to seize the steering wheel and push the other man out of the car, to beat his head against the window. He waited for his uncle to say a word, just one word to justify a response, but instead Nawaz spoke only to himself, under his breath, as they drove back to the house.

The other cars from the funeral cortège disappeared on the motorway. Just below the crest of the hill, on the hidden side, a cargo train was floating into the countryside, a line of long, thin rectangles which were dark paper against the horizon.

With the traffic the journey back to Westville took a good while. There was a call-in programme on the Indian radio station but the volume had been turned down so far that the speech was as indecipherable as his uncle's conversation with himself. Sharky concentrated on the rain marshalling over the city. It had spread from Clare Estate and Brooks Road to the Berea, doing nothing to reduce the malarial heat.

It was worse for many. One was constantly reminded of this South African fact. On the stony hill alongside the road an informal settlement clung to the slope. The plywood houses huddled back to back, like a crop of mushrooms, surrounding the big concrete base of a relay station. There was a concrete apron around one side of the station. It was fenced off by parallel lines of barbed wire.

A young man was bouncing a bicycle down the hill, staying impossibly upright after each collision, carrying a stack of newspapers in the basket. In the opposite direction an old man in a wheelchair proceeded up the snaking path, his muscular arms cranking away.

You could almost see the curve of his biceps from the road. He had tied some cartons of maize to the back of the wheelchair and was presumably going to sell them to the shack dwellers on the hill.

Many people at the bottom of the economic ladder supported themselves in this way. They sold, traded, bartered and haggled with people just as deprived as themselves. They got a few rands of profit.

Even the poorest had life. This obvious truth hit Sharky with the force of an explosion. Even the least of the least had energy, motion, breath, the vim to engage in commerce and thus to better their lot by some infinitesimal fraction.

Was it death which was the more terrifying to him, or was it poverty? Which was it that triggered the sensation of falling in his soul? Given the choice, would his father have moved to this lunar hillside rather than to the cemetery in Brooks Road?

Best that nobody was offered such a choice or we would all move into a slum, into the withered form of a paraplegic old man, into the brain of a millipede, rather than surrender all feeling. We would curse ourselves to survive. We would fall through all the levels of being and, given a choice, would never consent to non-existence.

Therefore it was best that, at the last, nobody asked our opinion.

Maybe it was best that he hadn't arrived in time to interfere with his father's decision ...

Nawaz had something to add. He had been preparing it, as seemed to be his usual practice, for several minutes.

"You must remember that your father, Shakeer, was a significant force in the political development of this country. People who had knowledge of the whole picture ranked Arif very highly. The shame of it, I must say, is that in this last year he was so bitterly disappointed with the condition of the country. My point, however, is that your father stood up when everybody was too frightened. This is still Africa, after all."

Nawaz checked in his mirror and frowned. Then he went on. "In that way Arif stood for all of us who have kept our eyes open and who have refused to be deceived by the superficial changes. It's still a small group of people who run things. Before it was white. Now it happens to be mostly black. Your father was the first in our community to understand that fact. I believe that this is what undermined his peace of mind. Towards the end he was not a happy man."

To his surprise Sharky now found that he didn't mind talking to Nawaz about his father, even in the past tense, because any possible conversation he could have with his uncle would be unreal.

As long as he was talking to Nawaz his father was still waiting in the bedroom for the car to arrive from the airport. As long as they could keep talking the past would not have hardened into permanence.

The past was a final draft, fixed on the page, but its completeness could be contested. The atmosphere of unreality around his uncle extended to his own thought and actions. No words which passed between them had been uttered. No event which one discussed with Nawaz had truly come to pass. Compared to this privilege politics was no obstacle.

Against his wishes Sharky admitted what had been troubling him. "I worry, Nawaz, that my father had fallen into a trap. I mean, the trap of beginning to hate Africa. He couldn't bear the pronouncements of people in government, particularly the ones he had once been on friendly terms with. Hundreds of thousands were dying as they came out with their debating points. He referred to what the President was doing as rolling the bones. Was it a slur? I don't think so. Bones were actually being rolled."

Nawaz smiled. He rolled down his window and then, when they came to a stoplight, reached over and rolled down Sharky's window as well.

Nawaz said, "Arif was critical because he had high standards. You know, he hardly spoke a word to me for ten years because I ignored his advice and didn't go for my accountancy certificate. That is when I left Standard Eight to earn for myself. But I never should blame him because you cannot blame somebody for their sense of disappointment with you. Everybody will say about your father that his love of the ordinary man, rich or poor, was immense. Not that he would make a parade of his feelings, of course. Not for all the tea in China."

"Yes. That's the odd thing," Sharky continued on a different line of inquiry. "He rated his own suffering very low on the scale. That rules out the possibility of his harming himself in any way."

Nawaz said, "In these cases the family is the last to know. Suicide is a great sin, as I said, according to our religion."

Sharky resolved something that should have been obvious from the minute he'd entered the bedroom. He hit himself on the forehead. If he had bothered to call Ginger she would have talked him down. It was just that they had been on the scene, and had been carried away by Nafisa's conviction. His mother had suffered through the past years. Therefore she couldn't see the facts of the case.

"But it wasn't suicide. It's psychologically impossible. My father was energised by the opposition of the government, despite the post-op complications. As you know, he was a natural stoic. He wouldn't take a Panado if he could avoid it. Think about the things he went through, our entire family went through, under the old government."

Nawaz offered no resistance. "No, I am sure you are correct. I am not going to argue with you on a day like this."

"I know that I am right. I am going to prove it."

They said nothing more. Nawaz went up the hill when he got to Argyle Road and the car skidded to a halt at the robot. Halfway up the bombed-out old suitcase in the back came undone. Old clothes spilled out onto the floor between the seats. Sharky reached back and tried to stuff them back in.

It was to no avail. The clothes were bundled into stacks that had slid under the seats. He saw a pile of schoolboy shirts, buttoned to their tough white collars and tied with string.

Something about the sight reached into him. It must have been the evident devotion with which the shirts had been strung together. Someone had gone to the trouble of tying them up. Someone, Nawaz, had expended his day on the shirts. It was breathtaking. Sharky pitied his uncle. He wasn't sure he had convinced him but he pitied Nawaz nonetheless.

At the same time Sharky waited for the opposite reaction. It didn't arrive. His pity was steady. He didn't want to avoid Nawaz as he had the cripple beside the Thomas Cook building. Nor did he want to push him out of the car as he had wished to do an hour before. Something quite different had happened. He was overwhelmed by the most profound sensation of reverence for his uncle.

The man did nothing, said nothing, to deserve his reverence. Yet Sharky felt that his uncle, his mother, his mother's family in general, possessed some store of Stone Age wisdom which let them manage the unalterable facts of birth and marriage, of illness and death.

They weren't entirely stupid. In fact they were entirely wise. Nawaz, amazingly, was a proprietor of this secret wisdom.

Yet his wisdom was unconnected to truth. For Nawaz wasn't accurate in much or any of what he cared to state. Nor was he necessarily sincere. It was difficult to judge the degree of insincerity in Nawaz's tone, as in his mother's, but it was undeniably present. No wonder his father hadn't spoken a word to Nawaz in so many years.

The issue between Nawaz and his father wasn't emotional. It was acknowledging a fact. They were no further apart now, with one dead and the other alive, than they had been a day before.

There was no point trying to communicate to Nawaz his realisation that the last thing his father would have done was shoot himself. Sharky saw it in a moment, just as his mind had changed about Nawaz. Some other person, for some other reason, had pointed that gun at his father. Only his mother, with her dark consciousness, imagined otherwise.

Beetles in her Head

~

IT WAS THURSDAY MORNING. NAFISA WAS AT ODDS WITH HER son, her worker, with Jadwat.

Between her and Shakeer was their disagreement about what had happened. Shakeer insisted she reconsider the circumstances of Arif's shooting. She was not prepared to do so. She couldn't believe that some unnamed person could have harmed her husband. Shakeer couldn't believe otherwise. But then her son had no real understanding of what had transpired the previous year.

Between her and Estella there was the need to test the girl. It had been her husband's wish that she get Estella on treatment if necessary.

Estella's chances weren't good. The numbers in this province for sexually active black women like Estella were the worst in the world, one in two. Nafisa wasn't looking forward to the conversation.

Between her and Jadwat there was Jadwat. Moreover there was some new sensation in her mind she couldn't completely identify.

The morning was busy. Life, or some weird imitation of it, was calling her. She was going back to the practice for the first time since the funeral. Kader, the accountant, was about to appear with a set of papers for her to sign. Govin Mackey would stop at the house on his way to work and drop something off.

Jadwat was returning to Richmond for the week. He was downstairs folding his shirts and packing them methodically into his old corduroy-skinned suitcase.

Like Jadwat Nafisa was packing, stacking her shoes in the boxes she had kept. When she was finished she would move them down to the bedroom at the bottom of the stairs.

Since the funeral she had been unwilling to return to her old bed. She couldn't imagine getting into the bed without Arif on the right-hand side. His weight on the mattress had reassured her. Without his presence the bed itself was unbalanced. She feared that she would fall off.

One of the nights Nafisa had tried to sleep beside Shakeer but the arrangement was unworkable on a twin bed. Neither had obtained a minute of sleep. It was her fault, not Shakeer's, who was not a restless sleeper. The odd sensation in her mind had kept her awake the better part of each night since the funeral. She couldn't work out what this sensation was.

Nafisa examined the heel of each shoe, putting aside those which needed to be mended. Several had to be restitched by hand. Some of the heels were missing or worn down. Estella could take them to the Greek shop in Davenport Centre next time she was in town.

The shop was presently run by a Pakistani man. The name people used had remained the same, as if it was a buoy held in place in changing water. The Greek had returned to Cyprus, Nicosia, after independence in 1994.

Nafisa missed his crusty character and, even more, their relationship. For the Greek had been affectionate towards her, fond of relating the one bit of wisdom which he had brought from Cyprus to humanity. If you keep a shoe in good condition it will last a lifetime ...

Suddenly Nafisa was certain that, at this moment, her husband was downstairs in the kitchen, murmuring through his piles of results and studies. While she was busy with her shoes he was applying his mind to a document on the laptop, pouring the first of his unending cups of tea from the kettle.

When he was concentrating on his writing Arif was in his own space. He refused to hear the doorbell or telephone and failed to see her if she appeared beside him. She could stand beside him for ten minutes and he wouldn't register her presence.

Now Nafisa's conviction strengthened. She was relieved to identify it at last. If she were to hurry through the house she would discover Arif beneath his crown of white hair, impervious to the kettle whistling, to the telephone ringing, to the dog scampering under the table, and to the beggar in a Muslim cap who came to the gate on a Thursday. She pushed the idea out of her mind.

She opened another box. It contained a packet of old banknotes. Its origin escaped her. She couldn't remember putting it there in the first place. The bills were printed on the bark-brown paper of the early 1980s.

In 1983 Arif had started talking against the government at meetings under the auspices of the United Democratic Front. Their home telephone had been tapped by the Special Branch. You could hear the clicks when you picked up the receiver. The police raided the house at five in the morning. They had confiscated all the books in the study. Nothing had been certain; whether Arif would be detained in a week, or whether she would go to work at King Edward in the morning as if she was any other doctor in any other part of the world.

In reaction – an odd reaction she couldn't explain to herself – Nafisa had started to collect *ooplung*, her black money which was coloured brown.

She put the packet back in the box. By dictate of the Reserve Bank the old currency was no longer legal tender. It was useless brown paper.

This fact, she decided, would have made her husband merry.

He made fun of money. Arif was an innocent but he had a great sense of the ridiculous. With such a side it was hard to understand how he could harm himself. He would have some motive beyond what was evident to her.

In other boxes there had been numerous mothballs, too many to hold in her hand. She would have to go down to the kitchen to dispose of them. Of course she didn't believe Arif would be there. She merely wished to replace the picture in her mind, in which he sat at the high table peering into the enchanted mirror of the Toshiba. The computer had gone to Jadwat.

When Nafisa went into the kitchen she went straight to the bin. She washed her hands to clean the traces of the mothballs. The soap was cold on her hands. She looked around the room which Estella had yet to clear up.

There was, of course, no beggar at the gate, no telephone call, and no sound from the kettle. The dog wasn't nosing along the bottom of the security gate, offended by the appearance of the bent black man who presented a cloth book in which he recorded each donation.

The beggar was a constant in her Thursdays. He produced a hardcover book for her to sign for each week's contribution. This volume, she suspected, was modelled on the Book of Deeds which would be proclaimed for each soul on the Day of Judgement. It declared the sum of one's positive and negative actions.

The absence of the dog struck Nafisa badly. She had fed him faithfully each morning, a brown stew which came out of a tin. His name, an Urdu word, had been given by Shakeer. He was a thick-bodied dog, short-furred except around his neck, and not noticeably affectionate.

After the funeral the dog had been carried off by Jadwat to his cousin's yard in Parlock. Jadwat had said that, at such a time, after such a thing, the house was no place for an animal.

Remembering these words choked Nafisa. Nobody listened to a word she said. The decision to cart the dog off had been made almost without the show of consulting her. But the creature was her first and only line of defence. They had no alarm and you couldn't rely on the security company to come when you called. She had been distracted by the funeral arrangements or she would never have permitted the dog to be taken away. Shakeer should have prevented it.

Nafisa held her son responsible. It was meaningless to blame Jadwat for this atrocity. He was merely an expression of the force which, given time and a free rein, would demolish everything permanent.

The Zulus, like Estella and Rose in the ward, would call Jadwat a tokoloshe. For who was it who changed the route of a river, who milked the cows in secret, who visited the virgins on the eve of their weddings, who riled up the bulls when their minders slept? But it was unfair to laugh at Jadwat. It was always unfair to laugh at a living creature.

Suddenly, with all her might, Nafisa missed the dog, the beggar, the drone of the kettle clattering amorously on the stove. They would never return. Her headache was stronger than ever.

She was about to do the logical thing and make a cup of Five Roses when Estella marched in. Nafisa didn't care to ask where she had stayed the previous evening.

"I thought I heard you laughing, Nafisa. I thought it was very strange. So soon after the funeral ..."

"No, I did no such thing. But there is a good deal of work to be done. I have just about finished packing my shoes. So, if you have a chance during the day, Estella, you can put them in the downstairs cupboard."

"I can swear somebody was laughing, Nafisa."

"Not in the least. I was here. You were not."

Nafisa couldn't recall laughing. Moreover it discomforted her that her interactions with Estella, despite the circumstances, verged on comedy.

The desire to cry turned on like a light at the sight of the girl. Their relations had changed. For what had Estella lost?

Estella was intact while she, Nafisa, was splintered. Her life had been punctured. In confirmation of this fact her headache sang loudly, an alien music in her mind which had become not one degree more familiar since it began playing in puberty. It was hurdy-gurdy music that made her want to cry out ...

"Do you know what I was thinking about? I was mad to let them take the dog to Parlock. I grant you, Dr Jadwat himself, who organised it, is as mad as a hatter. I never noticed it so much before in Jadwat. What do you say in Zulu about a person like that? I thought Jadwat was a tokoloshe."

"No, not that." Estella considered the question. She seemed pleased that they were able to talk. "You could say he has beetles in his head."

"Where did you hear that? I've never heard a Zulu person say that."

"That was the favourite expression of my grandmother. She stayed in the king's house at Nongoma. She was very dignified but she wasn't fond of children and the messes they created. When I did something wrong she would hit me on the head, not too hard, and say, 'Ukukwelwa amabhungane'. Which means, there are beetles in your head!"

"That's the perfect expression, Estella. I will remember it."

It was the perfect Zulu expression. She had never heard it before. Then the Zulus and the Indians, two cultures set side by side in Natal and once governed by the British, were deaf to each other. In this province, KZN, they were neighbours, their lives were entangled, yet they were as far apart as any two points on the globe.

There was nothing to be done about it; proximity only went so far, in life, and it wasn't so very far at all.

Nafisa opened the refrigerator. "Wait here a minute while I see if we need to defrost the fridge today. It's become worse than the garage."

You could hear the machinery starting up in the fridge. The light in the door blinked on, casting a glow on her hands. Nafisa compared it to the unholy glow inside a photocopier's lid.

Something in this glow, which heated the impasto strokes of her make-up, reminded Nafisa that she and Estella had hardly exchanged two words in a row in so many weeks. They hadn't attempted so much as the stub of a conversation. They had once been close – and how horrible to be further apart under these circumstances!

Nafisa knew that she was a bone in Estella's throat. She was tired of being a bone!

But there was one thing incumbent on her. She asked for Arif's sake ...

"Estella, don't you want me to do your bloods when I get back this evening? I can bring the injection. After all, you are a sexually active female in the most affected region of the continent. There is no shame in finding out if you are infected. Quite the opposite, in fact. Arif would tell you himself. If something is wrong we can put you on treatment."

"Why do you think something is wrong? I have not complained to you about anything, Nafisa. It is not your right ..."

"I don't think anything is wrong. Nothing is wrong. Of course nothing is wrong," Nafisa replied, feeling the insincerity of her words. "But I have learned, it is always better to be safe than sorry."

Estella too! The temperature between them rose so quickly. It was startling to see how angry the other woman was. She was so conscious of her right. For a moment Nafisa was frightened that Estella would hold her by the hair and force her into the open refrigerator. She felt the heat rise in her countenance.

This face! It stood between her and the world. It was the cause of half her disagreements with Estella. She blamed this face and would have liked to tear it off ...

Nonetheless Nafisa went on. Even as she spoke she saw that, as Arif had warned, she had waited too long to deal with Estella. She couldn't infuse her words with the necessary urgency. She was merely reciting them. In the past she had been too cautious to deal with Estella when her feelings were aroused. She could never be firm around Estella.

"Because God knows, we have no excuse not to test, not to know. Unlike the majority who exist in bewilderment – no thanks to the policies of this government – you, Estella, have the privilege of working in a medical household. If something were to happen, if tomorrow you were to develop Kaposi's or drug-resistant TB, think of how embarrassed we would be!"

It was Nafisa's final attempt. Yet with this statement she was aware that they had reached their usual impasse. She couldn't force Estella to discover her status. Estella couldn't force her to drop the question. The stalemate could go on forever. Strange as it was, there was some comfort in returning to a fixed position. They would always have each other!

Instead of pursuing the argument Nafisa stored the mail, Arif's mail, on top of the refrigerator. She recognised the journals by their covers: *The Lancet*, *SAMJ*, *Nature* and *New England Journal of Medicine*. Arif would have read them on the afternoon of their arrival, lying on his back on top of the quilt. He would relate the gist of the interesting articles to her. She couldn't bear to have them in the room.

After dealing with the mail Nafisa brought out the chops from the freezer. The packages were sealed, fogged by ice from the inside. The meat was grey. It wasn't in good condition.

How long did it last? It had been in there longer than she cared to remember since Arif had been mostly vegetarian since the operation. It might have to be thrown away. She sensed the not-yet-rubbery sensation of the meat through the clingwrap.

She handed each package to Estella. She didn't want to relinquish the topic entirely. But she dropped her head.

"Medicine has really changed since I was an intern. In the past five years alone, since once-a-day Sustiva appeared, our treatment options have improved. Today, if we know, we can do something. Even I take two capsules of Lipitor per day for my cholesterol. So it's up to you, Estella. Meanwhile, hold these. I want to have something defrosted for when more visitors come. One of these days it will be time to clean out this fridge."

The doorbell rang. The sound was so far away it belonged to another house in another district of the city.

"Nafisa, should I get it?"

"I'll go. It's probably the Thursday beggar."

Govin Mackey stood at the door. He was delivering the tupperware with a light blue lid that his wife had prepared. His wife had called ahead to warn her.

Nafisa was relieved to see Govin. His neat beard and haircut were as reassuring a presence as Shakeer and Estella. His eyes didn't quite focus on you as he talked. One looked here and the other looked there. They were almost grey, unusual in an Indian.

Govin was handsome in a way that men and women didn't resent, as if there was no masculine component in his character. At some point Nafisa couldn't define, Govin had graduated from being Arif's star student to being a member of the family.

Govin lifted the corner of the tupperware. "I don't know exactly what my wife sent, Nafisa."

The traffic of these pots and containers between Durban households was a good part of what created this current of family feeling. People cooked for each other. They sent things around.

Govin's wife's gesture affected Nafisa although she couldn't imagine putting a thing in her mouth. She had been light-headed for days but had managed to avoid people's efforts to make sure she was eating.

She took the tupperware in her hands and could feel that its contents were warm. There was some yellow rice, some potatoes, some kind of stew.

"You won't come in, Govin?"

"Unfortunately I have to be in court. I have to drive slowly because I don't want them to stop me and give me a fine. You know what the students did to my car week before last. I haven't had the chance to take it in to be fixed."

Nafisa said, "It's disgraceful what's happening in our country. Arif would say that to me almost every day until he could no longer bear to read the newspapers. Is there anything in them but misery and suffering?"

"And half of it is what we do to ourselves. More than half."

Then Govin was gone away and replaced by the Thursday beggar after all. The beggar stood there at the gate writing in his book while she went downstairs and rewarded him for his appearance with one of Arif's tattered old Pringle jerseys which had new leather elbows attached by Estella. Her husband never threw anything away if its usefulness could be extended. It was a point of difference in their marriage.

The beggar, who had hair like white grape leaves pressed close to his forehead, took the jersey doubtfully. He didn't try it on. Instead he folded his book into the red wool.

Nafisa said, "See if it fits first. I'll have more clothes for you when you come next Thursday. But I don't want them to be wasted."

On Nafisa's instructions Estella had aired out the cupboards and was going to take the professor's suits to the dry cleaner on Marbury Avenue, or the one in Davenport Centre.

Nafisa wasn't sure where or to whom to give her husband's clothes but she wasn't going to send them anywhere until there was not one button missing, not one unlaundered collar. The time had long passed to return things to their original condition.

The Thursday beggar vanished from the gate. She could hear him complaining outside the house as he pulled the jersey over his head. Estella had already gone down.

After a minute Nafisa followed her to her room. How stern she was!

"I forgot the ointment for your daughter. I picked it up yesterday. Bactroban, fifteen milligrams. It's the standard dose. And don't worry. I have already ordered the new course of tablets for the epilepsy. It's a good course. You'll notice that she hasn't had a fit in a long time."

As Nafisa handed Estella the Bactroban she noticed the handbag open on the bed.

"Do you have those shoes in your bag? As I have always said, our feet are the same size. You could have taken an old pair of mine – one I don't use, mind you – and saved yourself the money to spend on something better."

Nothing had changed ...

Since the funeral the house had been topsy-turvy. There had been no schedule, no rhyme or reason to the hours at which a parade of well-wishers had arrived at the door.

At first Nafisa had even been grateful on their arrival. The cares, small needs, and desultory conversation of the guests kept other thoughts from her until it was time to go to bed.

For she feared going to bed and avoided doing so as long as

possible. Lexotan did nothing to put her under. The guests distracted her from the prospect of sleepless hours. Somebody needed to fetch a child from Overport Secondary. Somebody had a rash on his neck and required an anti-histamine.

The house had cares of its own. The light in the garage had burned out, damaging the socket. Jadwat went to the Hypermarket to buy another and had promised to install it.

The key for the small telephone had been misplaced. It was only recovered after a lengthy search when Estella emptied the laundry basket, while doing the washing, and found the missing key at the bottom.

For the first time, after the appearance and disappearance of all these guests, the house felt deserted. Shakeer had stayed overnight at a friend's house in Pietermaritzburg. It was just the one evening he was away. Shakeer wasn't heartless. He hadn't abandoned his mother and would never abandon her. He had wanted to take some photographs of Oribi Gorge. She was happy that he had gone for a short time. He should be back at some point in the afternoon.

Nafisa found that she wasn't looking forward to his return. She didn't want to argue with Sharky about how far to prod the police in their investigation.

Was it better, somehow, if it was murder? Was it better if it was suicide? These were terrible questions to have to ask.

Her thoughts weren't consistent. She had her doubts about Arif's state of mind and wasn't ready for anybody, least of all her son, to push her into any conclusion about what had happened on that afternoon. At the same time to disagree with her son, to disagree with any person, was terrible.

The accountant, Ismail Kader, came by punctually at nine fifteen. First Kader had her read the terms of the death benefit provided by the staff medical aid. She hadn't known of its existence. It wasn't a large sum of money.

Nafisa could scarcely make out the type in the box on the form which was reserved for office use. It floated past her eyes and couldn't be resolved. Her dyslexia had gotten worse, not better, with age.

Nafisa had to concentrate to tell a *b* from a *p*, an *r* from the letter *t*. They turned around and gave the form the look of something which had been printed in a foreign alphabet. But the world was printed in a foreign alphabet ...

Kader noticed her expression. He was a tiny man, as sharp as a needle when it came to business, yet somehow always tired and dark underneath the eyes. It was true, she noticed, this early in the morning.

Nevertheless he said, "I can come to your practice at lunchtime, Nafisa, if it suits you better. Our offices aren't far apart since I moved. It can even wait until tomorrow. Or we can meet at Suncoast Casino. Have a look through the papers at your own pace, by all means. You read slowly. It isn't a sin."

He showed her where to sign. "Afterwards I can work out what is in your joint account and what money you have access to right away. I can give you a better idea of the lay of the land. When the tax guys come in I will have a formal response prepared. We don't want them to lay a claim against the house. But if you'd prefer I can postpone?"

She managed a smile. "No, Ismail. Like you, I'd rather have it finished and done. After all you took the trouble to come out."

"I think it's wise."

When Kader left with his papers the smile remained uncomfortably on Nafisa's face, as if she had wrenched her jaw out of shape. The same sensation accompanied her difficult exchanges with Estella.

It reminded Nafisa that she had been just as incapable of crying as of sleeping. It was a strange impotence, like being unable to sneeze, yawn, or hiccough. The tears had again built up behind her temple and caused her headache.

The memory of a black-and-white movie entered her thoughts. Many years before, in the afternoon, she had watched *Dam Busters* in a Knightsbridge guesthouse around the corner from Harrods in London. No doubt it was a trick of the mind yet she had no knowledge of harbouring this memory. It was a surprise to recover the recollection.

Arif had been detained at a seminar at Great Ormond Street. It was early in his career as an immunologist and he had come to Britain to report some interesting results about measles in African children. This was long before he became famous by isolating an African strain of the virus.

The film, to which she paid half her attention, portrayed the ragtag British bombing campaign against the Germans in 1943. One sequence struck her in particular. It showed the German dams faltering behind the detonation of the airborne mines and bending so slowly outwards, like a bow pulled back.

Michael Redgrave played the doctor attached to 617 Squadron. He was assisted by several British boffins, armed with slide rules and protractors.

When Arif returned from his seminar Nafisa was pleased to describe the boffins to him. It was something that interested her husband. He criticised the presentation of scientists in movies. It was a paradox. For all intents and purposes science was closed to non-scientists. Yet scientific research was the closest approximation to reality.

Therefore the advance of knowledge excluded the majority. If their condition was not blindness then it was like trying to see in an unlit passage.

According to Arif this fact explained the disappointments of democracy. Democracy didn't necessarily work. In the space between the people and the truth a thousand and one superstitions might be constructed. People would die on account of their superstitions. Yet, as far as he knew, not one man had sacrificed his life to determine the charge of the electron. It explained the last ten years of this country's history.

Nafisa had new doubts about Arif's theory. She wanted to convey them to him. But these doubts would remain with her. A marriage, her marriage, for all its faults, was a conversation which included all the topics of existence. One could not imagine such a conversation to be temporary, something which might one day run to its length like a tape measure.

She sat down at the table, feeling that she was about to be submerged by an angry tide. Let it take her. An image came of this ocean surging across the point where she had once stood. But now, what words had Estella used? She had beetles in her head ...

As if to prove it Jadwat came upstairs. He was carrying his suitcase with difficulty. The joints in his shoulder were inflamed again. It was too soon to inject him a second time. You erred on the side of caution when employing steroids. He was a diabetic, of course, which complicated the management.

Jadwat was returning to Richmond during the week for work reasons. His surgery had been shuttered for too long and his patients were making appointments with the other general practitioner in town. They were both going back to their patients who longed for them.

"Nafisa, why are you smiling?"

"No, I didn't realise I was." She got up from the table. "You are fully packed, Jadwat? You don't want to take some more food? People have brought so much that even the second freezer, in the pantry, is packed out. Govin just came with another tupperware."

"My trunk is full. I am going to have to put my suitcase on the passenger side. I don't like to put things on the back seat, Nafisa, because they will spill." Jadwat clapped. "Then you can forget it. You are finished when it comes to the resale."

They walked out to his car, which was gleaming. Jadwat had taken advantage of the idleness following the funeral to have the Mercedes polished and waxed by the dealer in Umhlanga Ridge. Nafisa compared the orange cheeks of Jadwat's car with the glow of a young woman wearing too much foundation.

The trunk was occupied because Jadwat had loaded it with the numerous studies and journals from Arif's office at the university. Metzger, appointed as director of the institute, had called for them to clear out Arif's property soon after the funeral. Shakeer had convinced Jadwat that something of interest might be found in these papers.

Although they had said nothing explicit about it in her presence both men believed it was impossible that Arif had taken his own life. They imagined they could figure it out before the police.

So the police were pretending to investigate. Let them pretend!

For who, without Nafisa's singular experiences, could imagine such a thing about Arif? Shakeer had not been around, could not calculate the effect of the operations on his father's spirits. And there was nothing Jadwat could calculate ...

In general the subject of her husband's death was too hot to touch. Nafisa couldn't approach the minute in which Arif had taken the pistol from her car. Was it coincidence? Could he have intended it to be their final conversation? She got there in her mind, got nervous, and turned away. She would think about it in a day, a month, and a year.

This year would be long with her thoughts. Shakeer, with his insistence, didn't understand her situation. Each day was long enough as it was. Each morning she was disturbed to wake up because it seemed impossible to get through the length of the day. There were too many hours.

Jadwat stored his suitcase on the back seat, strapping the seatbelt around it. He came around to her, hesitating before he got in.

"Yesterday, as we packed up Arif's office, Shakeer printed out for me all the emails and other files in Arif's document folder. When it comes to computers, you know that I am entirely useless. In that respect I am a man of the past." Jadwat was disconsolate, as tired behind his spectacles as the accountant. "I want you to know that I am going to pursue the story behind this wherever it leads."

"Read to your heart's content," Nafisa returned, closing the door.

"You'll greet Shakeer for me? If I find anything that bears on the case, that can give us some explanation of this catastrophe, then you and he will be the first to know."

"Tell Shakeer directly. If you think about it for a minute, Jadwat, no matter what you find in the documents folder, no matter what secret there is, Arif is gone."

She glowered at Jadwat, bracing his small legs inside the car. Who was he to exist?

Nafisa wanted to slap him so hard that his skin should redden after the blow, as if for once he was blushing.

But she mustn't judge. Jadwat, after all, was a midget. He was equipped only with a midget's understanding by which he reduced all things to his own dimension. There was nothing large in his soul. He hadn't loved his stupid and beautiful wife, as he had confessed, on their wedding day. One had to be big enough to love, as big as a barn ...

She said, "Make sure you call my secretary when you get to Richmond, just so I know you made the trip safely."

"I will call the minute I get in. I am going directly to the surgery in my tracksuit."

They parted on this unsatisfactory note. Nafisa watched the orange Mercedes make the turn onto the road with mixed feelings. It was true that on every subject her feelings were mixed but about Jadwat her feelings were especially mixed.

Shame! His life had been narrow. Jadwat didn't own the sheets on his bed. If a lady friend visited Richmond he put her up in the Montrose Guest House. He stayed overnight with his visitor in the single room without informing reception. In the morning he packed his corduroy suitcase full of bedding and took it out of the back door. Property, as he had often joked, was theft.

Nafisa smiled again, surprising herself, as Jadwat's car disappeared, testing to see if the discomfort in her jaw returned. She wondered what else travelled in that corduroy suitcase to Richmond.

It took Nafisa a while to remember where, weeks before, she had abandoned each of the items she would now have to take to work, as if she were resolving a picture in her mind which had been broken into pieces.

The Dewar flask stood on the wardrobe. Sharky had bought it on the internet from a distributor in Rhode Island in America. It accompanied her to the Afrox plant on Umbilo Road. They asked a fee of forty rand to refill it with liquid nitrogen.

She inspected the flask with a pang. It didn't hear. It didn't talk, cry out. It was immortal!

The liquid nitrogen was an everyday necessity in her work. It was used on imperfections and discolorations. One applied a drop to a patch of rough skin and could peel it off two minutes later. Half her job was mechanical – burning away a cancerous lesion, a thin brown wart or nodule, or scissoring a mole.

She had never enjoyed staying at home and could never have been a housewife. Work was interesting, more often than not the best hours of the day. She liked the flow of one patient, one small problem, into the next patient and next problem.

Nafisa supposed that this pleasure, like all others, belonged to the past. She couldn't say when the sunshine – Durban's unending tide of light from one January to the next – had last registered on her skin, or when something she put in her mouth had tasted of anything but cardboard. Music, which stimulated her feelings, was painful to hear even if it was playing in another room.

Indeed, when she changed and came down, she could hear that Estella had switched on the radio in Sharky's room while ironing. It was one of the African stations and, like Radio Lotus, the announcers had gaudy voices. Her father would say that such-and-such a person had money in his voice.

Nafisa found herself panting. She hadn't been steady in the face of music for more than a year. But she wasn't up to telling Estella to switch it off.

Estella had been preparing something for her daughter in the kitchen. There were several little pots on the boil on the small stove in the scullery, one filled to the lid with tomatoes and shedding the dark scent of sardines as if it was shy to do so. The brazen smell of the sardines reminded Nafisa that the house did not belong to her after a certain hour of the morning.

Nafisa's surgery was located on the seventh floor of Durban Medical Centre. From her office she could look out on Beatrice Street and the surroundings, from the racecourse to the Hindu temple, cellphone shops, and the hospital where ambulances were deployed at right angles inside the gate.

She had missed this view while she'd been away. It was full of activity. Vendors unloaded Cadbury's bars, packets of cigarettes, combs and magazines on blankets beside the gutter. She had often thought of buying a plastic comb from one of the sellers and presenting it to Jadwat when she was angry at him. What would he do with a comb?

When, on rare occasions, Nafisa walked out of Medical Centre she was struck by the smells of wet paper and urine hanging over the gutters. She paused to give coins to the beggars who set up camp in front of the garage and was reliably rewarded with smiles and prayers.

God created beggars, she imagined, to have one class of person who remembered his existence. Beggars, after all, were the only people who counted their blessings.

Below her surgery window the kombis sped through traffic, stopping instantaneously between robots to take on new passengers, shouting at pedestrians. She could almost hear them although she was too high up, on the seventh floor, for sound to travel.

On the corner the China New Territories fireworks importer had moved its crates onto the pavement. The green and white tubes of Catherine wheels, the gunpowder rockets bound in their dozens and sparklers in their wire cages were visible from the seventh floor.

Diwali was around the corner. Fireworks were legal again.

Only a minute was given to take in this scene. There was a phalanx of patients in the waiting room. Their ranks would never be exhausted. Their intent was to wear her out.

Patients would keep coming in, scheduling appointments, keep pressing against each other on the old leather settee even after she had passed on. Some young specialist would buy her practice, the patient list, and keep the settee in service. They would replace the legs of the settee which had mysteriously become stumps. The leather had once been black. Now it was almost brown. One day it would be white with age.

Her secretary came in.

"Nafisa, there's a patient who was waiting here when we opened the door. A Mrs Dhlomo. You saw her recently, before everything, and you had her tested. She is quite eager to get her results."

"Medical aid?"

"Her medical aid is through her husband. A Mrs Dhlomo."

"Yes, I remember. Would you bring me her file?"

"The file is right here." The secretary gave it to Nafisa. "You're sure you're ready to begin?"

"Of course."

The secretary said, "I can ask her to wait."

"Bring her in."

Nafisa read the file. The lab report was unambiguous. Where to begin? When she had started in practice her cases had been, eighty percent of the time, skin deep. She treated brides on their wedding days and B-movie stars, like Barbara Carrera, who were filming around Durban and had developed rosea or some other rash to be concealed from the camera.

The twenty percent of serious cases ranged from psoriasis to certain drug reactions, as well as the melanomas one found in fair-skinned Durbanites because of the sun.

Nowadays the ratio was reversed. The pattern of diseases was more racially pronounced than before. Eighty percent of her African patients tested positive. The corresponding figure was two percent for her Indian and few white patients. Before, in the old South Africa, race had been politics. Now race was medicine. And medicine was race, medicine was politics.

She felt the particular expression, which accompanied her words to this eighty percent, hardening on her face. It was as heavy on her as a mask.

"Mrs Dhlomo ... Millicent ... On the form you say you have been married for twelve years. Can I ask, do you have any children?"

"I have three in all, doctor. The oldest is eleven. My daughter is seven, and my youngest son has just entered Grade One."

"Your husband is close to them?"

"My husband sees us twice a year, doctor. On Christmas Eve he comes up from Durban with presents and stays until Boxing Day. Then on Easter, Simon – his Zulu name is Sipho – arrives in the evening and leaves the next morning. Would you believe, the past few weeks I have been staying with him in Durban, when I haven't been well, and that is the longest stretch we have been together since our marriage?"

"Is that so?"

"Even when I fainted Simon was very insistent that I do not come and see a doctor. He doesn't think anything is wrong. I hope the medical aid does not notify him."

Nafisa said, "It's a private consultation. As far as I'm concerned there is no need for your husband to be informed. Personally I believe that each person who comes forward and gets tested is doing a service for the country at large. I wish I could convince my worker to do the same as you have, Millicent. People won't listen. With the right attitude we could change this country overnight."

Mrs Dhlomo reminded Nafisa of a Victorian lady, with her bearing and the maroon scarf she wore across her shoulders. She couldn't have been more than thirty. She was nicely dressed to come to a doctor's office and hear her results. She wasn't like the usual Zulus who, in Nafisa's experience, were the roughest, the toughest, the proudest group in the country.

The Zulus were different from the Xhosas, Swazis, Tswana. They were conquerors. They had the rough attitudes of conquerors. Then, of course, as her patient proved, there were always exceptions to any rule.

Nafisa thought how Mrs Dhlomo, in her remaining future, would look back on this interview and recall the face of her doctor. She, Nafisa, would be seen as the representative of a terrible force ... someone who paid out her knowledge sentence by sentence instead of transmitting it at once.

But that was the fate of doctors. They brought messages. There was no right method to deliver such a message. There was something in this point which Nafisa was about to apply to her experience.

She consulted the chart instead. There was a protocol to follow.

"When you first came to me it was about the rash on your chest. I gave you cortisone, to assist the healing. I also suggested some tests. Given your history, given that you've been faithful to your husband throughout your marriage, it was only a precaution. Now the laboratory has come back. I am very sorry to say that your results are positive. You have been infected."

Mrs Dhlomo sat perfectly still. Then she put her handbag on the desk and opened it. She searched, brought out a polaroid.

"These are my children, doctor. My oldest son, the eleven-year-old, Godfrey, is on top. What will happen to them?"

Nafisa took the photograph. "Your children are almost certainly not infected because this infection is of a much more recent date, otherwise we would not be sitting here discussing it. This is not a death sentence for you, Millicent. We have good drugs to manage it. We are in a far better position than we were just two years ago. At St Augustine's they have money from the European Union to fund anti-retrovirals, once we get you on the list. I have to ask the same question again. Is there anyone besides your husband?"

Mrs Dhlomo shook her head. "My husband is the only man I have contact with, once in six months." She took the photograph back, put it into the handbag, and replaced the bag on her lap. "To be honest, this news does not come as a surprise. I knew Simon was not faithful. I am very angry with Simon. I am very angry. But I am not surprised."

Yet Nafisa saw no sign of anger. You might imagine there were many reactions to such news. Under most circumstances the endless variety of people's minds presented in her surgery astonished Nafisa.

In this one situation, however, she saw nothing to distinguish one from another. It was not an individual predicament. Every person who stepped into her surgery knew ahead of time what she was going to announce to them.

The laboratory merely confirmed what was understood by subliminal means. The Day of Judgement would also be devoid of surprises.

She asked, "Are you going to pick up the prescription now?"

"I might as well, doctor. I don't know when Simon will bring me back to town."

"In that case I will come with you downstairs. Here's a good chemist in the building. Many of my patients use him."

Abandoning her other patients Nafisa walked Mrs Dhlomo down to the chemist on the ground floor. If she went along she ensured her patients got a discount or, if necessary, she could credit their purchases against the samples she collected from Novartis and Glaxo reps and gave to Moonsamy to sell or use in his own business.

She wasn't systematic about whom she helped by going down to Moonsamy's; sometimes she chose one person who was less deserving instead of another. Arif was better, a rationalist, who thought about people in their tens of thousands rather than one by one.

Moonsamy's assistant, a boy in a long blue shirt and denims, unlocked the grille to let them in. He locked it behind them. The two fluorescent bars on the ceiling flickered in unison. Pressing on her handbag, Nafisa wrote out the prescription on her official pad.

As she finished she noticed a gun kept on a shelf behind the counter. The presence of the thing irritated her. It was an insult. She could only think of Arif in the bedroom.

What had her son said years ago? If you put a gun into a play the gun is sure to go off before the end of the play. It was a principle of composition.

"Should that be lying around in full view, Mr Moonsamy?"

"On the contrary. It's intended to be in full view of everybody. After all it is there for deterrent effect."

The pharmacist was a short man who hardly appeared above

the counter when he was at the back of the shop. His head was large, leathery, coloured a rich brown on top.

Nafisa was struck by how earnest Moonsamy was. He had come to the house after the funeral, managing to be more grave than anybody around him. He was overly solid, especially compared to her. She was volatile. His mood was inertial, refusing to move off in any direction.

Nafisa associated the man with his name. She often thought, in her surgery, of his head shining above the counter many floors beneath her. Moonsamy possessed a lunar complexion, with a scattering of discolourations on his cheeks. She had offered to treat him many times but he declined.

Moonsamy talked as he mixed chemicals for Mrs Dhlomo's prescription behind the counter.

"I keep a gun in sight out of necessity, although it is not strictly part of my religion and my philosophy of life," he explained. He was drawing the liquid out of a vial, squinting to see the fine grey lines on the side. "Day before yesterday, Nafisa, was the third time I have been held up since the start of the year. Three times in three months, can you imagine? The prisoners stroll freely through the gates of Westville Prison. These people know that they have nothing to fear. They can be out in a week if they bribe a guard. That's if they do not have DStv already in their cells."

Moonsamy paused and then, as if the conclusion was original, repeated words she heard once a week from somebody or the other. "Nobody is looking after things, Nafisa. In our country nobody is in charge. Therefore I have to be prepared to defend myself. I am sure you can sympathise with my feelings."

She was more interested in the gun which seemed to look in her direction. "You know how to shoot, Moonsamy?"

"I haven't bought the bullets yet. As I say, it's for deterrent effect."

On a whim, not wanting to return to her surgery and feeling unexpectedly attached to her patient, not wanting to let her go, Nafisa walked Mrs Dhlomo to the corner of Beatrice and Pine Street. She had the same impulse around her patient as sometimes overtook her around her son – she wanted to maintain the same distance between them, no more and no less than was comfortable.

They waited for a kombi in front of the Kennedy Fried Chicken, which was a local imitation of the international chain. A customer opened the door to let a tide of hot air bearing the odour of heavily salted and cured chicken rush upon them. It was strong enough to make her gag.

It was unusual to be outside in the midst of Durban. In common with the other doctors in the building, Nafisa didn't often set foot on the street. It was too dangerous, too disordered, too African.

Instead she drove into the garage beside her office and drove out by seven in the evening when the guards went off. She tried not to stop on the corner of Commercial Road where once, while waiting at a red light, her window had been smashed and her handbag seized right out of the car.

Twenty years ago it had been safe to do errands around town. She'd paid in cash for the mains at the municipality and deposited the receipts from her practice at the Barclays branch without fear of interception. Today reality was larger, more sour, more unpredictable. Reality was likely to push a knife between your ribs.

Things were bad. They were very bad in Durban. Equally there was always someone worse off than you, in Durban, in Africa, not a stone's throw from your present location … some someone without legs, hands, a face, someone without a minute of life remaining. All conditions were relative. This fact meant Nafisa would not be comfortable in London, Perth, or San Diego, destinations to which many of the local doctors had emigrated in the past few years.

At the same time she was at a loss to put into words what

consoled her about this ladder. She could no longer be sure of her position on some particular rung. Why had she been sure that she was near the top? Why had she banked on it? For there was the certainty of dislodgement. Indeed she had been dislodged ...

And it was Arif who had dislodged her. Nafisa felt the keen edge of her shame. It rose inside her. She had been waiting for it to appear since before the funeral. She would never be free of this shame because her husband had murdered himself! His action had brought her low, lower than Estella or Millicent Dhlomo, and lower than Moonsamy himself.

Now she understood. It was impossible that Arif would so have disfigured her existence. He wasn't such a person and didn't contain such an action. What was wrong with her? What was wrong in her view of her husband? Was it, in fact, her view of herself which was cockeyed?

Shakeer was correct. He had been right to argue with her. She should have understood this as soon as she had entered the bedroom. She would have to inform the police. They still had contacts from the old days.

Nafisa went over her instructions.

"Two sulphur tablets, twice a day, and two tablets of Bactrim in the mornings, until your next appointment. Meanwhile, Millicent, you'll speak to your husband about the situation. We need to find out when he was infected and who he could have passed it on to. Believe me, I know it is a difficult conversation to have. But, in my experience, all real conversations are difficult."

A kombi found them and braked. The driver rolled down the window on their side and exchanged a few words in Zulu with Mrs Dhlomo. He instructed one of the passengers to slide open the door.

There must have been eleven people in the back of the kombi. Nafisa noticed the loudspeaker mounted on the roof of the vehicle, as if it were a goddess on the prow of a ship. Wires ran from the speaker along the roof and into the cabin.

"Get in. Get in. We don't have time to spare." The driver inspected Nafisa. You couldn't see much of him behind his big brown sunglasses and Clicks cap. You couldn't even tell what race he was. But she could see that he was as small as a jockey. It was appropriate given his occupation. "You, madam, are you coming along for the ride?"

"No. I was just waiting with my patient."

He waved her back. "Then step away. I don't have time to spare."

The dented doors of the kombi had nonsensical slogans and boasts painted in silver strokes: "Dr Death's Mad Hatters", "Just for Pleasure Call 079 1454 ...", "Lion Roars ...", "Oscar's Party", "Umzinto Spa" and, in much smaller lettering underneath the driver's door, "Hubcaps Available at Cost. Enquire within."

Kombis and coffins were the most ornate objects on the continent. The drivers, or owners, decorated them to death. It made sense. Arif had often said that, given the way the taxis drove, they were interchangeable with coffins. Coffins and kombis took you to the same place. There were shootouts in the taxi ranks between rival companies.

Mrs Dhlomo got inside and sat on the bench. She touched the cross which hung around her neck. She was a delicate woman in a van of tough passengers. It was astonishing that she was allowed to live.

"Thank you for all your help, doctor. I will talk to Simon. I am sorely tempted to kick him yet I am a peaceful person."

Nafisa shook her head. "Husbands are very difficult."

She couldn't say what prompted her to make this remark. However she didn't think Mrs Dhlomo had heard what she said. The kombi disappeared into the traffic going up the hill.

Nafisa walked back to her surgery past the arcade lined with carpet shops and travel agents. A cellphone vendor was installing a neon sign above the narrow entrance to his store.

In the Indian quarter, Sharky said, Durban had the feeling of a souk. He had once tried to take photographs of this section of town but he couldn't make them specific. The shots resembled nothing so much as Tunis or the black and Arab marketplace in Zanzibar. It was not surprising. Religious men in white caps stood arguing softly in the doors, and bullying their shop boys. They recognised her, nodding their heads.

Nafisa paid them no attention. Her conversation with Mrs Dhlomo had stimulated a surge of anger inside her. It was directed at, of all people, her husband. She was suddenly white with fury against him. Her hands trembled with rage.

But what reason did she have? Well, what reason did Arif have? Could he have shot himself? He could never have done such a thing to her.

True, Arif had been supremely bad-tempered since his last operation. He was certainly apt to do stupid things when he was angry. During his preparations for the law suit, Arif had argued with her instead. It was uncharacteristic. Clearly his mood had been disturbed after the surgery. She should forgive ...

But in this looking-glass world how did you forgive the dead for being dead? How could you forgive the sick for their sickness, the poor for their poverty?

It was part of human nature, she suspected, to punish weakness in others. The dead were merely the weakest of all. They had lost their place. For this it was difficult, if not impossible, to forgive them.

In her office, before she could collect her thoughts and begin with her next patient, the phone rang. It was Kader, the accountant.

"You have a minute? Here's an interesting question which only you will be able to answer. The tax guys came back to me, Nafisa. It seems that in the past few months, especially with all the concerns about terrorism, our Receiver of Revenue has begun to share information with the banks in London and vice versa. As far as I can tell, that seems to be what triggered the investigation into you. It goes back to that. They are interested because all the money in your London account – which you weren't supposed to have there in the first place, needless to say – was withdrawn as one lump sum."

"I don't understand."

"If the transaction goes over a certain limit then the bank is obligated to send a notification to the regulators. And that notification is what came back to Pretoria and raised a red flag in the tax office."

"No, that's impossible. Hold on a minute, Ismail." Nafisa paged through her chequebook for want of something to do with her hands. If it had been any other day in her life she would have been sick at the disappearance of so large a sum. "Nobody even knew of the existence of that account besides Arif and myself. As my husband, certainly Arif had access but he was not interested in money matters."

"In any case could it be Arif?"

Nafisa said, "But he hasn't been in London this year. How could he travel, sick as he was? Besides, if I gave Arif money, he would have lost it, or given it away, or lent it to somebody at the university by one in the afternoon. Then he would have to borrow money for a sandwich in the cafeteria. Arif would always leave money matters up to me. Frankly, Ismail, I can't make head or tail of this. I don't get the statements sent to me directly anymore for the obvious reason. If it's not sitting there somebody must have taken it, which is impossible."

"The tax guys want some explanation," Kader said. "But if it wasn't you it was Arif. Only what use could he have had for it? As you say, the man could live on the smell of an oil rag."

"No, it's impossible. The one thing can't be connected to the other."

Kader said, "Well, we must come up with something to tell the tax guys that they are prepared to believe. They don't like to see money vanishing into thin air. It's their professional religion to follow money from place to place. Now I don't mean to intrude into your affairs, Nafisa. I have always maintained the policy that what you decide is my business, that is my business – and what you don't tell me is your business entirely. In this country can an accountant believe anything else? But we must have the facts."

"We all want the facts, Ismail."

Kader went on. "One more thing. It only stands to reason that this would be connected with Arif's death. I am starting to believe Jadwat was right to argue there was something untoward about this. Nafisa, we must find out about that money and who has got their hands on it. Fifteen, twenty thousand pounds ..."

The trapdoor in her looking-glass world opened again, underneath her feet, and Nafisa saw herself spinning head over heels into another tunnel.

Fool's Mate

~

THE POLICE WERE PRETENDING TO BEGIN THE INVESTIGATION. Two constables from the Westville station were rounding up the usual suspects. They parked on the driveway of the house while they interviewed the servants in the nearby residences.

The police, under a new government, thought along the old lines. They planned to question the black workers in the neighbourhood, their families, friends, and boyfriends. They canvassed the bus station, the taxi rank beside the motorway, tea rooms, and spaza shops.

The police pretence, the irrelevance, disturbed Shakeer. They didn't connect the facts. There was no relationship Shakeer could see between the London bank account and the workers in Westville.

Looking outside Shakeer resented the presumption of the white police van with its rusted and barred windows. It intruded on him. They should have put it on the road.

The Opel was a tiny van, hardly taller than a child. It was a toy van compared to the officious Ford Explorers which transported guards around San Francisco's dockland. One couldn't take it seriously as a vehicle of authority.

The modest size of the van disconcerted Shakeer. His heart sank to look at the thing. It involved him in a vulnerability he didn't wish to admit. If it was there, in the driveway, should it not be more imposing? If the police were pretending to authority, shouldn't the pretence be more absolute?

Time improved nothing. If anything the situation was more cruel in its action upon them than it had been a week before. The uncertainty about his father insinuated itself into every other fact in their lives. His own feelings, as much as those of his mother, found no definition so long as their subject was indefinite. In this way the obscurity surrounding his father's actions had surrounded Nafisa and him as well. It prevented some image from developing beneath his eyes.

The doorbell rang. Not wanting to see anybody Shakeer went on the veranda and then into the garden. There had been five minutes of rain just after the constables had arrived. But the clouds, if there had been any to bring the rain, had burned into a long blue sky.

The jacarandas along the side of the garage looked fresh. His mother had replanted them when they moved to Westville. Nafisa hadn't wanted to leave them behind in the yard of the old house. This action struck him as representative of her character.

After a few minutes Estella followed him outside. She was wearing an old apron of his mother's. It had rubber loops over the shoulders.

"Sorry, Shakeer, they are asking me to go down to the police station. They want to take my fingerprints."

"They can't be serious. What do you have to do with all of this?"

Sharky went to the front door to argue with the constables. There was a young white man in charge. Although he was not impolite, he refused to budge about Estella.

The young constable had a pompom of yellow hair, rawhide complexion, and spoke in an Afrikaans accent, unusual in Durban. He must be from the South Coast, perhaps Pennington or Amanzimtoti, or from as far down as Shepstone. He couldn't be older than twenty-five.

Not for the first time it struck Sharky how young such white men could be in South Africa. They had no knowledge of another country, and another politics. They had lost privileges and recreated their innocence. They were the lucky ones. The accounts had been cancelled.

Even while Shakeer was irritated he wanted to take the constable in his arms. But it would be too great a surprise.

"The superintendent, Mr Gumede, gave us the instruction to bring her in. He specifically wanted to talk to her. If you would like, you can come down to the station and lodge a complaint. Or you can make a telephone call."

"Well, maybe I will do just that."

"Maybe you will."

Estella didn't object any further to the proceeding yet it was painful to watch as the other constable, a black woman, loaded her into the back of the van. Estella had been a favourite of his father's. He would be horrified to see this happen as a result of his death.

How stifling it was, South Africa! How repetitive! Middle-class opinion held that, in every case, there was always somebody on the inside. Somebody opened the gate to the intruder. Somebody gave away the location of the safe. Yet this somebody, this white Opel van, these interviews around the neighbourhood, had no application to the matter of his father's death.

In life, his father had been protective of Estella. The professor had extended his interest to her daughter whom he had recently diagnosed with epilepsy. While in hospital, waiting for a kidney donor to turn up, he had read up on the new guidelines for management of the disease in children.

The professor was jealous of his work. Estella was the one person who had been allowed to sit opposite him at the table as he typed on the computer, his countenance crisscrossed with thoughts.

Even in St Petersburg, where he once stayed in the student hostel of a mathematics institute, Shakeer had never met another man who thought into reality with such great concentration. Whereas his own attention tended to wander from subject to subject and then right into the blue.

No wonder the old man disapproved of interruptions! His father, in his sixties, had been in a hurry. His research was years behind schedule, centuries behind the progress of the epidemic. Hundreds of thousands of preventable deaths and a greater number of preventable infections occurred annually. The Health Minister held up experiments through the Medicines Control Council. She argued that the idea that there was an African strain of the virus was defamatory of Africa.

The government blamed the International Monetary Fund, the Central Intelligence Agency, centuries of racism, for the epidemic. But they hardly expected their excuses to be believed. They were simply in a position where it was not important what others believed. This was an intoxicating position.

To cap it off the Minister of Health, in cahoots with Sekolo and Metzger at the university, had filed a defamation suit against the professor. The first hearing had been scheduled for the week after his father's retirement. It had preyed on the professor's mind. Doctors didn't like to be mixed up with lawyers.

Nafisa complained to her son in Papua New Guinea that, on occasion, her husband mixed her up with the Minister of Health. Sharky could well imagine his father's arms stiffening and colour coming up in his cheeks.

Unlike his mother, Shakeer couldn't take such expressions of a bad temper seriously. There was nobody he wished to vanquish. The idea of winning his point against another person dismayed him.

However, there was one argument Shakeer would have liked to have won. He would have liked to convince his mother to stay away from work for a longer time.

Nafisa was already back at her surgery, seeing twenty and thirty patients in an afternoon. Despite his objections she preferred to be busy. It wasn't a good idea. A doctor's work was demanding, mechanical, tough on the mind.

His mother was not a psychological person. She refused to step back and survey the canvas in its entirety. Each minute of life some small worry came along, occupied her attention, and prevented her from seeing the main point.

Sharky called her at work.

"Can you believe the police are taking Estella's fingerprints? They are scarcely running an investigation of their own. All they have figured out is what we told them in the first place. They know a sum of money disappeared in London. What do they think she had to do with it? Do they suppose it's a red herring?"

His mother's response surprised him. "They have to do their job. Let them, Shakeer. Since they know about the money they have every reason to investigate. Estella will survive. You know, and I know, and they know, the police are useless in this country. If they ever find the right answers it is by accident. I wash my hands."

"How will Estella get back here?"

"She will walk back to the house when she finishes. I don't believe there are any taxis which come in our direction. Estella is used to it. You forget how poor people live in this country."

"Yes, but it's hot outside. From the station it's almost two miles."

There was a call on the other line. Nafisa said something to her secretary. Then she came back.

"Three point two kilometres. Look, Shakeer, if you don't want her to walk, then by all means pick her up from the station. You can see MacDonald Gumede when you are there. Give him my regards. You don't remember him from the old days? He will remember you. Take your father's car. Jadwat was the last to drive it when his car was still at the dealer. I believe he left the keys in the drawer. Just as you enter the house, on the left, that cupboard."

He asked, "Work is okay? You're all right otherwise?"

"I am quite well, thank you very much."

He saw that his mother had repelled his question. In all this time she hadn't said a meaningful word to him about his father and about the investigation. It was as if she didn't care about the mystery of the shooting.

In general Nafisa didn't want people to be concerned with her feelings and would not allow them to be tested. If one were to set a mirror before her she would immediately shatter it. In this way his mother typified the country. It resisted self-consciousness.

Shakeer drove down to the station on Beech Street. It was surprising how deserted the suburban streets were in Durban.

There was a car guard, a young woman, wearing a padded orange jumper to signal her occupation. She wore canvas shoes which were taped together at the toe. The lapels of her shoes had many holes but no shoelaces.

Shakeer waited until the guard came over to him. He noticed that the car guards were everywhere now in Durban, from the beachfront out to the northern suburbs and surrounding towns like Hillcrest and Kloof. It wasn't bad to have them. In their presence you were less likely to be accosted, have your wallet snatched, a screwdriver levelled at your neck, or your car taken at the point of a gun.

He gave the woman a two-rand coin. He noted her reaction, then added another coin. She must have children at home. To him the coins, thin as cheese parings, were as meaningless as words in a foreign language.

"You will take care of my car? It belongs to my father and I don't want anything to happen to it. I am nervous leaving it out here in the first place instead of in a parking garage."

She smiled and he saw she was missing her front teeth. "Don't worry, sir. It can be here for a thousand years and nothing will happen to it. You can rely on me. I am a Christian."

Sharky was going to say, "I don't know if a Christian is necessarily the right person to defend a car," but he thought better of it.

He walked along the block and went into the station. There were a few policemen standing around in sagging dark blue uniforms, looking bored or talking on the telephone. One prisoner was being held in shackles. No one was attending to the man. Sharky didn't see Estella.

Without being challenged Sharky followed the sign up to the superintendent's office on the second floor. MacDonald Gumede had been placed in charge of the investigation.

Sharky had only the slightest recollection of the man although he knew something of Gumede's career. In 1988 Gumede went into exile in Lusaka. He was just in time to participate in Operation Vula, the last effort the external wing staged in the closing days of the old government.

Vula was a plan to seize power in case the transition was delayed. Gumede, who had been a printer in Empangeni, had disappeared on the morning his illegal printing press was discovered by the Special Branch. He fled to a safe house in Maseru until amnesty could be arranged. As a reward for his service Gumede had subsequently been appointed to the position of inspector and then Westville Superintendent.

The new superintendent seemed pleased to see him. There were old loyalties to his father. Gumede's office was sparely furnished. An electric fan stood unplugged beside a socket. A transparent runner had been placed over the brown carpet.

Gumede filled two glasses of water from a jug and moved one over to his visitor.

The superintendent had prepared a speech of sorts. "I believe they have finished with your worker. She is in the charge office. I understand you were displeased that Estella was brought down here but it was only procedure. So long, let us take the opportunity to become acquainted again. What do you say?"

Shakeer nodded.

Gumede said, "Before I used to be very close to the professor. Most of what I understood about scientific socialism I learned from Arif. I mean Marxism."

"But he was never a communist. People misunderstand that fact. He didn't like the leap of faith. There was no positive evidence for communism, as opposed to socialism and parliamentary democracy."

Gumede said, "Well, you couldn't be open about your principles in those days, whether you were a communist or not a communist. We can agree that, with his political ideals, it is unlikely he should have taken his own life. Ultimately I must convince the attorney of this province to open a docket. But I am starting to believe that the facts are on my side. If you look at the powder burn there is some suggestion that your father was not holding the gun."

"I have no doubt in my mind."

Some signal Sharky couldn't decode flashed in Gumede's expression. "You know that I met you once when you were still a teenager? In fact you beat me at a game of chess."

Sharky didn't remember the match. He said, "I don't often lose."

"Oh, I can believe it." Gumede leaned back in his chair, more comfortable at the turn he had engineered in the conversation. "The odd thing is that I was not a bad player, those days. When I was very young – I am speaking about the time before I started in the printshop – I spent more than a year in detention where we had nothing to do but to play chess and talk about Marx and Engels, Lenin, Fanon. You must know the cliché that detention was the university of the movement? We argued for hours about the merits of Flight Lieutenant Jerry Rawlings who was then President of Ghana. After the discussion I would take out my chessboard, a travelling set with magnetic pieces."

"And so?"

"Today, Shakeer, the very guy on whom I sharpened my chess skills – who was a devotee of Lenin and Kropotkin – that same fellow keeps a Bentley Spirit in his Houghton garage. However, if you ask that guy, he will tell you he is still a dialectical materialist, that not for a minute has his faith wavered. Your father was correct to say that, after the changeover, we allowed the system to make us in its own image. I agree with many of his criticisms, many of them, although I may not have made them in the same tone of voice. But here I am rambling on."

Sharky had become increasingly impatient. "Do you mind if we talk about the case? It would be convenient for the powers-that-be to publicise this as a suicide. My father, as you know, had powerful enemies."

"None that I know of," Gumede replied quickly. "However, I take your point. The one thing I want to convey … Just because the police force is now run by Africans, do not assume we are incompetent. One lesson we can take from our history is that many people, even certain black people, cannot stand to live under a black government. There are too many stereotypes of Africans afoot: that Africans plunder, Africans rape at the drop of a hat, Africans cannot be trusted to control our instincts. That is what our real struggle is against."

"I would have thought your real struggle is against murder. Incompetence doesn't have a colour."

Gumede said, "But when we see incompetence we must ask ourselves why we notice it, after all, how we identify it, what are its distinguishing marks. It's not as if the old government was any better."

"There we can agree."

Gumede produced a binder from the top of his desk. He opened it and sorted through the contents, taking out various documents and photographs, sliding them over to Shakeer as if he were moving a bishop down the board.

Sharky examined the fingerprint charts, telephone logs, notes on the scene, and the coroner's report. He wanted to vomit. Anywhere else in the world, even in Oakland, California, you would scarcely be sorting through the file concerning the death of a member of your own family.

But this was a looking-glass society. Nobody and nothing was in charge. His nausea dissipated on remembering this fact. Shakeer saw that he had never been truly at his ease anywhere else on the planet ... in Guadalupe, Mauritius, Mexico City, in Santa Fe, wherever else his assignments had taken him.

He didn't like to be under somebody's thumb. Some people were born through the looking glass.

"What's this supposed to be?"

Gumede looked at the print as if he was seeing it for the first time.

"This is the impression we took of a footprint from the driveway. Of course, being Durban, the property has tyre marks and footprints which it would be futile to investigate. That one I discovered out of the way, across from the pool, where somebody, at some point, could have jumped over the wire."

Gumede turned the photograph around so that it was facing him. "Looks like a woman's shoe, doesn't it? Could be nothing. Could be vital information. Could be Estella's." Gumede looked over his spectacles. "Let's say we rule out suicide, then do you have suspicions of your own? Who do you think benefits?"

Sharky didn't think he could say a word to the superintendent. He didn't want to argue, to stand up for himself, to supervise the interest of his family in pursuing the investigation. He was unalterably weary and could scarcely respond to the other man's questions. He wanted to lie down at the foot of Gumede's desk.

He went back to something. "I really can't let you get away with something, Gumede. You will admit that my father had enemies. I would put the Premier on top of the list. Then there's the vice chancellor who prosecutes professors for criticism. I mustn't forget the President who, apparently, wants to be a medicine man for the country, who doesn't believe in logic and science, only in politics and magic. Did you think he was going to forgive my father for pointing that out?"

"Let me ask one question since you're here. You have a good relationship with your uncle? I mean your mother's brother."

"Nawaz is from another planet. The laws of his self-created world are crazy to begin with. But do I think he has anything to gain? No, I don't. He had no involvement with the London money. Nobody did, as far as I know. In my opinion it's an absolute red herring. This has to do with politics."

"In that case let us continue."

They went through the rest of the folder in ten minutes. There was little which Sharky had the training to understand. The pathologist's report was detailed, with a photograph of the wound clipped on the corner and a handwritten note on the deceased's medical history.

The report was signed by Chris Labuschagne, a name Sharky remembered without being able to place the man. Had Labuschagne worked with his father on purifying the virus? His father and Labuschagne, if he remembered correctly, had been the first to isolate the variant of the virus which was heterosexually transmitted in sub-Saharan Africa. The government objected to the experiment. The President believed there was no such virus in the first place. But the President had no control over his own beliefs.

Gumede continued. There was a note on the bullet's trajectory in small and painstaking writing, a photograph of the gun which was framed in the shot by two rulers, a photostat of the licence, and a printout from Barclays on his parents' account. Sharky had little sense of his family's financial arrangements.

Neither did his father. It wasn't like the professor to handle money in any form. Once, when they had happened to be in London at the same time, Sharky had needed to take the Underground across the city, from Shepherd's Bush to King's Cross, to rescue his father who didn't have the money to buy a ticket. Finding his father in King's Cross station was a trivial task, by virtue of his unearthly mop of white hair. There was nobody in the world whose hair was that colour.

Across the table Gumede put on his hat. Sharky saw that the man was restless. Something which had been troubling him came to consciousness. The policeman, clasping his beribboned brown hat, reminded him of Morgan Freeman.

The resemblance, now he identified it, was striking. It made Shakeer uncomfortable to have found the comparison. He wasn't taking the situation seriously enough. He had lost a father and was therefore without a protector in the world.

Gumede began to replace the photographs in the folder, checking the numbers in the corner of each one against the notations in the folder.

"You know, Shakeer, I have remembered the circumstances of the game of chess I said we played so many years ago. You must have been thirteen, fourteen, at the time. Your father was high up in the movement, meeting in secret with Senator Edward Kennedy and the bishops. That was the eighties for you. I was a mere organiser. Your parents said for me to stay in the house because the Special Branch was looking for me. You beat me in three minutes straight and with a fool's mate of all things! I have a bone to pick about that. When you are dealing with an experienced player, isn't it considered to be an insult to attempt a fool's mate?"

"I always try it first," Sharky replied after he had a chance to think. "If it doesn't work, then I try something else."

Gumede rose to his feet. He was, for no obvious reason, radiantly happy, as if he had heard some piece of news for the arrival of which he had been desperately hoping.

He shook Sharky's hand, and said, "You would make an excellent policeman, my friend. I wouldn't have been able to say the same for your father, who had no cunning in him whatsoever. That may be what caused his disillusionment in later days. Also, apologise to Estella for the inconvenience in coming here. She is quite beautiful, isn't she?"

"You won't get anywhere with Estella. She likes younger men."

That evening an old friend of his mother's was celebrating a *mawlud* in Stanger, forty-five minutes outside the city.

The ceremony was bound to be raucous. It marked a Muslim saint's birthday and there was likely to be heavy music, singing and even dancing.

Nafisa's friend, and her family, were sufis, Muslim mystics, or called themselves such at any rate. They spoke Urdu rather than Memon or Gujarati and derived from an entirely different section of the subcontinent. Their customs were distinct, more musical and more ecstatic than their fellow believers.

Sharky wouldn't have thought of attending such a ceremony under ordinary circumstances. But his mother could use the company. She could use the change.

Since the funeral, after all, her mind had only been running in certain channels. With no certainty about his father's death it was hard to divert her into other channels. For it wasn't certain what event they were mourning.

Moreover Shakeer was curious about the sufis. They established their own relationship with the cosmos. Was there some secret he could learn?

His responses to religion were inside out. He feared the observant more than his father. Yet he longed for the reassurance of their doctrine. He had been desolate to abandon his father to the custody of the imam, as big as a doorway. Shakeer hadn't spoken to anyone, particularly not to his mother, about his misgivings on this score. In general he felt that he was continuing something on his father's behalf.

They drove up to Stanger just as the evening descended. It astonished Sharky to see how rapidly the north side of Durban, past Glen Ashley and La Lucia, was succeeded by a patchwork of beach towns and then by countryside.

One hundred yards back from the ocean there was almost no sign of development besides agriculture. Even that was sparse. He could see tractors and cantilevered carts parked on the sides of the hills.

Some small dams had been built out of concrete and appeared as black rectangles on the land. They became more and more difficult to make out until they had entirely dissolved into the evening.

A long line of cat's eyes condensed from the dusk around them. The studs along the road were orange. The reflectors had been coloured green when he was a child. Who had changed them from green to orange?

Sharky turned on the radio. There was nothing but static from one end of the dial to the other. He turned it off again.

"We should be there in half an hour?"

Nafisa said, "Less, maybe, at this speed, assuming we make it intact. Stanger is not that far. But be careful, Sharky. This is a bad stretch of road. Remember you are not in California. Terrible things have happened here."

Some trucks were riding slowly up the incline. They went so slowly that each ghostly chassis seemed stationary in the glitter. Otherwise, for ten minutes at a time, Sharky couldn't see anybody but themselves on the road.

The route wound along the border of the higher land, cutting off one's view every minute or so, and ran across several inlets and small river mouths. The trestles of the bridges were unsteady beneath the car.

He imagined one of the poles giving way and plunging them swiftly into the water. If it happened at the right time nobody would be any the wiser. Nobody, perhaps, would be any the worse off.

He said, "Money doesn't disappear like that. Whoever closed out the London account, he or she, must have had at least a power of attorney. To do that one of your signatures would be necessary on that very form."

"If you are asking me to explain it, Sharky, I just cannot. Arif couldn't travel at the time. According to Ismail Kader the branch in London accepted your father's identification book as proof of identity. Ismail doesn't have the full details as of yet. Of course the truth will eventually come out. Not that it will do us any good."

Sharky turned to his mother. He had avoided looking at her for a week. It was as if they hadn't spoken about the situation for fear of making it permanent.

There was nothing exceptional in this iron rule which had been applied to them. It was an insult to their freedom. Freedom to do what? To have one's thoughts filled with scorpions! His hands trembled on the steering wheel.

"Terrible things happen everywhere, particularly in this country, isn't it? You don't even have to open the newspaper."

Nafisa didn't look away from the road. "I just had a patient who was infected by her husband. Didn't I mention it? Men in this country don't think twice about the consequences of their actions even when the consequences alter many different lives. What do I tell this lady? When I tot up what your father did for this country and what gratitude he received in exchange ..."

Sharky put on the brights and peered into the long columns of light. Far away, left of the road and some distance below it, there were some houses decorated with strings of multi-coloured bulbs.

His mother continued. "When you stop to think, it is better not to have been born in the first place. Isn't that exactly what your Greek philosophers and playwrights have to say? You told me about them during your first year of university, before you failed your exam and chose photography. I never dreamed they would apply to myself. I used to enjoy those conversations." She stopped, pointed to the ramp he should take, and summed up. "No, if you want my opinion, it is better not to have been born in the first place."

To this remarkable speech Sharky couldn't find an answer. Luckily they were already in Stanger.

The *mawlud* was in full swing. They had taken longer than expected to get there. Nafisa was led away to the women's section where the women wore bright green and blue scarves.

Shakeer found himself cross-legged amongst the men. There must have been two dozen in attendance. Someone passed him a cap which he fitted on the top of his head.

Carpets had been hung on the walls and over the windows. At the front of the room was the party of musicians. Like all the men they were dressed in long white robes.

Some of the musicians wore red and white *kaffiyehs* around their shoulders. They sat on a long mat in front of several microphones which, Sharky decided, had the form of flowers he had seen in Namaqualand. His first commercial photographs, as a student, had been of these annual fields of flowers.

One immediately saw about the main singer that his features were unusually refined, suggesting he was perhaps Ethiopian or Somali. Indeed many of these groups were international, comprised of Pathans, Yemenis, Hararis from Ethiopia, and Balochis, *mujahers*, not to leave out Sindhis from Pakistan and Ibos from Nigeria.

It was only in the last few years that such mixed parties had been coming to South Africa. How greatly the place had opened up! How remarkable, how trivial it was, to belong to all of mixed humanity!

The performance was thrilling. The subject might be religious but the drumming was frantic. The singer, whose beautiful brown face gleamed, called out to the members of his party who responded with shouts of their own.

Sharky had first listened to *qawali* music in a club in Los Angeles, one of the roundabout routes by which he approached what, he decided, belonged to him. His father had been a devotee of the Sabri Brothers, Abida Parveen, Nusrat.

At first the religious music had been difficult to like. Your perception of time and octave had to change. Your mind, more than your ears, had to adjust because the proportioning of time in a *qawali* was closer to classical music than pop. A piece might take three quarters of an hour to develop from the slurring introduction.

In this instance several minutes went by while the singer crooned delicately at the audience. He looked at the audience in an insinuating manner. Then he sped up, bringing his party of musicians to an ecstatic froth, slowed them down, and sped up again.

The tabla player was hunched across his instrument, beating it so efficiently that the room filled with clicks and bangs. There was some truth which had taken shape in front of them that couldn't be parsed in words.

At the height of the recitation the men standing against the walls clapped vigorously. Sharky couldn't identify his mother amongst the swirl of scarves on the far side of the room. The women, sitting in a block, were as intent on the ceremony as the men. You could see it in their necks.

Afterwards the singer read a religious text. When he finished the room cleared without applause. Soon Sharky was in the garden.

His feelings were strangely neutral after the performance. He felt clearheaded and refreshed, as if a window had been washed. The coloured lights he had seen from the highway had been strung around the house. They dyed the white costumes of the guests with red, green or yellow.

People streamed from the back door, talking, activating and checking their cellphones for missed calls, congratulating the players.

Sharky didn't recognise anyone around him. He shouldn't expect to. It had been several years since he had been to a function in Durban. He hadn't remembered how unfamiliar they could be. The city, the greatest part of it from the townships to the English suburbs and the Indian sections like Overport and Reservoir Hills, was foreign to him.

On a picnic table were two-litre bottles of Coke and Sparletta, plastic cups, plates and bowls of crisps. He poured a drink.

He turned to a man beside him.

"So what's the occasion?"

The man looked angry. "It is the Prophet's birthday, *sallallahu-alayhi-wa-sallam*." He translated, "Peace be upon Him. Every year we celebrate on the twelfth of Rabi'-ul-Awwal. Why are you asking such a question? If you are here, you should know the basics of the religion."

Sharky didn't reply. He didn't reject the criticism. He was sure the man was correct to be angry. The man had been right to see something disharmonious in his presence at the *mawlud*.

Shakeer walked over to the embankment and looked across the street at the ocean. The tide surged onto the beach, sliding in crab fashion almost onto the road itself. The moon hung like a lamp in a quarter of the sky, gilding the ocean all the way in to the breakers. It was as if a woman's hand had touched the nearby water.

Further back, about two hundred yards, the sea was an absolute black ... the black of the universe. Its movements suggested the rugged back of a bear. Sharky felt the thrill of its magnitude – and then came his familiar wish to be extinguished in the shortest moment.

When he thought about the end of his life, ever since his schooldays, Sharky wanted to be annihilated down to the very last atom ... for this alteration to proceed in a split second so that he would have no knowledge of it and feel no pain, make no prediction. Hiroshima was his idea of a happy exit.

Here he remembered his father, and how, when he went in behind Nafisa, his father had been curled up on the big bed as if something singed him. The evidence of that curl, the sensation it dramatised, made Sharky feel the stupidity of his fantasies about extinction. And, generally, he was as stupid as a block. He was as stupid as a paving stone.

On his way back to the house he spied Nafisa on the veranda. In company, as he had hoped, his mother was back in her element. After all, she was a sociable being and was comfortably conversing with a number of the other women.

He was glad to see it. Whether the women were offering their condolences to his mother or whether they were asking her for medical advice wasn't immediately clear. He saw his mother rubbing one hand over the other and guessed she was explaining where to apply a lotion.

Nafisa complained about the people who came up to her at a wedding, or a function, or even a funeral and showed off their rashes and blisters in the hope of obtaining a free consultation, and perhaps a prescription.

Before he got to the veranda he was stopped by a touch on the arm.

"Shakeer? Oh, you don't remember me? Well, I don't blame you for that. It has been many years. I came to the funeral but we didn't have a chance to talk." The speaker paused. "You remember now? I haven't changed so much."

"Of course. Leila. In Arabic it means ..."

"You have it."

They shook hands. It was strange Leila assumed he wouldn't recognise her. She was making some point. For he knew her well. They had known each other as teenagers, when she had studied to be an accountant at university. Indeed Leila had been almost a girlfriend at a certain point in his life. She had been over at the old house a good deal and had become popular with his parents.

For some reason which Sharky could not immediately bring to mind, a relationship between them had never entirely crystallised. Perhaps it was because Leila was just as tall as him.

Sharky decided that Leila was far more beautiful than he recalled and in the very same moment he observed the wedding ring on her left hand.

But then his estimations of things were wide of the mark. Since his father's death his reactions to others had been unbalanced. Either he was irritated, couldn't wait to flee their company, or he was transfixed by some unearthly quality in their composition, as he had been by his mother, by Estella, now by Leila.

"You're married."

"And I have a son, and a daughter," she said, raising her eyebrows. She pushed her scarf back, freeing herself. "One of each. I thought your mother would have kept you abreast. As for you, Sharky, we hear a lot. My husband, Omar, does a good deal of business with your mother's brother. Nawaz, your uncle, is the one I mean. They know each other because my husband is also a *hafez*. They can both recite the entire Qur'an but their profitable work is mostly these property investments. You know with the market going up as it has been, twenty, thirty percent a year."

"Nawaz has property? I don't believe it."

"I don't get involved in the details. You can ask Omar yourself. They put some money together into that new shopping centre in Tongaat, or Isipingo. Anyway, Sharky, I keep up on your progress through Nawaz. Ask him and he will confirm it." Her expression changed. "I was so sorry to hear about your father. Do not allow the police to get away with classifying it as a suicide. They only want to save themselves the work of investigating. You saw me on that day? In fact I wanted to come to the house the next day again, to greet you, but my son was running a fever. I'm so embarrassed."

"Don't worry. The house was overpopulated."

Leila seemed to peer at him. She must have been surprised at his tone. "I thought you would be completely American by now. But you hardly sound American at all. On the other hand you never sounded completely South African either, even when we were on campus already. You left before you got your degree ..."

"Well, I've lived everywhere in the world. Last year I was in Papua New Guinea and for an entire month I had to live on cassava. I still have not recovered."

They talked for a few minutes. Sharky wouldn't have been able to say what they were discussing. He was entirely distracted.

When they had been very young he had liked Leila well enough, to the degree he was able to like anybody. But now he was bewitched.

Yet it was unquestionably the same person. Nothing had really been added, nothing subtracted. She had the same straight eyebrows and the same thin shoulders inside her shirt. Only her hair, tinted reddish brown, had changed.

Leila's gestures, her tendency to nod violently when she agreed with some statement you had made, the current of excitement and joy which surged into her shoulders and face ... these facts were familiar to Sharky but they took on some vast new significance in his mind. It was as if a lens above Stanger had bent all the light in the vicinity upon her.

In his present state Sharky knew that he was unusually susceptible. Yet he had long been susceptible to women. He was the sort of individual who fell in love in ten minutes flat. He could predict, even as it was happening, that he would long remember each detail of their conversation and, in particular, Leila's way of concentrating on you as if there wasn't anyone she would rather be with.

"Well, Sharky, let me go and collect my boy," she said finally. She touched him on the arm again. "My daughter is at home with Omar. It was lovely to run into you. And I will come to the house. Although I did ring I must convey my condolences to your mother at greater length. You must visit us. Omar, my husband, will be only too delighted to make your acquaintance. You can tell us about your wife then, how that story came to an end, and everywhere you've lived. But it's really been too long, Sharky."

They also shook hands again. Sharky watched Leila collect her son from around the house. The ceremony was coming to an end.

One of the organisers was paying the musicians, peeling notes off a wad of money in his hand. The players were busy loading their instruments and microphones into the back of a kombi. The singer wasn't helping. He was carefully combing his hair while gazing into the window of the van.

Two black women started to clear the tables. After a while the outside lights were shut off. The sufis, Sharky noted, were business-like. People drifted to the groups in which they had come. You could see the line of cars in convoy moving down the beach road in the direction of the city.

On the way home Sharky questioned his mother about Leila.

Nafisa was happy to talk. It was the first time Sharky had seen her so animated since before the burial.

"You probably know as much as I do about Leila. People say she's not happy, Sharky, although she has always been clever. You know she changed her course from accountancy to psychology? When your father was ill last year and you were in the jungles of San Salvador, we couldn't reach you to let you know. During that period Leila came to talk to your father every morning in the hospital. Your father became very fond of her."

"Dad was consistent. He was very fond of her when we were young also."

Nafisa said, "Everybody knew, about your father, that he would never change his stripes, not in the big things and not when it came to the little things either. But, as for Leila, they say her husband doesn't treat her well. Your father was most upset when he found out. He insisted on talking to Omar, and promises were made, but today what are promises worth? Then we talked to Leila, to persuade her to leave, but no dice. At that point she couldn't contemplate going against her family."

"You're sure about Omar?"

Nafisa put on her seatbelt. She was cold in the car and turned on the heater. "It's what I hear. I have no basis to say that I have witnessed anything untoward. Leila herself hasn't said a word to me. Even in Standard Nine she was extremely private about the goings-on in her family. And what a family it was! Why are you so curious about Leila?"

"No reason."

Nafisa said, "There is always a reason."

"I don't think that's true."

They were back in the city. The roads were silent. People didn't like to go out late in Durban if they could avoid it. You were more likely to be hijacked waiting for the garage door to open.

The huge apartment buildings in Umhlanga were dark. There was one chandelier burning right at the top of a house beneath the ridge, but the room it illuminated was empty.

They passed Virginia airport where there was a double line of red lights marking the runway. One of the big airport sheds was open. Behind its long door was a propeller aeroplane with two engines.

Sharky recognised it as a turboprop de Havilland, assembled in the 1950s. It was one of many such aeroplanes lovingly preserved at Virginia. During the day a succession of light aircraft skimmed along the highway en route to the runway.

Once a year, as part of the Virginia airshow, Fifteenth Squadron ran a flight of Impala jets out of the airport. They trailed streamers of red dye along the shoreline and carried out aerial acrobatics, loops, and other manoeuvres in formations which changed so rapidly they resembled the shifts of a cloud of swallows.

Sharky had once been in one of the larger buildings in Umhlanga on the morning of the Virginia airshow and had been startled to find a jetfighter suspended at the level of the eleventh floor window.

He was still surprised to think that these aeroplanes belonged to his own country, to his own government, and even more surprised to think that there were individuals in Durban who could afford to operate an aeroplane for pure pleasure's sake.

Who were the owners? Where did the money come from? And was the pleasure only the purer because of the surrounding poverty?

Nafisa said, “Leila is very beautiful.”

“She always was,” Sharky replied. “I have a separate question to ask. Leila mentioned her husband and Nawaz were investing in some property development together, somewhere on the South Coast, she thought. Where would your brother have the cash to go in with a guy on that level?”

“Nawaz doesn’t have a cent to his name. Leila must be confused.”

“She didn’t sound confused.”

It was rare for Nafisa to be angry with him but then all the rules were suspended in a looking-glass universe. When his mother did happen to get angry, it happened more quickly than one could anticipate. Her mood changed as suddenly as a chemical reaction in a beaker. The water was white, then it went cloudy.

“Shakeer, if this is what you have the audacity to ask me, then I can guarantee that my brother would never take money from Arif. Nawaz has a great deal of pride. He wanted to be independent from the day he left school to support himself. He would never be mixed up in anything untoward. So please don’t let me hear another word. My brother is my brother.”

Sharky didn’t trust his mother’s assurances. She had offered them too spontaneously. But they were turning onto Rhodean Avenue and he didn’t want to push the conversation. He wasn’t sure how tender his mother was. Nor did he want to find out. She might disintegrate in front of him. Ginger had done it to him many times.

It was odd that his mother was so protective of her younger brother. They had nothing in common apart from the physical side. Their personalities, their philosophies, were utterly distinct. Nawaz dwelled in one world, underneath one world, with his graveyard clothing, and Nafisa in another.

For himself, hardly connected to his hands on the steering wheel,

Sharky couldn't say about himself that he was alive in any of these worlds. He pinched himself, very hard, on the arm, to make sure.

Yet there was some invisible link which bound him to Leila, as if he had noticed some insensible perfume in her presence, which he couldn't communicate to his mother. He could not calculate how this link could bind him so strongly just a fortnight after he had stood in the cemetery.

Therefore he had no right to this steep sense of excitement which rose into his head. He could hardly look at his mother for fear of revealing to her this blasphemous sensation.

Black Swan

~

THE HOSPITAL'S SETTING WAS SOMBRE, ABOVE A SOBER HARbour, its name imperial.

Nafisa had spent half her lifetime in the wards without once associating the name of the hospital with British royalty. King Edward made an empire in its own right. It had its own monarchy, its subjects. New residents arrived in ambulances while others departed in an unpretentious mortuary van to Red Hill. Now Nafisa felt that a second half of her life had elapsed since she had last been through the gate.

From the entrance on Francois Road you saw that the power plant, behind Casualty, flew a kite of white smoke deep into the sky. The spectacle reminded her of the signal sent out by the Vatican on the election of a new pope.

Some years ago she had travelled with Arif to a conference in Rome coinciding with the papal election. She had been seized by the strange conviction that the smoke was crematorial; the ashes of the old Pope announced the choice of the new man.

She nursed a similar suspicion about the King Edward power plant. Many of her patients had disappeared from the wards over the years without a word of explanation.

Despite the sombre setting there was a jazztime energy about King Edward that was irresistible to somebody, like Nafisa, prepared to recognise it. She was surprised to find that it still claimed her attention. Trucks went in and out of the gates. Discharged patients hobbled across Francois Road to the tea rooms on the opposite side. There was motion and energy everywhere.

Orderlies, nurses, constables and doctors swept between the red buildings. Taxis queued at the entrances, hawking out their destinations like fish mongers. Below them, along the waterfront, the barbed-wired warehouses of the shipping companies were entrenched.

Nafisa's heart sped up. Her grip on her husband's absence, a black pearl held tightly in her hands, went slack. Even in heaven, or in hell, she thought, in the minute before a great catastrophe, an African would be making a plan, boarding a bus, tying a shoelace, repairing the heel of a hand-me-down shoe, and making do. Everything was bent on his destruction. It wouldn't occur to him to harm himself.

The boom was just off Francois Road. Nafisa was waved past by a sentry who sat on a stool but sprang up to lift the pole when he recognised her disc. On the front of his ears perched a pair of ramshackle spectacles. While he replaced the pole he motioned to her to wait. Nafisa opened the window.

The guard put his hand on the door. It was bony, dark, purple at the bone. Nafisa saw what must be a keloid on the thumb. She should tell him to go in for treatment. These things could grow.

She thought better of saying anything. She didn't like giving out free medical advice. It was a shortcut for people. Let them discover their troubles in their own time.

"Doctor, I have heard about your husband, the professor. The report came in our newspaper, *Ilanga*. I was very disappointed to hear it." The guard removed his hand but wanted to prolong the conversation. "Your husband was a good man. A fighter. For all of the people. I remember from the old days."

"Yes. Thank you."

"Please, my regards to your family at this time." He hesitated, and said, "You have never forgotten our Christmas."

Nafisa parked in the slanted bays outside POPD, thinking that the difference between life here and, say, Melbourne or Toronto, was that here, whatever one's place, one was attached to a thousand contrary souls and conditions.

Economic facts were relative. If Nafisa didn't tip the guards by the second week of December they asked for their Christmas. So did the man who delivered the newspaper and the woman window-washer who appeared outside her surgery Wednesday mornings in her winched and cabled basket.

At King Edward her peers came and went. The doctors and nurses Nafisa had worked with in the old days were long gone, to retirement, private practice, private hospitals. The only faces which struck her as familiar were those of the children on long-term treatment in the renal unit.

Children, like cats, were eternal. The same children, with the same concentrated expressions on their small faces, had been here since Dingaan and would be there until the end of time. They sat against the building, sunning their brown legs out of their green hospital gowns.

Passing them Nafisa was conscious of her starched white coat. It was freshly laundered, yet it was an anachronism. Only doctors of the old school wore white coats. Most of the others wore casual clothes, never ties, or stockings and skirts. Nafisa disapproved of the change in the dress code.

The pride she took in her work, in her standing, was a family trait, not snobbery. During the forty years her father worked as a cashier in a dusty corner of Gaborone he had suspenders on his belt and a crisply ironed Greenacres tie around his neck. The material of the tie was as thin as a sheet of paper.

The daughter inherited her father's disposition. It happened like that in families; sons were like their mothers. Nafisa, much more than Nawaz, had her father's temperament. Until the last year she had always been conscious of her exceptional good fortune.

Her father talked of his good luck in life. He counted his blessings as if he was counting money into the Siemens cash register. Yet it wasn't obvious about her father that he had been in any way fortunate.

Even after the first of his strokes, and the second, and the third which rendered him immobile, her father insisted he had been granted special privileges by providence. He allowed nobody to sympathise with him.

It was a puzzle to Nafisa. Could she call her father unlucky if he didn't see it that way himself? Could you ward off misfortune by refusing to meet its stony gaze? All the success in the world, she knew, could leave you unfortunate and unhappy. But could you be fortunate in spite of every calamity?

On her way to the ward Nafisa ran into two of her colleagues. David Gerson and his partner Govin Mackey, formerly Arif's student, were surgeons and thus on a last-name basis with the world.

The two surgeons had moved into private practice, and to the private hospitals like St Augustine's and Umhlanga. The fees were too low in the public sector. It was unusual to run across them at King Edward, which was run by the province. The two men had operated on her husband the previous year and, in all probability, saved his life. And for what?

Govin Mackey had been at the house several times since the funeral. David Gerson, from what she understood, had been out of the country until the last week. Nafisa didn't want to go over everything that had transpired in Gerson's absence. She was used to having gaps between herself and other people. She preferred not having to fill them in.

She said, "I heard you were overseas, David. Last year, if I remember correctly, you were content to let Govin travel to all the international conferences. You're well? You were in Israel, I understand?"

"I was," Gerson replied. He nodded his head vigorously. "And I am very well. Very well indeed."

She could see that Gerson didn't want her to go over the story either. He wasn't good at courtesies.

They stood outside the rubber doors of the ward. Gerson trembled a little on his feet. He was a good deal older than Arif yet showed no sign of wanting to retire. Gerson was defensive about his age, health, and energy level. He hadn't taken a day off in thirty years.

His life was at work. Doctors, especially surgeons, formed strong bonds. Gerson's principal attachment in the world, Nafisa suspected, was to Govin, his former houseman.

Their bond was more than emotional. It was rumoured that, because of Gerson's developing tremor, Mackey did the delicate work with the knife. Gerson, however, did the talking. It was rare for Govin to say a word in his presence.

In many ways, Nafisa supposed, Govin Mackey was still the shy Indian boy, the first son of a poor family from Reservoir Hills, who had been her husband's number one student before he was Gerson's.

It made sense for Gerson to rely on Govin's hands. Nafisa wished she had a younger colleague of equal value. It would be a pleasure to rely on another's competence. Govin had perhaps the finest touch with a blade in the entire country. For relaxation he was a fly-tier. He went up to what had been Eastern Transvaal to fish. Was it now part of Limpopo?

"I didn't expect you to be working so soon," Gerson continued. "I hear you've even reopened your rooms in town. My dear, you should be at home with your son. There will always be work to do at King's. You know perfectly well that the patients will never stop coming, Nafisa. Go home."

"To be quite honest, David, I don't want the time to think. My mind fills up with junk. Shakeer takes care of the practicalities, the legal details, and so on. It's a blessing to have him around. Meanwhile I have a patient in crisis here, a Mrs Dhlomo."

Gerson raised his eyebrows, pushing his spectacles back on his nose. You had to know the man in detail to know what it signified. It meant he was thinking, not that he was surprised by what had just been said. Gerson's gestures were legendary amongst the doctors.

Nafisa knew Gerson wrangled prolifically with his son and daughter-in-law in San Diego, with the hospital superintendent, with newspapers, journals and the editor of the South African Medical Association quarterly, in a series of letters composed on an old metal-keyed typewriter.

Because there were so few Jews remaining in Durban Nafisa considered David Gerson especially Jewish. She admired his method of lunging at something internal whenever he spoke. As he turned aside to think his piebald head passed beneath his massive spectacles as if it were the subject of a slide under a microscope. Gerson's manner, which was rough and sweet simultaneously, struck her as Jewish in type.

Was it fair to categorise, to classify? Was it not a mark of inexperience? Meet one black swan and imagine that the world contains nothing but black swans. It was a novice's mistake. Yet Arif had often said, about his work, about science and discovery, that life could be summed up as a search for one black swan.

As they were standing and talking a nurse went past them and into the ward, pulling an enormous cart loaded with sheets and blankets. The nurse was a towering woman in her short-sleeve uniform. From the huge pile of washing emanated, for some reason, the smell of burned wood.

Nowhere exercised Nafisa's nose like King Edward: the jelly and custard smells lingering around the paediatric ward, Omo detergent in the sinks and basins, the odours of toasting bread and talcum powder, peaty pink bottles of antibiotics, sickly sweet Erythromycin syrup in orange tablespoons, the vapours of mop buckets, and soiled and spattered sheets.

It proved you could be nostalgic for anything. How odd!

She had never thought to ask another doctor, not even her husband Arif, if they shared this same experience. It was as if, for twenty years, they heard the same piece of music in the morning, and had never thought to mention it to one another. But then, it seemed, there were many things she and her husband hadn't mentioned to each other. Their marriage, to go by what had happened to Arif, had been mostly silence.

Gerson resumed the conversation. "Well, Nafisa, if you can find pleasure in your work, let me be the last one to disallow it. For me the joy of the thing went out of it years ago. The challenges were different when we, even Govin, were in medical school. Medicine was a different kettle of fish."

"You're quite correct. It's not the same as when we were in training."

"As surgeons, the working conditions are worse than they have ever been. We have to suit up in theatre, wear gloves and a mask, spend the whole day drenched in blood which is full of virus particles. How many times haven't I cut myself? You know the minute there is the risk of exposure they put us on an emergency pack, and that has major disadvantages. Grown men will weep on the emergency pack. Ah, I wouldn't advise any young person today to train as a surgeon. Thank goodness we two are almost at the end of our careers. Govin is the one I feel sorry for."

"Come to the house, David," Nafisa replied. She feared that her eyes were filling again with tears. "It would be nice to meet."

Gerson brightened. "Yes, of course. You know my daughter is visiting from overseas. She has been after me to bring her to you. She has some condition on her arm she wants to ask you about. She says no doctor in San Diego can catch you."

Going upstairs Nafisa wondered if Gerson was more withdrawn than was ordinary for him. It must have to do with his and Govin's court case. She had heard that their defence against charges of organ trafficking was proving expensive. Legal fees could eat up everything – your house, your savings, your insurances.

The same could happen to her. Kader had warned her that she should expect to spend between a quarter and half a million in her own dispute.

The sheer sum of money at stake between her and the government astonished Nafisa. It was astonishing that a poor society could be so wasteful ... that it could squander its rich people like that ...

She was delighted that she hadn't told her husband about the Receiver of Revenue. She had saved a good deal of consternation. She had delayed telling Arif until the matter never needed to be handled.

Just as suddenly, just as perversely, Nafisa realised that she had a piece of news which would remain with her rather than being passed on to Arif. She was an atom where once she had been part of a molecule. Even as a girl she had never been an atom. The thought was terrifying; at the same time it thrilled her. She had been atomised. She took some strange pleasure in having thus ceased to exist.

A different possibility came along. She had observed that Shakeer had enjoyed Leila's company at the *mawlud*. Nafisa had long viewed her, despite her marriage to Omar, as the kind of girl she would want for a daughter-in-law.

Leila reminded Nafisa of herself but without her cargo of unnecessary knowledge. Nafisa was too old, too sore, for vanity, of course, and yet she could not easily imagine a higher recommendation.

There were complexities in things which only someone like herself, someone as tough as Leila or Nafisa, far tougher than Shakeer, Jadwat, David Gerson or Mackey for that matter, could hope to meet. Women were the tough sex. The idea pleased her. She was like a cockroach and could survive a nuclear blast.

In the ward Nafisa collected her patient's chart from the nurse. She took a syringe and needle absent-mindedly from the supply cart while she read through the indicators.

On her approach, in deference to her white coat, the patients returned to their beds. Several Indian patients were playing tunny on one of the beds, their hospital gowns hitched modestly above their knees.

One old woman, plainly deaf and dumb, had been positioned in a wheelchair in a square of sunlight and continued to sit there unawares, her gumless face baked into a smile. It was impossible not to smile in reply.

One ward contained every variety of life and death, pain and pleasure. Nafisa found a chair and moved it to her patient's bedside.

Mrs Dhlomo, as the head nurse had warned her, was not in the best shape. Nafisa was taken aback. At first her patient didn't greet her or seem to recognise her. She was curled on the bed, a bigger and more awkward creature than Nafisa remembered. She was moaning.

She was obviously running a fever. Her head was gleaming at the front. She was partially alert, partially responsive, with a gaze which settled on her visitor and then passed back to herself. It was rare that somebody deteriorated so rapidly, but it happened. Given enough time everything that could be came to pass.

With so much disease, an infinity of disease, Durban doctors were seeing cases that should have been one in ten thousand, one in a hundred thousand in the textbooks, on a daily basis. These Durban doctors, herself included, were epicureans of disease.

Nafisa couldn't tell if Mrs Dhlomo would understand what she was saying. She had to take blood. The laboratory would come back in a day or two with the numbers.

She decided to do a lumbar puncture as well. It was better to be on the safe side. She took the woman's arm, pinched it, looking for a vein.

"Millicent, I have to do some further tests and investigations, which may be painful for just a moment." She looked around for a nurse. "I am going to take care of you from now on. You have other choices, if you prefer, but I was the specialist who made the diagnosis. So usually it would be me."

To her surprise Mrs Dhlomo said, "I am not sure if the medical aid has an opinion on the subject."

"Let the medical aid and your husband fight about it. Let's do your temperature. With the nurse's help I can do the bloods."

As she inserted the thermometer Nafisa saw that, at the back of her patient's mouth, was a whitish net of thrush across the tongue. It was no thicker than a spiderweb. You wanted to sweep it away with a toothbrush.

The first time she had treated a patient with thrush Nafisa had been horrified how difficult it was to scrape off the white deposits. Today it was a routine occurrence although she had nightmares about developing thrush herself and being unable to swallow, to talk, then to breathe. It was the closest approximation to hell. She didn't want to displease God. He could permit terrible things.

She held Mrs Dhlomo's arm as tightly as she could while she screwed on the needle. She motioned to the nurse to hold the patient steady on the other side.

Nafisa moistened a swab and cleaned a square on Mrs Dhlomo's arm, inhaling a suggestion of the alcohol in the sterilising solution. She liked to work with her hands. So much of the knowledge of her profession was carried in these hands.

As she was preparing she talked. "Millicent, I forget if my secretary asked, and I wouldn't have the paperwork on me in any event, but you work for the municipality? That's how come you have insurance?"

Mrs Dhlomo shook her head. "It's through my husband." She looked very hot, shook her head, and lost the thread of the conversation. Then she said, "Sipho, Simon, is supposed to be here today, for the visiting hours."

"Good. I have to speak to him. It's become urgent. Your husband has to go on treatment if he wants any chance to survive. If I don't see him today I am going to write my number down here. You see over here? Tell him to telephone me."

Mrs Dhlomo supported herself on her elbow for a moment and asked, "Doctor, do I have something to fear?"

Nafisa said, "We all have something to fear."

"But for me is it something soon?"

Nafisa paused. Something about her patient sitting cornered in the narrow hospital bed reminded her of a boxer pushed into a corner of the ring. For once in her life, she decided, she would tell somebody what she thought.

"In my experience, no matter how much of a distance we try to put between us and what we fear, when it finally catches up, it happens far too quickly. Be prepared, whatever good it might do for you. There is an independent value in being prepared. But you must also be prepared for the fact that preparations are useless. Something will just punch through them."

Before she even finished Nafisa knew that this speech would have no discernible effect upon the listener. Wisdom, she had found, whatever wisdom she calculated for herself on the basis of her own experience, was of no utility to other people.

After a minute Mrs Dhlomo lapsed into unconsciousness. Sweat poured from her. Soon she was moving uneasily inside the bed. Nafisa battled to draw blood from her arm, fighting against her own tremor which was usually under control at this time of day.

She succeeded in getting the blood which she drained into a specimen bottle. The lab required only a drop.

Thirty years ago, when testing had been a matter of brute force, she had taken half a pint of blood if there was more than one test to run. The pallor of her patients would change before her eyes. By the time she had filled the bottle they would be grey from their tongues to their hands.

David was correct, she thought. Their training was as out of date as applying leeches. Twenty years ago the nurses boiled trays of fat glass syringes overnight. Today you chucked a syringe in the bin after one use. Or you chucked away a human being. The majority of people had always been disposable here. Now, the difference was, everybody was disposable.

Mrs Dhlomo looked to be fast asleep. The first nurse had gone off to the kitchen. Nafisa went across to the nurses' station. For some reason her heart turned over when she saw Rose, an apprentice nurse. Rose had been around in the ward since January. They didn't get along.

Nafisa dismissed the sensation. Even before her great new store of unhappinesses – before Arif's illness, before the defamation case brought against her husband by Metzger for denouncing his unscientific views, before Ginger had left Shakeer, before the letter arrived unannounced at the accountant's office – her emotional responses had been disproportionate.

Now, for instance, considering the young nurse, she discovered she was unable to breathe. She struggled to keep calm.

"Rose, I do need your assistance. I want to do a lumbar puncture on my patient. I don't want to miss anything obvious that a biopsy will reveal. Sometimes it happens, you understand. You miss a pneumonia, or some other infection. By the time you catch up it's too late to do anything. I don't want to take chances. So leave your tea for the moment, if you don't mind."

Nafisa wasn't sure why she was explaining. Rose was a sulky young woman. She had unusually strong arms which she kept folded in front of her when she wasn't drinking.

Without necessarily agreeing to help, Rose put down her cup and saucer carefully on top of a blood pressure monitor. Nafisa saw that the nurse had stacked four Marie biscuits in the saucer.

Rose coaxed Mrs Dhlomo onto her side. Mrs Dhlomo's hospital gown was open at the back where the puzzle pieces making up her spine were prominent. The green cloth was as thin as a handkerchief. Nafisa felt that the open gown made a patient vulnerable as a child. They were made for easy access, not to preserve a woman's dignity.

She prepared the injection. She blew at the needle as if she was blowing out a candle. The needle you used for a lumbar puncture was thick, almost a centimetre of grey steel at the base and not much thinner at the top. It reminded her of a flute.

"Rose, make sure you've got her tight. It's a tricky operation. I don't want you to slip."

"No, I have her properly, doctor."

"Be sure."

As she inserted the needle into the spine Nafisa observed that underneath the ear Rose the nurse bore an elongated scar which was pink on the rim, rough-grained, contrasting with her cheek which was as dark as tarpaulin.

The scar must be the result of something sharp, a knife, or the edge of a tin, but Nafisa didn't ask. Rose was a black swan. So was

Millicent. So, for that matter, was Estella, her black swan. They all had something to tell her. Everybody had a story from the Cape to Cairo. It was best not to ask about it unless you had the time and sympathetic energy to hear them out, from start to tragic finish.

Here Nafisa saw that she had a story of her own to tell. Why, she could outdo Rose, exceed Rose and her scar, Estella and her daughter. She was almost proud. When it came to the quantity of tragedy, for the first time, there was no clear and bright line between her, her family, and the rest of the continent. There were no exemptions. How much of her life had proceeded on the assumption there were?

This thought occurred to Nafisa just when there was a motion in the bed. Mrs Dhlomo was awake, stampeded, with a terrified white look in her eyes, the white and blanked-out look of a horse about to rear. She was awake in the bed, not aware.

Nafisa felt, without seeing, the woman's body thrash underneath her. Rose hadn't been anticipating anything and had relaxed her hold on the patient's hips.

Rose, Nafisa noticed at that moment, wore a disgusted expression, distant from the proceedings, as if she couldn't be expected to put up with such nuisances. It struck Nafisa that the hospital was full of nurses who wouldn't put up with patients, doctors who wouldn't put up with patients and nurses alike. The patients didn't put up with each other. Nobody, in this new South Africa, was putting up with anything.

She couldn't complete the thought. Mrs Dhlomo's arms swept down the bed, dislodging the syringe from her back. When Nafisa looked down she saw the needle was holding fast in her own left hand. The syringe stood by itself on her hand.

She removed it immediately, without thinking. There was no pain, not even the friction which told you that a needle had inserted itself under the dermis.

If you didn't know precisely where to look there wouldn't be a puncture mark. Through such a small portal, as small as the eye of a needle, a life was altered. How many doctors had been infected in this fashion? Govin, she remembered, had once been on an emergency pack until he was sure he hadn't converted. Nafisa put down the syringe and looked across at Rose.

Apparently the nurse hadn't seen what had happened. She hadn't seen Nafisa remove the needle. Yet there was a smile, a coarse smile, on Rose's countenance.

Nafisa had never seen the sulky young woman smile before. It made her wonder if Rose had figured out what had happened. Rose was smiling, for all the world, as if the distance between them, between nurse and doctor, had collapsed.

Rose's smile was shining, like a dark torch high on a mountain, directly into Nafisa's soul. But what message did it bring?

"I am sorry I couldn't hold her. Are you okay, doctor?"

"Why shouldn't I be?"

Rose was still smiling. She said, "Can I fetch you a cup of tea? Doctor, you look as if you have seen a ghost."

"I don't believe in ghosts," Nafisa said quickly. "Rose, I will have coffee in the staffroom when I go down, so don't bother. As for Mrs Dhlomo, she seems to have calmed down. Keep her on the antibiotic. Vanomycin is a big gun." She was talking, she thought, so as not to allow her mind to enter her circumstances. "One of the interns can do the lumbar puncture properly tomorrow. Their hands are better than mine are. I have a congenital tremor. It has only gotten worse with age. I can't rely on my hands anymore."

Rose continued to smile as she made the bed around Mrs Dhlomo. She didn't say anything more about what had happened.

Nafisa wanted to jump on the young woman in front of the ward and rest on top of her until her breathing stopped. She wanted to suffocate Rose, to tear each one of her petals with delight and

break her stem. The desire passed. Nafisa was left with the curious sensation of having burned herself very badly yet being unable to determine the pain which had resulted.

Something like this had happened to Nafisa once when she had burned her hand on the stove and yet had continued talking to her husband in the other room. She had been suspended between receiving the wound and accepting it, seeing the large burn with her eyes before she could feel it on her nerves. It had been half an hour before the flesh had begun to send back pain messages.

On her way out of the ward Nafisa saw that pain was something which required calculation and recalculation on the part of the sufferer. If she never did the numbers, if she never worked out the end result for herself, it would never take hold of her.

It was a task to maintain her sense of violation in the steady sunshine on the roads, made more difficult by the controlled lighting inside Musgrave Shopping Centre.

Nor was it possible for Nafisa to believe, on the escalator in Musgrave, that some enormous force had been released with her name on its lips. Everything could happen in a hospital but, by definition, nothing transpired in a shopping mall.

So much of life, in South Africa, was conducted in shopping centres and yet one couldn't take them seriously as places in which life, death, love, happiness could be at stake. They were outside of history.

Some time ago, visiting Shakeer in San Francisco, Nafisa had seen *The Terminal*, the Steven Spielberg movie. The story of a man trapped in the wing of an airport, surviving on scraps from the chain restaurants and literature from the airport book store, applied to the airtight existence of middle-class South Africans.

There were many such new centres in Durban. You could be sealed inside Musgrave, La Lucia Mall, The Wheel, The Pavilion,

or Gateway for a lifetime. During this lifetime you wouldn't bleed. You would not suffer. You would not age a day, or live a minute.

Should she say anything to Jadwat about what had happened in the wards? Should she ask his advice?

She felt that to alert Jadwat was to confirm the shock of the needle finding its unerring way into her hand, as if an arrow had been shot into her. So long as she hadn't said anything nothing would have happened. Besides, there was a high probability that nothing had actually happened. An emergency pack would make her weep.

And she didn't want to listen to Jadwat's advice. Sometimes she didn't want to hear a word out of his mouth, or anybody's ...

For a Marxist, Jadwat liked shopping malls, Musgrave above the others. He admired its restrained décor and dimensions. When the public library had been open he would spend an entire Friday afternoon reading books and pretending to shop for suits at the Italian boutique. But he wouldn't buy a pair of underpants at Musgrave prices. He shopped wholesale from Rex Trueform; his cousin worked in the factory shop and got him clothes at a discount.

Once the municipality shut down the library Jadwat moved to the coffee shop on the second floor where he pecked at his cellphone and offered his opinions to the waitresses.

Today, though, he was waiting for Nafisa in the parking lot, patient, very comfortable, running the air conditioner in his Mercedes.

She looked in the window to discover Jadwat in a state of suspended animation, his short legs trembling, but otherwise as still as an alligator, to all intents and purposes asleep while a Dunhill smoked itself in the ashtray inside closed windows. Yet Nafisa guessed he was quite conscious of the surroundings through those heavily ballasted eyes.

She knew Jadwat would remember and have something to say

about every person who had walked by his Mercedes, every car which had gone in and out of the lot, since he had entered hibernation. He was a car spotter, the equivalent of train watchers from the UK. He prattled about the resale on the Fords, the Kias, the Subaru he had spotted, all the new brands which had never been heard of before in Durban.

It was hard to hold in one mind the idea of reselling a car and David Gerson's warning against emergency packs. Jadwat was simply irrelevant.

She didn't know how her husband put up with it. It had been impossible to pry a critical word out of Arif where his old friend was concerned. The closest was his observation that Jadwat had the eyes of a sultan.

Of course Arif was loyal to a fault. He was loyal to people who, in her opinion, didn't deserve loyalty. This was surely the reason he had opened the door to whomever had appeared on that Friday afternoon.

Nafisa was now convinced that a murder had taken place in her house. Rose, the nurse, had convinced her. It had taken her all this time to change her mind, or to adjust it to the circumstances.

As yet she couldn't conceive of a killer. She couldn't allow for the existence of such a person. To have taken her husband was gratuitous. No one benefited.

Jadwat was the opposite. He was in fighting form and could conceive a thousand possibilities. He had been reading through the documents and was convinced, first of all, that the university was bound to pay out the full amount of the life insurance, not the reduced sum for which Kader made her sign.

Nafisa hardly knew what to say. The point was irrelevant. Money was as unimportant to her existence as music. It could only put her off her balance.

"Nafisa, I have been reading the notes Arif was intending to turn into an editorial about Metzger's doings. You remember that Metzger is the principal complainant in the defamation case against Arif. I am sure he was the prime mover. Arif discovered his laboratory got illegal funding from the Health Ministry. Money in suitcases. That's how this country operates. And that, my dear, is what Arif wanted to write about for *The Lancet*."

"He didn't say anything about it to me."

Jadwat, Nafisa thought, had been correct once before. He had seen that Arif couldn't have harmed himself. Maybe he was now correct about Metzger's involvement.

Metzger, like Sekolo, was certainly unscrupulous. She had met the foreign scientist now and again at a university function and disliked his manner, to say nothing of his pseudo-scientific speeches and papers on the epidemic which were distributed by the vice chancellor in Durban as well as the office of the Presidency in Pretoria.

Yet she couldn't bear the thought of confronting the creature. To do so would involve Metzger in their sorrows.

Jadwat went on. "It could go very high up. As we know by now, these people accept no limits to their power and to their supposed wisdom. They thought they went on the track to an instant cure. They thought overnight they were going to validate Africa in the eyes of the world and bring about the new millennium. If they had to circumvent medical and scientific protocols, so be it. That is the lesson of the years between 2000 and today, and until we can change the class basis of this leadership."

"It's Africa, Jadwat. After a point what can we say? We live here by choice. I can't imagine they would go so far as to threaten Arif. There's a point beyond which even the people in the government are not prepared to go. We still have newspapers. We still have courts. We are not like Russia. They are not going to assassinate us."

"What nonsense are you talking? I am quite certain they would."

The two of them walked along the corridor and towards the

shops while Jadwat chattered on about this and that. Nafisa tried to listen, then gave up and became entirely detached from Jadwat's arguments.

She was feeling that her presence, whatever she did in the world, meant zero without the possibility of its drawing her husband's attention. He had been the kind of husband who took pleasure in hearing each day about her doings. Her day was incomplete, in the ultimate sense, until she related its happenings to Arif. There was no one else to whom she cared to report, Jadwat included.

The one thing she and Jadwat agreed about was the value of Musgrave. The shopping centre had also been her beloved place since it had opened more than twenty years before, an oasis of shopping in which everything was safe, orderly, and foreign.

Yet today the ease she took in the place evaporated. The watches in Cardin's Jewellery Bazaar gazed back in her direction, their faces deep in gold and silver shadow.

The papier mâché dummies in the men's boutique, it seemed, had entered into a conspiracy. They tittered at Jadwat. Their lumpy white shoulders and necks, in some of which the wire netting was showing, struck Nafisa as unpleasant imitations of the human form.

Ordinarily the Italian shoe shop on the second level, next to the dry-cleaner, was sure to cheer her up. The ranks and columns of shoes were drilled into colours and shapes.

Each shoe, as she had often noticed, was beautifully tailored down to the last Milanese stitch and button. Their insides were as expressive as a musical note. Yet on this encounter Nafisa was gripped by the image of all the pairs of shoes surviving her in the upstairs cupboard. They would linger long after her.

The image was confounding, to say nothing of the fact that Estella would be there to strut about in them. Given half a chance Estella would stride around in her bedroom and take her shoes back to the township. She would show off to her men in Nafisa's Italian-leather shoes. Some betrayals you could predict with one hundred percent certainty.

Nafisa saw that purchasing each new pair was merely a means to accelerate one's own passing. All those shoes! Those cork heels! They would dance on her grave. For the first time she understood the significance of leaving the world without possessions, wrapped in a sheet. The tradition was a contrivance of great wisdom.

She was going to go back to Westville and start giving things away. She would give away the carpets, the bracelets she had from her mother, gold and silverware, crockery, blouses and shoes. She would burn her envelopes!

Soon enough, nothing would be left. She would have the house emptied out in no time.

Jadwat noticed her interest. He put his hand on her arm.

"You want to go in? I can take you. You want to shop?"

Nafisa shuddered. "You must be crazy to ask such a question. Let's go for a coffee."

They went up. This coffee shop, at the top of the escalator, was designed, like much, if not most, of Durban, according to the taste of 1970 in Edinburgh or Glasgow. The panelling, uncomfortable straight-back chairs, and high wooden tables must have been someone's idea of a gentleman's club. Compared with the hall outside it was kept dark and cool.

They sat there amongst talking couples and a few individuals reading magazines and newspapers. There was a block of light beneath the counter where three shelves presented the three-quarter and one-quarter circles of the cakes. The espresso machine hissed in the background.

It had been weeks, maybe months, since Nafisa had eaten anything much. She was hardly able to swallow. She had lost three kilograms.

Now she ordered a slice of lemon cake as well as coffee. Jadwat was paying.

The waiter brought back their orders in no time. The floury fragrance of the cake, the sour and bitter coffee, penetrated her mind. She remembered that, more often than not, coffee gave her a headache. Her hand, her head, throbbed.

Through this Jadwat had been quiet. He picked at her slice of cake, smiling at her whenever she looked across. But he was an odd bird! He was preposterous!

Nafisa considered the possibility of Jadwat having her in his sights. It was established he had a fixation on widows. Nor was he a man to be deterred by good taste.

But was he so preposterous? Did this Jadwat know limits? It was impossible to say. Where human beings were involved there were no rules. There was nothing to prevent Rose the nurse from murdering her that morning in slow motion. So there was nothing, in concrete form, to restrain Jadwat's loving disposition wheeling in her direction.

For herself Nafisa would never entertain the thought of another man. She had always criticised the speed at which some women, particularly English women here, remarried over the graves of their husbands, in a matter of six months, nine months, two years. Who gave them the right to restart their lives?

It wasn't mere considerations of age and dignity which applied. Her husband's disappearance, she felt, had plugged her up for good, as if a stopper had been inserted in the mouth of a jug. Her mind had been just as securely plugged.

Without her husband she had no entitlement to a future. She was hardly touched by what had happened to her London money. It had become as irrelevant as she was. She should vanish. In this looking-glass world, with its blank and impermeable prospect, she was unable to look into a mirror.

"There's been something I wanted to ask you," Jadwat announced. "I went to talk to Ismail Kader, on your behalf, this morning. Anyway my good fellow Kader, the arch-capitalist, has been doing some research on your brother's doing. Sharky asked Kader to look into the matter. It takes no time to send a lackey to look up the records held by the municipality. Apparently Nawaz has invested in some property development down the coast. So Nawaz has money to burn. From where?"

"You mustn't blame my brother."

Nafisa couldn't get angry about it again. She was too confused to be angry.

She said, "I have heard enough of it from Shakeer. Even if Nawaz and I do not always see eye to eye, even if he has gone further into religion than I am comfortable with, he would never be involved in anything untoward. Durban is a village, as you know very well, Jadwat. We are consumed by gossip. We live and die by rumours, if people want to get at somebody or if they develop some petty jealousy. Leave my brother out of it, please. It only hurts me in the end."

"You never asked your brother anything of the kind, about where the money is coming from? You didn't ask Arif?"

Nafisa was irritated. She said, "Don't be ridiculous, Jadwat. Things were very bad after the operation. We didn't have the luxury of conversation. Since you are so clever you can explain to me what I am supposed to say to my brother. I am supposed to ask him if he stole from my husband. Should I also ask him, while I am at it, if he picked up the gun and shot Arif in the chest? Maybe you have a better idea?"

Jadwat stood his ground. "So you think if you never mention something it will eventually vanish?"

"Everything will eventually vanish. You don't have to be an Einstein to figure that out."

Jadwat was no Einstein. He saw her implication immediately and was crestfallen.

He dropped his head as if she had successfully scolded him. Nafisa saw that he wasn't completely bald. He had a fine crest of hair, she saw for the first time, along the top of his head.

Nafisa was immediately sorry for having chosen these particular words. It was careless. The sentence had been a commonplace of her husband. Why, this country was full of people who were no Einsteins. Each time Arif had said so he was surprised at the observation.

There were things to which even these no-Einsteins could hardly close their ears. In the townships the coffin-makers were flourishing. It was impossible not to know the cause and yet just as impossible to know. You pushed things to the margin of consciousness where it could do no harm. Her mind would never return to the existence of Rose the nurse and her morning in the ward which had stuck her in the arm.

It occurred to Nafisa that this strategy was a form of witchcraft. To refuse to know, to postpone comprehension, was to obtain a hold over things. Life, love, music, just because they penetrated us before entering our understanding, were modes of sorcery.

Why, it was a feat of conjuring that the atoms which made up Jadwat should assemble every morning. If she were Jadwat, caught on her glare, she would have crumbled into dust a long time ago.

On the escalator to the ground floor she turned to him on the higher step. "I didn't mean anything by it, Jadwat."

He waved his hand at her. "Oh, I've forgotten about it already."

She had had her fill of the man, of course. This had been true for many years. Perhaps she had not had her fill of having her fill. But this was the kind of observation her son used to make before his recent unhappiness.

She didn't sound like herself. Often Nafisa couldn't recognise her own voice in what she said. She saw herself in others more easily. Estella, Shakeer, Rose the nurse and Millicent her patient, her black swans, were closer to her than herself.

Nafisa couldn't tell what she had become, in the past week, in the past month, or year for that matter, or was in the process of becoming. There was some transformation underway even before the accident in the morning. She could sense it inside herself. There were enormous forces in motion. They were a tide which ran against everything which had conspired to take Arif's life away from her.

Vanilla Essence

~

ON THE WEEKEND JADWAT DROVE DOWN FROM RICHMOND, bringing pastries in a shoebox. Richmond was famous for its pastries which were made only in private homes. They were not available in shops.

An association formed in Shakeer's mind between these pastries and his new sense of freedom. Since meeting Leila he had been keenly aware of new possibilities in life.

Each time Sharky saw anything of the pastries he was reminded that, in his father's absence, he could do anything he chose. There was nobody to whom he should answer, nobody to whom he could appear inadequate.

This sensation of freedom was exhilarating but it was also disorienting. He was unsure of what to do with it. Sharky scolded himself. It was illogical. He had been at liberty as a photographer from the age of twenty. Why was he now more free?

Jadwat unpacked the pastries himself. He couldn't eat them because of diabetes. Instead he put them around a plate for the visitors while he spoke inconsequentially to Estella. Each was decorated with something individual – a button of apricot jam, a silver star made from shortening, or a date from which the stone had been pressed.

Thanks to the shoebox the house was full of the unlikely scent of vanilla essence. The vanilla blended into Shakeer's new feeling about himself.

The incongruity of Jadwat as a figure, everything he said and did, struck Shakeer more than ever. The guy kept a lazy eye on the older women as he served the plate of pastries to the visitors in the lounge.

That it was a funeral house did little to dampen Jadwat's mood. Indeed he exuded a palpable satisfaction at his state of health.

The exception to his good condition was his crook shoulder. Jadwat winced when something caused him to pull on his shoulder.

When it happened again, as he was bending to retrieve the empty plate, Shakeer stifled a laugh. He was overcome by a rush of superiority to this imitation of a man. Liberty was a precious gift. He could say anything to Jadwat, treat his father's dear friend badly, and it wouldn't matter. He could ask him if he needed a comb and laugh in his face ...

The impatience, Shakeer knew, was displaced. It was his mother who was the cause of his frustration.

Despite his new awareness of strength Sharky couldn't approach Nawaz in his own right. It would shame his mother. They would never speak again. Instead, twice as impatient with her, he touched Jadwat twice as hard on his afflicted shoulder.

Jadwat was alarmed and sat down in the kitchen.

"You won't call your mother? It's time for another injection, I believe. This shoulder has the tendency to act up during periods of stress. Nafisa administers a steroid to settle the tissue down. I rely on your dear mother. Contrary to popular belief a physician cannot heal himself."

"I think she's busy with the insurance agent in the upstairs bedroom. I would inject you myself although my hands aren't steady."

Jadwat sloped back on the high stool. He watched Shakeer mildly above his spectacles.

"I had better wait for your mother. Is it Kader again who is in with her? Is it again this problem of the taxes? If you make any money from your photographic hobby, Shakeer, I'll give you some advice which may be warranted. Keep anything you make overseas. Don't bring it back into this country. That way the government knows nothing about it and if you have to go, you can go."

"Photography is not a mere hobby, Jadwat. It's how I make my living, here and everywhere. And I don't have to leave the country. I don't live in the country."

Jadwat didn't register the objection. "Well, I hope Kader makes quick work of his business with Nafisa. I don't know how much longer I can endure."

Shakeer wanted to shake him by his injured shoulder. He wanted to hear this being squeak. Jadwat was an absurdity, an anti-tragic force. He put himself at the centre of everything. If he had not yet desecrated the house then he had tried to disenchant the spell of their mourning. By mere existence he undermined sacraments, contracts, and promises.

It was a mystery, Jadwat and his father, both doctors, both products of a similar society and education. All the things his father had approached in a serious light, as a serious man and a researcher, Jadwat dissolved into his levity.

Friendship, of course, had reasons an outsider could not penetrate. For his father and Jadwat had been inseparable, by all accounts, since first-year anatomy class in Bombay. They had both been studying overseas because Indians had been almost entirely barred from tertiary education in South Africa.

Bombay was decisive. Jadwat and his father liked pretty much the same movies, books, Indian music of that era like Kishore

Kumar and Mohammed Rafi. So much they had in common. Nor did they necessarily disagree about politics.

Yet there was no sign, apart from the uncertain testimony of his shoulder, that the disappearance of his friend touched Jadwat more deeply than a cloud passing in the heavens.

If anything, he was in good form. He had taken the job of answering the intercom, travelling back and forth to the door in men's stockings when the buzzer rang.

When Nafisa was not available Jadwat settled the new arrivals in the lounge where he crossed his short legs and scored political points. His faith in Trotsky was undiluted. And he re-proved his theorem of political science step by step to the visitors. He demonstrated that no society in history had attempted the construction of a socialist system ... except, perhaps, Albania under Enver Hoxha.

From start to finish it took Jadwat about fifteen minutes to arrive at this conclusion. Shakeer had timed him.

If Shakeer had any sympathy with the new arrivals he would have saved them from Jadwat. In fact his feelings were quite the opposite. The visitors were intolerable, more intrusive than the two constables from the previous week. They made it impossible to think.

Shakeer wanted to push each new arrival back into the road. With his new sense of freedom he wanted to pick on their deformities, to seize them by their collars, and shove them out of the door. They were worse than Jadwat.

Relatives arrived at any hour of the day or night. Friends of his mother turned up after work, mostly professional connections – the doctors who referred patients to her, specialists to whom she referred, the drug reps who were often waiting in her rooms.

Then there were the nurses with thick arms, largely but not exclusively African, with whom Nafisa worked at King Edward. His father's co-workers from the departments of biology and virology appeared in the evening once their laboratories and classrooms were locked up.

One person did not appear. The only person Shakeer wanted in his neighbourhood had vanished from the planet. Each time the intercom pealed he hoped it was Leila. She had promised to come to the house again.

Moreover he had a hundred things to tell her about his father. She would understand because she and his father had been close. Only Leila could relieve him of his memories. He could almost make out her face at the gate even though it was never her standing there. And each time it was somebody else, he was disappointed.

Leila was elsewhere in time and space. At two o'clock she would be picking up one of her children at Carmel College. At seven in the morning, in all likelihood, she would be asleep in her bed.

That wouldn't have changed. After all, Leila had been a late sleeper in school and through university. She had never made it to early lectures. She preferred to lie in bed until her father insisted she get up. Happy bed!

Somehow Jadwat, still waiting in the kitchen for his injection, touched on the theme of Sharky's thoughts …

"So your mother tells me you ran into that old girlfriend of yours at the *taziya* in Stanger. I recall that she was a very lovely girl. Her mother was lovely also, in her day, and her day may not be past. The daughter's name is on the tip of my tongue …"

Sharky didn't help. He didn't wish to hear her name on the other man's tongue. To have it spoken would establish some unwanted complicity between the two of them. Whereas it was vital that he exist on another plane altogether to Jadwat.

His ferocious old wish to differ and to be different, never to be absorbed into all the superfluous old flesh in the world, rushed into his head.

"It wasn't a *taziya* in Stanger, Jadwat. I know the ceremony you mean, as it happens, because I once photographed a *taziya* in Madras. They used to hold them in Durban, starting by Wills Road and ending at the Umgeni River. Now, of course, it's a dying ritual. It's interesting. *Taziya* was a Shia procession originally. It is meant to teach religion to an illiterate audience. They build a replica of Imam Hussein's tomb which they carry through the streets. Then they chop it up with axes and throw it into the river. It's all modelled on the non-Muslim festivals in that part of India. In Stanger, by the way, it was a celebration of the Prophet's birthday, a *mawlud al-nabi* – and also with music, which the orthodox believers criticise."

Jadwat waved away his explanation. "I don't know about any of that, Shakeer. I left religion behind a long time ago."

That evening Jadwat had a second chance to disembark his opinions. In the living room there was a heated discussion about the recent policies of the government and the university.

Whether it was by chance or design, several of the guests on this particular evening belonged to international organisations. Their groups were based either in Basel or Geneva, or across the Atlantic in Bethesda, Maryland.

The foreigners had a sense of proprietorship in his father and, more particularly, in his research into the biochemistry of the disease. The professor had eventually been able to isolate all the important strains of the virus which were more common in sub-Saharan Africa and, with the assistance of a computational biologist and Labuschagne, establish the patterns of genetic change in the virus. The equipment came from overseas, as did a number of outside researchers and technicians. But Shakeer disliked the foreigners' tacit claim to ownership. They were muscling in on a national disaster.

His dislike was unfair. The international funders had supported researchers inside the country when the government halted all the tests of new vaccines and retrovirals. The Health Ministry argued that drug trials violated the dignity of black Africans.

But dignity, pride, self-reliance were mysterious facts. You could never tell where they would land you. You could never say what they would allow and what they would forbid. The Health Minister promoted African dignity by passing suitcases of illegal money to Hansel Metzger at the Union Buildings. She ensured African dignity by drinking herself into a public stupor by lunchtime on a working day. But dignity, dignity, dignity forbade counting the numbers of the dead.

This at a time when the epidemic was the worst in the world. Over the decade, mortality had increased by a thousand a day.

The government, of course, objected to these terms. First of all, who was counting? Second of all, who were they to define a day? Why should we simply accept the European definition of a day? It was the logic of the looking glass.

Compared with the government, therefore, the foreigners were a blessing. Yet Shakeer couldn't choke down his distaste. Unlike South Africans, they were half sincere. They were half absent, only half present in the house.

Shakeer went outside to catch his breath only to discover two of them speaking softly on the stairs beneath the garage. The man and woman seemed to be flirting.

He didn't know their names and didn't greet them. Instead he went back inside to find others, in the lounge, bent painfully over their telephones typing messages to contacts in other time zones.

At one moment they were divided into a dozen times, places, and purposes. Why, they were too busy to be alive!

What bothered him? Sharky decided there was something light-hearted in the attitude of the foreigners towards the circumstances, far more light-hearted in essence than Jadwat. They were here in spite of themselves. They cared to possess his father, not his father's family. Whatever his deficiencies, unlike the foreigners, Jadwat had given himself to the occasion.

There was, however, an interesting conversation in progress. The foreigners were discussing the government with a few members of the university staff. Because they were from outside they were uncertain of how firmly to couch their criticism.

The news was disturbing. They had heard of the racial polarisation at Howard College and amongst the medical faculty. The administration and the bulk of the students were black, African, while many of the staff were Indians who had not yet been pushed out.

Shakeer listened to the conversation from the doorway to the lounge. He didn't want to sit down and end up saying something in his own right. His new freedom was also the freedom to listen and not to be committed.

At some point Jadwat had moved from the kitchen, bringing another plate of pastries with him. He appeared to sleep in the armchair, his short legs, in their long stockings, drawn up beneath him.

There was just the suggestion of a smile remaining on his mouth ... like one of the sleepers piled on each other in the crocodile farm on the old route to Pietermaritzburg. It indicated, Shakeer knew, not so much consciousness, or even its absence, but a readiness to strike.

The conversation turned to the difficulties at the university. A dozen Indian members of staff at the medical school had been suspended from their jobs pending an investigation into allegations of racism.

The lecturers had refused to pass certain black students on the supplemental exams. One of the students had belonged to the Student Representative Council and had lost his bursary as a result of his failing mark. Demonstrations had been organised against the Indian staff members. The new vice chancellor, from Zimbabwe, had participated on the side of the students. Several cars had been turned upside down. Others, including the surgeon Govin Mackey's, had been damaged.

Amongst Indians in Durban, who reserved the admiration for physicians once allotted to holy men, the controversy was considered to be the beginning of the end. For them the end was always beginning.

Sharky was irritated by the imprecision. People's fears, in South Africa, had the conformity of their hopes. They wouldn't check the facts for themselves.

Jadwat pricked up his ears. He lit a Dunhill cigarette from his pocket. Then he put his spectacles on.

After a minute he rose in the armchair, extending his legs. "My friends, I must remind you that the students have chosen precisely the same members of the academic staff who, in former days, were involved with the United Democratic Front."

He sipped at the long beige filter of the Dunhill. "So the mob targeted the very people who were true-blue socialists and communists. They chose the ones with integrity. Arif, I will have you know, was very concerned. He had begun to write a letter to the newspaper on this very subject."

Some in the room nodded. Others were indifferent, or, Sharky thought, unsure of the stakes, and the drift, of the conversation. It was tough to criticise in Africa; one consented to a good deal simply by living here. One consented to the chance of sudden death.

Jadwat looked over his spectacles which, Sharky noticed, were bifocals, thick as the bottom of a mug. The glass looked white from the side.

Jadwat paused, then went on. "So they have been charged. So they have been charged. That is the story of our revolution. Instead of class politics we are the victims of a certain romantic view of the continent. And who benefits from the ensuing confusion? Trotsky would not have been deceived. My friends, we have sold out to international capital."

Somebody said, "You are talking through your hat!"

"But you must really inform yourself if you want to make such a statement," Jadwat returned without impatience. "Unless you have specifically read 'The Zimmerwald Manifesto', then I am afraid there is absolutely nothing to discuss."

Shakeer heard the telephone ringing in the other room. There was no one to pick up. Estella had gone to the tea room on the corner to get milk. His mother was busy with somebody in her bedroom. He went into the kitchen.

The call was for Nafisa although Shakeer had doubts about calling her to the telephone. On the other end there was a very angry African man who wanted to talk to the doctor. They had a short conversation.

"Unless you give me a good reason I am not going to put her on the phone. This is a doctor's house. Unless we set some limits people call here twenty-four hours a day."

The other man made an effort to explain. "The doctor admitted my wife, Millicent Dhlomo. I want the doctor to sign the form so they will allow my wife to go out of the hospital. There is nothing wrong with my wife. She has no other boyfriend. There is nothing wrong with me either. When my wife can come out I am going to take her to the village."

"Why don't you leave her there in the hospital until she can be properly discharged?"

The man said, "There is somebody who wants to see Millicent in the village."

But who was this somebody? Where was this village? What was the urgency? Sharky didn't have the energy to resolve it.

He went to find his mother. She was hanging up her outfit for the following day in the small bedroom. She buttoned the blouse on the hanger before following him upstairs.

After she had exchanged a few words with the caller Nafisa banged down the telephone. She was furious and the skin under her eyes was very soft and black, like a bruised fruit.

It was odd. Sharky had never seen Nafisa do such a thing with a patient or the member of a patient's family. Usually she had infinite patience with her patients, one of the traits which made her a popular doctor. She would talk to reluctant patients for a quarter of an hour to get them to understand the basis of their treatment.

Perhaps, without her describing it in the same terms, his mother had contracted the same consciousness, the same disease, of her freedom. It struck Shakeer that his mother had no intention of being a widow in the ordinary sense of the term. She had always been the most determined member of the family. Her refusal to accept her predicament was at least as strong as his own.

Nafisa noticed his surprise and said, "This character Simon Dhlomo has brought devastation on his own family, and believes he has gotten away scot-free. We'll see. He's like Estella. He won't come in to get tested. Until he does he has no right to my patience. He wants to take his wife out of the ward and, I believe, take her to a healer. Where am I going to give him permission? This continent! People will not believe in the reality of sickness. Why, they won't believe in their own deaths."

"I don't know if anybody can. Our point of view only extends to the horizon of our own life."

Nafisa said, "Well, that's that, in any event. On another subject, Shakeer, do you think you could help? Bring my remaining things from the top. I am sure Govin would be pleased to assist. He is somewhere in the house, I believe."

Nafisa refused to sleep in the master bedroom. She was living downstairs next to Sharky and needed some of her clothes with her.

Shakeer and Mackey moved her boxes and cartons from upstairs into the kitchen. From there they carried them to the small bedroom at the foot of the stairs. His mother had stored her valise behind the door. The room itself had never belonged to any particular person. It was the one neutral room in the house.

Sharky unpacked some of the boxes. Most contained shoes and scarves, many of which were in their original packages, folded blouses faded before they had ever been opened with mother-of-pearl clasps that were still unscratched and looked unearthly atop the faded cloth, and Pringle jerseys, and women's cardigans. They had lived and died and faded in their boxes like butterflies discovered dead in their cocoons.

After ten minutes of work Govin showed Shakeer the contents of one box.

"Look at this, Shakeer. I am sure your mother must have forgotten this was here. It must have been here for over a decade. Nafisa might need to be reminded. She has always been forgetful at the best of times. But it's a good quality. She will forgive a grudge in two minutes."

"The one exception is Estella."

The box Mackey was holding open, a shoebox with painted sides, was filled with brown and red banknotes. The notes were clipped into bundles of equal thickness, and crammed into Barclays packets. To see them Sharky realised he hadn't seen the Barclays logo in South Africa in many years. He saw it around London when he went through Heathrow.

"Don't worry my mother, Govin. She'll find it if she wants to find it. If not, not. I believe she has currency from one of her holidays which dates back to when the Portuguese ran Maputo, Lourenço Marques. And the Portuguese have no plans to return and rule over us. Do me a favour. Put it with the shoes. I don't want to know anything about it."

Govin put the lid back on the box and placed it at the bottom of the closet.

"You mustn't apply standards from outside to here, Shakeer. Yes, we keep money away from the government, preferably overseas, because we are faced with such uncertainty. Your father, who tried to give me a broader education than simply medicine, was the first to say western standards don't always apply. He only insisted that we take our own standards seriously. The only problem is, we take nothing seriously."

Sharky didn't mind Govin's invocation of his father's authority. A not unpleasant sense of companionship had sprung up between them while moving the boxes.

It was almost the first time they had been alone with each other. Govin Mackey first came to the house when Shakeer was doing shoots around southern Africa for foreign magazines. Mackey had developed a relationship with Estella as well as with the various members of his mother's and father's family. One had the impression he would befriend anybody. If you left him alone in a room with a porcelain cat he would befriend the cat.

Govin, Sharky knew, was his father's one true protégé, the one student on whom his father doted. He had been a star at medical school. And he was still young, still thin, about Sharky's height, his age, but handsome, with thin hips and a natural air of authority, perhaps because of his short beard and appearance. His eyes didn't quite come together when he looked at you. It was curious. He was good-looking, and even authoritative, without seeming to assert himself.

There had been a great future in science ahead of Govin, a fellowship at Oxford or Johns Hopkins to complete a doctorate. Yet, to his father's disappointment, the young doctor married a relatively uneducated woman upon becoming a houseman. He soon exchanged research for a lucrative stint in private medicine.

Sharky thought, entirely without satisfaction, that despite his father's predictions, Govin had sunk himself entirely into the community. He had no wish to differ and be different.

Govin wanted the same Mercedes, the same unaffordable Crawford school education for his children, the same contribution at the temple, and the same steady band of the Rolex watch on his wrist. That was Indian materialism for you. This surgical genius had translated into nothing more outstanding than a large house, large wife, large car.

They kept talking as they stacked the boxes. It came out that, on his father's request, Govin had acted as the external assessor on the surgical examination. He had refused to pass two of the scripts, one of which belonged to a member of the Student Representative Council.

In consequence, in the demonstrations, Mackey's car had been singled out while he sheltered with the other lecturers in the cafeteria. When he came out, after Sekolo had returned to Howard College, he found that somebody has slashed all four tyres. One headlight had been smashed. Somebody had prised away the hubcaps. They would have been sold to the nearest garage even before he came out of the cafeteria.

The car was not wrecked but it was unpresentable. However the date of Govin's court case was approaching. He hadn't a spare afternoon to take it into the Audi dealership. He was, therefore, driving around with one headlight. People looked at him oddly on the motorway.

"Speaking of that, when we go upstairs, you can do me a favour," Govin explained, although he didn't specify the favour in question.

Shakeer locked the cupboards. They went along to the study to check if Nafisa wanted them to bring anything else down. There was nothing else. Nafisa disappeared into a conversation with Zuleika Mayat. The one woman was so small and the other so large that they hardly belonged to the same genus. Govin went on about the students for a few more minutes.

Sharky didn't mind listening to these complaints. Yet he had the sense the other man was pursuing an argument which had begun elsewhere. They stood in the study, Govin's strong but delicate hand holding the cold wood of the banister.

"Something I couldn't explain to your father, no matter how I tried, is that I enjoy collaborating with Gerson. It's not the money. Gerson is one technologist, a revolutionary. Always he is on the lookout for a better way to do procedures. And there is value in that. No wonder those who fear the future want to close us down. But thankfully, confidentially, Shakeer, we may soon have a settlement."

"I am glad to hear it. I wouldn't want you to lose your career over this."

Govin frowned. He was so earnest, Sharky found it painful. He sounded, for a moment, like a much older man.

"The real culprits in the affair have already skipped the country. Vishensky sits in Tel Aviv with his fortune in stock, protected by the constitution of Israel, while Gerson and I have given our homes as security. There's no logic. The world is upside down and back to front. Confidentially, Shakeer, I hear that Nafisa has her own points of difference with the tax guys but I didn't want to say anything to her directly. If I can assist ..."

Sharky said, "I don't know anything about that."

"No, it's just what I hear. Come, I'll show you the damage. It's quite something, the new South Africa, not what we anticipated."

They went out. Mackey walked Sharky around his car. It was a beautiful blue and silver model with a long bonnet. The damage to the car was extensive. Insurance wasn't going to pay out, given the political disturbances clause which had been written into every contract since Soweto.

The evening was cold for a change. The lights on the hill were unusually clear. The jacaranda trees were shivering black masses – women in black dresses, shivering in a black evening.

Settled on the gravel the Audi was beautiful despite the smashed mooring of the headlight, which gave it the startled expression of a chameleon. The inner rims of the tyres were exposed where the hubcaps had been removed. Each tyre was new and tarry, as if your hands would come off black where you touched them.

Shakeer was immune to the interest of cars. Yet he was touched, first of all, by Govin's melancholy, and second of all, by the association he made with the car's diminished beauty. It reminded him, in a way he didn't care to define, of his former wife Ginger. She had never been entirely the same, from the inside, after her miscarriage. Her wheels had been slashed also. It had been his responsibility also.

Yet, he knew, his guilt about Ginger was useless guilt. She had never been the same beforehand.

At this point Shakeer saw that Mackey was talking to him, unspooling his thoughts, as a proxy for the professor, his father. It was a false substitution. He was worse than bad. He was frivolous. Whereas in Govin's eyes, in Gumede's and Jadwat's and, for all he knew, Leila's, he had taken up the place vacated by his father.

It didn't matter to these people that he was undeserving. Govin, Gumede, Jadwat, were in need of something, and his own hair was turning white. Govin trusted him. Shakeer was ashamed that, in return, he knew at second hand about Govin Mackey's troubles. He should never read the newspapers.

The *Sunday Times* reported that the Attorney-General had charged

Govin Mackey and his mentor David Gerson on more than a hundred counts of organ trafficking. In a private hospital in Durban they had removed kidneys from Brazilian donors and placed them in Israeli recipients.

The fact that money had changed hands made the procedures illegal under international law. The two surgeons had denied any knowledge of the payments. His father had accepted Govin's excuse and had defended his former student in front of the Medical Council. It wasn't clear that his confidence had been justified.

Govin said, "Do me that favour, Shakeer? Call your mother from the lounge. She offered to complete a testimonial on her and your father's behalf. Your father hadn't finished writing it … When she's done I can then present the statement to the judges, if necessary, in mitigation. I should discuss with Nafisa what facts have to be put in, what is better left out. I would go myself but I saw that creature in there, holding court."

"Who do you mean?"

"I mean our Dr Jadwat, of course. Who else?"

It surprised Sharky to see how embarrassed Govin was. This embarrassment had stiffened his features as if a shirt was mixed with excess starch. With his starchy look Mackey loosened his tie with one hand.

Sharky noticed that his fingernails were nicely trimmed. He did have surgeon's hands, long, thin, yet strong, and finely articulated.

On his way to summon his mother Sharky began to imagine these hands of Mackey's on his young wife's back. Did a surgeon feel different when he touched somebody he cared about? Was there not some danger of confusion?

His mother was busy. She was talking on the telephone in the kitchen and mouthed a promise to find Mackey afterwards.

In any event Jadwat was nowhere to be seen. He was likely

busy in the bathroom on the mezzanine. That bathroom was almost a second office. Jadwat spent a great number of hours there, grumbling on his purple lips behind the door, inconsolable on the condition of his bowels.

Sharky asked about Jadwat when he went back outside.

"Ah, I have a little history with that fellow. We have a little history together."

"Keep going."

Shakeer was willing to press people, at certain moments, on certain questions. He had studied philosophy and classics at the university, before he dropped out, for a reason. They harmonised with some aspect of his character. They discontented you with the surface of things.

From his studies Shakeer had developed certain convictions. Reality was only too happy to keep you at the furthest distance. Reality – its endless sequence of doors which led inward – let you close only if you pushed past each door. It was a deliberate process, not something that just happened. It involved the will and, between two people, perhaps, a contest of wills to put down the illusions of one party. He was knocking on Govin Mackey's door ...

Govin, however, happily explained. "When my father passed on, fifteen years ago, you cannot imagine how relentlessly our friend Jadwat pursued my mother. We were poor people, very poor indeed. Even in the new South Africa, many things are a question of class. We were humble people. You won't necessarily understand what it meant back then, and what it means up to today, to be poor in a society which does nothing to protect people. Humility gives you a different perspective."

Shakeer said quickly, "It is not as if we were so rich."

"Well and good. I take your point. But your family were comfortable. You didn't always fear for the next month. That is to say nothing of the Hindu and Muslim divide between Jadwat and my mother. This was right after Jadwat's divorce so he had all the pent-up energy. I warned my mother. But show me the person whose heart is secure at such a time?"

Govin waited for an answer and then asked slyly, "When our mutual friend won her confidence what do you suppose transpired?"

"Do you know, I never imagined Jadwat had a separate existence from my family? Let's go in, Govin, and you can tell me the rest of the story."

They walked down the staircase and along to the house. They stood outside the security gate, looking through the open door into the living room.

Jadwat and the other visitors were nowhere to be seen. They must have left unannounced or gone into the garden.

Estella was moving around inside. She was collecting cups and saucers. It was late for her to be working. She didn't notice them waiting at the gate. Shakeer listened to the saucers ring against each other. They were like the keys on a piano.

After a moment he became aware that Mackey, behind him, was also watching Estella. She was beautiful. She was strong. But she wasn't for either of them. Estella belonged to the future which, in turn, was her property. Either she or her children would inherit this future when he and Govin were shadows, and when Jadwat and Sekolo were just stories you told to frighten children.

Govin said, "Even if you have trouble imagining it, it is quite an existence your Jadwat enjoys! In the end, with my mother, everything stopped in midair. He didn't deign to return her calls or, for that matter, my own. I swore, next time I ran into him, I would give him a proper hiding!"

The mixture of Mackey's tenderness for his mother and his resentment of Jadwat was ridiculous. It could even be perceived as insulting. Govin obviously had no grasp of the ratio of his troubles to the troubles of those around him.

But who did? This number, this ratio, Sharky thought, was a complex and imaginary fraction. Small difficulties provoked unending frustration where larger facts left no mark. Moreover this fraction's numerator and denominator were impossible to establish. The universe didn't want us to calculate in numbers.

Here Shakeer noted something quite different about their conversation. Govin was the brother, a fragile brother, he had never had. Shakeer was only sorry he didn't love the guy. His freedom was too big inside him for him to love Govin because it was an obligation. He refused to inherit such an obligation from his parents. Govin Mackey was on his own.

From nowhere Govin said, "I am saying, beware of Jadwat. Don't let it happen to Nafisa."

"She's in no particular danger. People don't understand, Govin, but my mother is the one with the strongest will of any member of our family."

Leila hadn't appeared. Shakeer missed her presence. The feeling between them was subtle and subjective. It would be too crude to call Leila because it would disfigure this very feeling.

They went inside and Mackey got into a conversation with Ismail Kader, the accountant. Kader had appeared as if by magic, and was mysteriously wide awake in the evening.

Later on, just before Sharky went to sleep, he heard Mackey talking to Estella in the corridor.

Mackey was saying, "If you ever want another job you can come to us, Estella. We need all the help we can get at home. Keep it in mind. The offer stands. But now is not the time to talk about it. So let's keep it between us."

Just when he had achieved his freedom almost everybody else was in chains. People had a different sense of time in Durban. The police had made no discernible progress in their investigation. MacDonald

Gumede refused to return his telephone calls. Leila had vanished into her own life and the chains she had chosen.

His mother was in no hurry to talk to Nawaz and find out what, if anything, he might know. In her condition it was impossible for Shakeer to hurry her up. She would have to come to the decision in her own time.

Only Jadwat, in Richmond, had advanced. He had been reading through his father's emails. They established the context of his father's work over the previous months. According to Jadwat the letter criticising Hansel Metzger's laboratory, if it had been published overseas in *The Lancet* or *The New England Journal of Medicine*, would have caused great difficulty for the university.

The university depended on international accreditation. Yet its administration, in concert with the provincial government, had encouraged Metzger's enterprise. Tens of thousands of patients had been taken off their drugs to prove Metzger's theories about African medicine and the non-existence of the virus. Many of these patients were already dead. The casualty rate had been hushed up.

Metzger's relationship with the university administration was still good. When his father, on the other hand, objected to the scale of death he had been forced to retire from the faculty by the vice chancellor.

With his new sense of power Shakeer decided to confront Metzger in person. Those tens of thousands of shades called for a tribune. Even if he uncovered nothing he had stored up a thousand insults. He would stub the man out like a cigar!

Shakeer didn't expect to see a familiar face on campus. His friends from those days were in Johannesburg, or in Melbourne, Swakopmund, Pondicherry.

The professors who once taught him had also relocated. Bernard Shumaker had retired to Milton Keynes, outside London, where he wrote letters to the *TLS* and was preparing for publication his lectures on Frege, Russell and Ludwig Wittgenstein. Shakeer visited him now and again when he passed through the UK.

Turner, the Latinist, had gone further afield. He had been shot at the wheel of his tractor on the farm inherited from a grandfather, Randolph, who served as governor of the then Natal colony. But the land and his library of Loeb classics had been left to the university which, at Sekolo's direction, had auctioned them off.

On his way up to campus Shakeer thought about Metzger, Sekolo, Shumaker and Turner, Gerson, Gumede the superintendent. He would take his chances against any of them. He was a conqueror ...

Then, when he parked in front of the main building, of all people he ran into Leila. He saw her first. She was going along the path in the direction of the library, a backpack on her shoulders as if she were still a student.

And in a way, Shakeer decided, she still was. She was untouched by her circumstances. Even if it was twenty years after graduation it was natural both of them should be there. Their potential was intact.

Leila changed direction and walked to him. She chose her steps efficiently. It brought out her tomboy character.

A current of joy ran into Sharky's head. He wanted to fall down amongst the students. No woman had ever seemed so beautiful. Yet nobody was that beautiful ... certainly not Leila. You couldn't quite say to another person what she looked like, or if she resembled anybody.

From a certain angle you discovered that Leila had a comedian's face, with a prominent nose and wide cheeks. She wasn't what you would call typically beautiful. He wanted to kiss her in plain view. He had the power to do so.

She gave him her backpack to hold.

Without lifting her eyes she said, "You must be here for the speech. I am glad you're staying around – for your mother's sake. You're not taking photographs for the occasion, I assume."

"I didn't know there was a speech. I haven't been able to pick up my camera in ages. It just feels wrong. What are you doing up here?"

"Well, I lecture every Wednesday to the second years," Leila explained. "Nothing special, because I am not on permanent staff. But I will go to the vice chancellor's lecture afterwards. He is apparently making some statement on African philosophy. You know how it is. They talk about Africa when they have nothing else in their heads. It's simply a way of excluding the rest of us in this country."

She pinned her hair in a barrette and took her backpack. "It used to be a good university. Who knows? Maybe it will revive."

He wanted to put his hand on her face. "I doubt it very much. Sekolo and Metzger are bad, no doubt about it. They will eventually go to prison, I suspect, or to a better university. But there's no reason to suppose their replacements will be any better. Humanity is a bottomless pit. We needed a new government to teach us that lesson."

Leila thought for a minute, as if she were puzzled. Then she said, "You are different, Shakeer. You are afraid of things now. I would always talk about you to the world as an adventurer."

"You're right. I'm not adventurous anymore."

Leila was right. His interest in the world had run out. In that way he was a lost cause. Was she being unfair in saying so?

Leila had the ability, as he remembered, to label people without being malicious about it. He didn't mind her saying whatever she wanted. For she was generally interesting.

Shakeer wondered again why he hadn't ended up married to Leila after he had left the university. But things were as they had developed rather than as they were intended to be. By the time you saw their drift the inertia was too great to move them back in a rational direction. He changed his mind again. He couldn't dream of kissing her.

She said, "You'll come then to the lecture? We can chat afterwards if you like. Gerson and Mackey are receiving an award now their case is settled. Govin is a true friend, one of the few people in Durban with whom I can carry on a conversation." She checked her watch. "And we are colleagues. Govin refers patients to me and I refer to him. Since he operated on your father, we have become very close."

His triumph carried him through the orange door of the laboratory behind the science building.

But there was no one to cow. There was no guard, no receptionist. The walls were nothing more than coloured panels. Indeed the whole structure had been put up overnight.

Sharky was looking forward to a confrontation. He wanted an altercation with a guard. He would have shouted at a receptionist who stood in his way. He would cheerfully pummel Metzger if the man refused to have a civilised conversation.

Yet there were only photographs to confront. In one, Hansel Metzger held hands with the President and Mugabe. In another, Metzger, in tails and a top hat, posed on the steps of the Constitutional Court. It was the day he filed his defamation suit. The costs of his legal actions were borne by the university.

A poster showed Metzger accompanying the South African ambassador to the United Nations. That was before the ambassador's speech to the General Assembly asserting the non-existence of the epidemic which filled cemeteries and hospitals. No wonder looking-glass creatures like Metzger and Sekolo set up shop in South Africa.

The photographs were framed and signed. From all of them the Viennese scientist was smiling out at Shakeer because he knew about Leila. Sharky blinked and the effect almost disappeared. Yet some sly consciousness remained.

At this moment Metzger stepped into the corridor. He was a man in his fifties, trim, with neat silver hair, wearing a red bowtie. Metzger had a large mole on one side of his head which, as if it was a button protruding there, one had the impulse to touch.

Sharky had the feeling that one of the photographs had come to life and was grasping him by the arm. He had the sense that, in person as in a photograph, Metzger was flat from the side on. If he turned to the side he would disappear altogether.

"I know just who this might be," Metzger muttered, as if the answer came with difficulty. "You are the splitting image of Arif, my great adversary. Not at all like your beautiful mother in appearance, so I judge. Ah, I have the memory of an elephant, Shakeer. Not an Indian elephant, which sits down for the rider. I mean an African elephant which nurses its grudges. Since you are here let me show you the scope of the project your father held up for ridicule."

Metzger walked him along the corridor, speaking sarcastically in a German accent. There was no occasion to punch him in the mouth. It was even difficult to make out what he was saying. For Metzger kept his own words at arm's length.

Shakeer closed his eyes to listen. Stupidity had its own music, organ-grinder's music. Metzger's voice reminded him of Jadwat's observation, which Jadwat made about every second man, that somebody must be holding him by the balls.

"... International Monetary Fund ... a virus which causes poverty ... Here, as our first priority, we don't impose a Western paradigm. On the contrary, as the President demands, we reach out to the bearers of local knowledge, African-inspired knowledge. You would probably dismiss it as witchcraft. I have even brought a herbalist on site. In fact Dumisani is moving into your father's old office, as we speak."

"That's why we had to pack up so suddenly, for Dumisani?"

Metzger looked around at him. "Don't mistake this for a petty academic feud. The stakes are high. Segregation in this country was, as I have shown in my book, a conspiracy of the pharmaceutical companies. I will give you a copy. Companies like Nestlé, Glaxo and Novartis created a defenceless population to experiment on. Anti-retrovirals arc simply more of the same. Why should we take Western technology at face value?"

"Nothing I could say would change your mind."

Metzger smiled. "Not a word. Your father did his utmost. Rationality, I believe, is the essence of the scientific method."

But reason was useless. The masterstroke of the looking-glass creature, Sharky thought, was to step from the mirror into the world beyond. Then, so long as it never looked behind itself, it could argue there had never been a mirror in the first place. But you could catch its image in the looking glass.

His father shied away from vulgar quarrels. His father had believed in principles ... and in fathers and sons. Whereas Shakeer was free to act on his own impulses. He was more capable of hatred. His mind was filled with scorpions. Finally these impulses, these scorpions, belonged to him!

He was led to the main office where Metzger produced cigars in a box. Sharky declined. Metzger clipped and lit one.

Sharky disliked the richness of the smoke in the closed room. He wanted to open a window but couldn't find one.

Metzger had been smoking himself, in his smokehouse of an office, as thoroughly as a ham. He would be smoked ... imperishable ... in his coffin. They would open this coffin in a thousand years to find him untouched by death as by life.

"I don't rejoice in your father's death, whether they are calling it murder or not. The violence in this country is the direct result of policies dictated by the World Bank. Therefore this university is taking a stand against Anglo-American multi-nationals. That is the step at which your father baulked. That is why he had no place at an institution which orients itself towards African scholarship."

The smoke from the cigar was filtering out of Metzger's mouth. The man was fat with smoke, and his hands cluttered with rings …

Shakeer asked, "Aren't you originally from Vienna?"

"Born in Basel, Switzerland. I spent a good deal of time in Nairobi. It's a beautiful city. To get to the point, despite your attempt to distract me, I would like to drop my suit. A simple statement of regret from your father's estate will suffice." Metzger put away his burning cigar in an ashtray which he placed in a drawer. "I am not vindictive. Although we had to prevent your father supervising research, I found, with Vice Chancellor Sekolo's assistance, another capacity in which Arif could continue as a member of staff."

"Selling textbooks in the science bookshop!"

"These days any kind of job is a luxury."

Shakeer stood up. He turned Metzger's chair forcibly around so that he was looking at the window.

"I want to get a mirror so that, instead of these portraits, you see yourself as I see you. In that mirror the thousand people who get infected per day, the other thousand who die, are waiting for you."

Metzger had begun to smile again. Somehow his smile had become detached from his features. Shakeer's freedom was powerful inside of him. He was going to slap the nonsense out of Metzger! He was going to slap the smile off his face!

Just as he was leaning over, Metzger put his hands up to protect himself.

"I don't blame you for being over-emotional, given what has befallen you. But I am merely a scientist doing my duty. In fact

I have a very profitable arrangement with a member of your own family. Nawaz is your uncle, I believe. Nawaz and his partner Omar are renting me space for my new laboratory on the South Coast. Did you know that? Despite Archibald's, the vice chancellor's, full support I can't keep my research in the Ivory Tower forever. I want to take it to the people."

Sharky felt as if a riddle was being posed. But he couldn't bear to hear the answer from a pair of Viennese lips. He was almost frightened. Even if Metzger was thin from the side he seemed to have grown much taller in his chair so that he loomed over Shakeer. It was inadvisable to hit him. One's fist would go straight through ...

The moment passed, the tension disappeared from the room, and they were again almost on good terms. Sharky again had the sense that Metzger knew about Leila. As Metzger handed him a copy of his book, he was smiling to wish him luck. Shakeer was too astonished to refuse the gift. Everybody seemed to know.

Yet there was no sign of Leila when he got to the auditorium in Shepstone Hall.

The lecture had begun. The slide projector was on, opening a pane of yellow light behind the stage.

A friendly-faced man in a flowing red cape stood behind the podium. It took a minute for Sharky to identify him as Vice Chancellor Archibald Sekolo. Sekolo was originally Zimbabwean.

In the darkness of the hall Sharky's indignation gradually subsided. He found a seat near the back. There was an odd sense of privacy which settled on him amongst the hundreds of other people in the audience. He was still a conqueror ...

Perhaps it had been a mistake, in his conqueror's mood, to talk like that. His father would never have done so. But what was Metzger doing with Nawaz and Omar?

After a few minutes Sharky saw that Leila had come in. She was sitting on the opposite side. He tried to attract her attention. She was clapping.

When he turned back Sharky saw Gerson and Mackey going up to the stage. They were collecting an award for bringing funds into the university. Long-legged Mackey loped behind bespectacled Gerson who wore a double-breasted white suit.

The vice chancellor had medals positioned beside him in red felt boxes. He took these, wrapped the ribbons around their circumferences, and presented them.

Sharky was distracted by being unable to get hold of Leila. At the front of the room the vice chancellor was talking. Sharky was conscious only of sections of sentences, as if logs had been broken up and were drifting downstream into his mind.

The vice chancellor reminisced about his days at Oxford. He had been the only black African in the biological sciences, excepting a pair of Senegalese twins who maintained the equipment in Rutherford and Czerniski's old laboratory.

At Oxford Sekolo had often been mistaken by his fellow students for a technician, a guard, a canteen worker, for one of the Senegalese brothers who looked nothing like him. On account of his complexion he had never been regarded as a fellow scientist. That was the colonised mind.

African scientists should understand that the sources of science lay in Africa – in Benin, Sudan, Great Zimbabwe. Shakeer saw that people wanted to clap. Yet Sekolo didn't stop for applause. He was making a case, not trying to impress an audience.

Sharky couldn't find it in himself to disagree with the vice chancellor. He saw things differently to his father. His father had been interested in truth, in Africa's miniscule contribution to world culture, in the continent's wells of self-pity and self-deception …

But what harm did it do to hear of the manuscripts belonging to the great collection of the library at Timbuktu? Those floating castles! Those imaginary laboratories! Those vanished colleges in the Malian oasis of Timbuktu! Who did they harm?

Sharky wanted to say something about this to Leila. He wanted to ask her about the connection between Metzger and her husband. When he turned around he could see, even across the hall, that she was disagreeing intently with Sekolo's propositions. After the lecture, when he tried to find her, Leila had vanished as entirely as a Malian university.

With his new consciousness of freedom he had been planning to kiss a married woman. He should never have dreamed of it.

But there was a trace of vanilla in the air which nobody besides him noticed.

Vancomycin

~

HER PATIENT DIDN'T RESPOND TO THE BIG GUNS: PENICILLIN, Vancomycin, and the standard course of Avelox.

Nafisa couldn't count the pulse in Mrs Dhlomo's neck, watching the seconds on the nurses' clock as she felt unsuccessfully for the change in pressure. You saw it every day. Once the powerful antibiotics failed to reduce a patient's temperature the result was pre-ordained.

Mrs Dhlomo had been non-responsive, lolling in the bed, producing black beads of sweat at the temple. At morning ward round the consultant could not revive her. Because she was listed as attending physician, Nafisa was called to initial the death certificate before the body could be moved to the mortuary.

Luckily she was already at King Edward. Some of the surgeons and other doctors were celebrating the dismissal of charges against Mackey and David Gerson in the Pietermaritzburg High Court. A deal had been struck between the two doctors and the province. The terms had not been made public.

The surgeons were in POPD staffroom across from the old red-brick wards. One of the nurses had put a banner over the door. David had brought a cake from home. But it was a sombre celebration. Today, doctors were sombre.

When the call came through from the nursing sister Nafisa excused herself.

She washed her cup in the basin.

"You don't mind if I leave you and go, Govin? I prefer to sign the certificate right away. I suppose that I am superstitious. Arif couldn't comprehend the fact that I find it easier to leave a living patient to hang ..."

"Go ahead, Nafisa. The only thing that remains is for the Natal Attorney-General to put the judgement on record. With people dying like flies, it is too late to be treating doctors like criminals."

She placed the cup in the rack and said, "I could not agree more. Arif could never understand why the new government treated doctors and scientists as the enemy. It was our government. For them to turn around and attack him as a racist, because he isolated the local strain of the virus, gave Arif the shock of his life."

"Without his presence I am often at a loss. Since then I haven't been myself for one hour of the day."

It was difficult not to admire Govin's open heart. Nafisa saw why her husband had been attached to him. She had been close to Govin only since the operation. Yet it was impossible to pinpoint when another person had become dear to one's heart. It seemed always to have applied.

Not long ago, but in another life, she had chosen curtains for the house. Her brother had brought a book of cloth samples to the surgery. If there were such a book for souls Govin would be the sample of a young man on which her attention would come to rest.

For Govin and Shakeer were a study in opposites. Shakeer was closed, concentrated, obscure. Shakeer had been given more security than was good for him. Whereas Govin's open demeanour, Nafisa sensed, was connected to the early loss of his father. He had been in Standard Six when it happened. Since then Govin had needed parents, patrons, people to look after him as well as people he could look after.

As if to coincide with her thoughts he said, "I have to thank you for Arif's testimonial. The judge specifically mentioned it. I must think of a way to express my gratitude. You must come to the house, Nafisa. We are expecting you."

"That will give me the chance to have a word with your worker. I hear you tried to buy Estella from me."

"But you know how people talk."

Nafisa didn't resent the transgression. Indeed Govin was one person for whom she could generally manage a smile. With his energy, his openness, he was a promise of some fact about life. In his company she foresaw that, on a given day, she would again be able to listen to her music, the *qawalis* and Bombay soundtracks of Lata Mangeshkar and the Sabri Brothers.

On this same day, far in the future, the mark which had vanished on her left hand would have vanished from her consciousness. She would be free of Rose, Kader, Estella. Govin reminded her of her independence from circumstances. Thanks to him her own day of liberation was coming.

By the time Nafisa reached the ward her elation had dissipated. The staff had pushed the bed into the corridor where it wouldn't interrupt their chores.

She felt that the small body, concealed in its sheet, communicated a reproach. This reproach was levelled at her.

At King Edward – it seemed of all the hospitals in the world – the nursing staff took pleasure in each deceased patient. The outcome proved to the nurses that the doctors knew no better than they did. Nobody, under the new dispensation, was supposed to know better than anybody else.

Without having examined the body under the sheet Nafisa saw

that it had a message of its own to convey. Soon, was what it said. Soon.

Rose the nurse was working on the ward list. It had to be updated every afternoon. She filled in the lines impatiently and didn't immediately acknowledge the arrival of the doctor.

Once she had underlined the date at the top of the ward list Rose found the certificate for Nafisa to sign in one of the drawers. She put it on the desk. The future, Nafisa thought, belonged to the Roses. She could hardly recall her last encounter with the young nurse. Trying to do so made her unwell.

"Were you working when this patient ..."

Rose shook her head. "When I came to work at eight o'clock she was already gone. If you have questions you can ask the matron. But she is on tea break now."

Nafisa took the certificate. Rose's assertion of superiority was tangible, as if she had placed an elbow in Nafisa's side.

This rudeness was not determined by the bad relationship between nurses and doctors. The nurses had favourites amongst the consultants and registrars. Rose, like the other nurses, lit up when David Gerson attended one of his surgical cases.

It was a commonplace in the staffroom that the nurses got on better with English doctors. Indian males were tolerated, on occasion, indulged. Whereas to be an Indian woman was to belong to the lowest of the low.

Nafisa didn't object to being situated on the lowest rung of this scheme of things. The way the Zulus saw her was as alien as the mentality of the Incas. They were entirely otherwise. At the same time they were as familiar to her as her own hands, familiar as Rose, Estella, Millicent Dhlomo.

Nine million Zulus shared a universe. That there were yet greater universes – a Swahili universe, Chinese universe – made her head hurt. It perplexed Nafisa to live amongst nine million beings, to treat them, to pay and be paid by them, to be buried in ground they claimed for their own, yet never to see how they should be so certain of their own place, and of hers. Yet they were certain and she was not.

In the action of Rose's bowed head, travelling across the big pages of the register as she checked the names of the patients, Nafisa sensed the assertion of this superiority. I know, said Rose's head with its caterpillar plaits. I know, it repeated as it circled the page.

On the one hand the statement disconcerted her. On the other hand, on different grounds, Nafisa was reassured by the sight of Rose's large arms. For Rose the nurse was awkward. She would be awkward in the arms of her lover ...

This youth, this awkwardness, precluded Rose's bearing any serious implication for her own existence. So far Nafisa was safe from Rose and the syringe which had slipped while they did the lumbar puncture.

She felt for the place where the needle had inserted itself into her mind. There was nothing. And there had been no consequence of the accident except her subsequent fever.

A fever meant nothing. A fever could mean anything, as Arif would have told her. Her temperature was hardly more than a degree or two higher than normal. She would be stupid to worry. It was no more relevant than Rose's hostility. But these feelings about the nurse, about her patient, about the hospital had no obvious relationship to each other.

"Do you want to bring me the patient's chart to sign? I might as well do it while I am here."

Rose brought it over to the bed, seeming to grumble. She handed over the chart and rolled down the sheet. The woman in the bed was far smaller, leaner and bonier than before. Something had dried out and, like the dairy powder distributed to clinics, would have to be reconstituted with a tablespoon of water.

Nafisa staggered, and wanted to retch. She held her hand to her neck until the impulse passed. A doctor's routine should protect against such sensation. Patients' faces and their complaints should vanish in the course of a ward round.

A recent image wished to emerge into her consciousness. She ignored it, concentrating on her patient. That lady-like manner had been marred. Now Mrs Dhlomo looked affronted. On her cheeks a slight black fur could be detected.

Nafisa could hardly stop her hand running along these cheeks. She wanted to slide her hand into the hands of the woman who had developed this soft black hair along the curve of her face. It was as natural as wanting to hold a child.

That change should continue outside of life! One's atoms would survive forever, or nearly forever, as Arif once explained. In the furthest future that science conceived, these atoms would themselves disappear in a pulse of energy.

"Has the family come? Are they taking the body?"

"Sister said the husband was coming to collect everything this afternoon. Usually the husband requests for the body to be delivered to the funeral home."

Nafisa signed the log, pressing on the bed. She gave it to Rose.

"Keep a watch on her possessions till then. Rose, I know things are not always kept safe and secure in this ward."

This world, the one and only world, was in the possession of the Roses. On her way downstairs Nafisa decided never again to set foot in King Edward. She never wished to see its corridors and canteens nor step on its linoleum floors.

Indeed there was no need for her to be there. Arif had wanted her to work, part of the time, in a public hospital, but the situation was untenable. The money from the province was laughable. Given a forty percent tax rate, the job didn't pay for her petrol to come across from town. She wasn't entirely a socialist. Nor was she a saint.

Soon she would resign her post with the province. Soon she would rid herself of Estella and Estella's troubles. She would unload all her burdens. She would sell the house and leave the country behind. She would find out who had murdered her husband. She was fed up with this in-between condition. In every direction she would push things to a conclusion.

Having made this decision Nafisa was about to laugh out loud in the parking lot. She stopped herself. It was embarrassing to laugh out loud. Fortunately there was nobody around.

She should laugh less, in future. It was an instruction she remembered from her *madressa*. In general *madressa* had not made a lasting impression on her. Religious school, which had been held around Gaborone in family garages and the back of tea rooms, had printed the invisible ink of its doctrine upon her brother instead. Of the two of them Nawaz had been the enthusiastic scholar.

Yet she remembered this one sentence from her lessons. One day, it was reported, Prophet Muhammad had said to his followers, If you knew what I know, you would laugh less and you would cry more.

Nafisa didn't regret her stern words to Rose on leaving the ward. When a patient passed away in the wards his or her possessions disappeared as completely as the atoms on that final day. Everything disappeared and no sign of its existence could ever be recovered. It was only surprising that more doctors didn't vanish in smoke through the powerplant chimney.

She could never complain to Arif about such a thing. He didn't share her dismal view of the nursing staff. He was angry if she said anything about them. It had been his article of faith that poorer people, darker people, were the more honest. Thus Estella.

Nafisa remembered, as some point on a line which had long been passed, the story of her Lacoste perfume and Arif's reaction to her discovery. Arif knew what he thought before he tried to think. He didn't give a minute to take her seriously!

She longed to be involved again in the small grievances she had accumulated against her husband. This longing was as great in intensity as a bolt of love piercing her heart.

She was looking forward to seeing Jadwat because of this pang.

Jadwat called to say he would meet her at the Botanical Gardens.

It was an odd choice of location, Nafisa thought, but then Jadwat, with his surplus of time, had endless quantities of information about places to go. If you had a free afternoon anywhere from Potchefstroom to Port Elizabeth, Ballito to Benoni, Jadwat would know the whereabouts of the halaal restaurants as well as the sections of town it was safe to visit.

As far as she was concerned the place itself was irrelevant. No, Nafisa looked forward to seeing Jadwat because of who he was, how he existed. Wherever he went he was always on the surface. Whether on a particular day Jadwat was pleasant to have around, or whether his presence irritated her in every detail, nothing about him reached any further into her heart.

Compared to her husband, compared to Shakeer, Estella, Leila and Rose the nurse, and Kader the accountant, Jadwat played a role in the creation which was as superficial as a butterfly. He didn't pray. He didn't go to the mosque, didn't give *zakaat*. He didn't connect to a community.

Should Jadwat die, it would be ridiculous to cry for him. The man wouldn't cry at his own funeral. Thank God for Jadwat!

Nafisa continued to be weightless as she drove up to the Botanical Gardens. Cowie Road ran along the hill and was a sentence punctuated with palms.

The alternation of light and shadow caused by the palms brought back a medical school trip to Uttar Pradesh with Arif. He hadn't yet proposed. Their train had passed beneath an uncountable series of rickety railway bridges on the way into the mountains ...

Such memories distracted her from the main event. If she wasn't careful to exclude them they swept her away from the present moment.

At the Greek café outside the Botanical Gardens Nafisa stopped and bought a Sprite. She hadn't touched a cool drink in years because she was also monitoring her sugar. She didn't want to wind up with diabetes.

Inside the gate, about twenty metres along the path, she found the spot Jadwat had mentioned. There was a small bench where she sat down. The Sprite, of all things, set in motion a tide of joy inside her.

The municipal gardeners were out in force. They wore orange uniforms and some were carting long hoses. Others knelt, shaping the soil around the trees with trowels.

"And how are we?"

Jadwat startled her. He had arrived from nowhere, silent in his orthopaedic shoes, listing to one side because of his shoulder. He was wearing linen. She noted that the jacket needed ironing. The yellow suit was tight at the chest and belly.

She had never seen him look so old. She had never seen him so much resemble the actor he had wanted to be.

He sat down beside her. "You're excitable today."

"Jadwat, I don't believe that I am."

"Let me pour you some tea."

For some unguessable reason Jadwat was carrying a Woolworths packet. He brought out a thermos which he unscrewed between his legs. He poured the tea into the top of the flask without spilling a drop and tested its temperature before handing it on.

In the throat of the thermos, for just an instant, Nafisa observed herself, very thin, with her arms in a tent, and stretched out to the width and breadth of the silver lining. Then the image was gone.

It occurred to her, for the first time in their long acquaintance, that Jadwat was probably a good doctor. He was no less methodical than Arif. No wonder they had been close in their student years. Both men went about everything step by step, pouring a drink or driving a car, as if they were putting the pieces of a jigsaw puzzle together. She was faster, like her son, and more prone to making mistakes.

"To be on your guard, to retreat from involvement ... but it's nothing to be ashamed of. Through my work as an actor, as quite a young man, I gained insight into the intricacies of psychology. I observe, for one thing, that you have internalised the turmoil of the last year. Not that I blame you. I really admire you."

Nafisa couldn't think of an answer to this strange declaration. It was a looking-glass speech, containing looking-glass sentiments that she could not immediately identify.

She gave him back the cup.

"You don't care for the tea? I filled it at the Greek shop."

"I'm old-fashioned, Jadwat. You should know by now. Unless I know who made it, unless I have seen the kitchen, I won't drink."

Nafisa was baffled. Jadwat's expression, flickering in his mutton countenance, was incalculable. In his face she couldn't immediately work out the proportions of jollity and solemnity.

Indeed, in so many years of acquaintance, she hadn't taken the measure of this man. Some people you could not fathom although they were not deep. For Jadwat was an enigma in her own mind rather than in himself.

Like clockwork, at the sound of his name, at the very thought of him, the same sensations rang out: her exasperation, her contempt for his mere existence, and, above all, the sense of a long and stale relationship which reminded her of opening an old packet of Tennis biscuits.

As if to reinforce the comparison, her companion brought out a packet of these biscuits. Nafisa was starting to be less confused. She had caught the mood of the occasion. Her companion was intent on re-staging the Mad Hatter's Tea Party.

Jadwat was the March Hare. For she was Alice and had been Alice from the first breath she took. The secret must be kept between them. If Shakeer discovered her in this situation she would sink into the ground.

Jadwat was ardent. The fact did not instantly displease her. Nobody had approached her in this interesting condition for so long that it took half a minute to find the word.

Had Arif ever approached her in this state? Had he ever been like this in Bombay? Was Arif ardent, for one instant in which their hearts stopped, before he proposed in Uttar Pradesh? She didn't recall. It was startling that on the very same day that Rose's certificate had been signed in King Edward Jadwat should be ardent ...

"I have to eat a Tennis biscuit now. I carry them because of the diabetes." He put his hand on her arm. He was short, of course, and his eyes burned into her neck. "When I feel my sugar is low then I take one. Can I offer them to you?"

"This is unexpected gallantry. Since when do you carry Tennis biscuits around?"

Jadwat put down what he held and took her by the hand. His voice settled down. Despite the wildness in his face he sounded just as if he was explicating some article of Trotsky's from the Civil War period.

"I just explained about the biscuits and my diabetes. Oh, you are a master at distraction, even from your own emotions. Yet even you, Nafisa, cannot prolong forever. Because people can talk a lot of nonsense. They say you cannot recover, will never recover, that you have changed utterly since Arif's operation. Oh, they say that you are on a downward slope. And what reply do I make?"

Nafisa was hypnotised by the stupidity of these words. Yet she didn't wish to forestall them.

For Jadwat's train of declarations must arrive at its destination. Something, some small difficulty, might resolve itself. Too often people glanced off each other at an angle. Nothing came to a head. Nothing was resolved, nothing discovered.

"Tell me. What do you say to them, Jadwat?"

"I say, I will cure Nafisa!"

Jadwat turned to her, perhaps hoping to put his arms around her shoulders. His short legs were raised slightly in his lap. The gesture reminded her of an expectant dog. Who was this man?

Nafisa stopped herself laughing although there was a joy in her as wild as Jadwat's. The cause of her joy was different.

"I will cure you, Nafisa! Allow me to cure you ..."

"Shut up now."

"Let me take care of you. Don't forget I have established a good footing with Shakeer. All I ask is that you allow me to contribute according to my ..."

She drew back on the bench. "I mean it, to shut up! This is not the revolution of your political fantasies. We are talking about human beings, about what is possible, and not possible, with human beings. Having a character means having limits. Respect them for yourself, if you want to be a real person for once in your long and drawn-out existence, Jadwat."

For a moment Nafisa wanted to call the man in front of her by his first name. She wanted to soften the blow they were both pretending to administer to him, but she had forgotten Jadwat's first name.

Instead of saying his name Nafisa shouldered her handbag. She had brought the green one to work. But she was always doing something instead. The word defined her existence.

She wasn't angry. She gave Jadwat a parting kiss, moving away so he had no opportunity to take her in his arms. She looked down to hide the fact that her eyes were filling with tears.

For she didn't want him to misunderstand these tears. She was grateful that Jadwat had pretended to suffer from this admiration. His cure was unlikely to take effect.

Between them Jadwat and Rose and Estella had created enough absurdity for a lifetime. They would never go directly to the point. Nafisa, on the other hand, had no taste for circumlocution.

She was finished with Jadwat, as he had perhaps intended. Her brother Nawaz was next on her list. She was going to discover whatever he knew.

It was her responsibility, Nafisa decided on her way back from meeting Jadwat, to probe Nawaz. She owed it to her son. For, she could see, the uncertainty about Arif had entirely unsettled Shakeer. It made less difference to her. Maybe it made no difference whatsoever.

Kader's documents arrived at Beatrice Street. Nafisa opened each folder on her desk while the telephone rang in the other room. She smiled at her secretary whenever she tried to enter and refused to listen to the noise in the waiting room.

While she was reading she called Kader, typing with one hand and holding the receiver under her chin. The switchboard put her on hold. She kept reading. This box of documents, it occurred to her, was a Pandora's Box. Arif had liked to say that all of human history had spilled out of Pandora's Box.

The new information concerned her brother. Kader's investigator had done his work on Nawaz. He had a copy of the receipt of Nawaz's air ticket from last year which went from London through Dubai and back to Johannesburg.

Nawaz had left a fortnight before the money had been taken out but that might suggest that her brother had found an accomplice in London. He had never mentioned that he had been in London – and for Nawaz, who sold clothes for a rag of a living, to be in London?

Her brother, it seemed, belonged to this world of shadows she had tried to neglect but which had conquered her previous life. Shadows had dissolved her good luck, but how? Isipingo? Dubai? Hansel Metzger? There was no obvious way in which these facts could be connected.

Nafisa was ever more convinced that Arif had not harmed a hair on his own head. Therefore he had not intended his act as a criticism of her. This certainty caused a current of such warmth that it was as if she were blushing.

Kader sounded as if he hadn't gone to bed in a month. "Obviously, when it comes to money overseas, you cannot complain to the police if it goes missing. Whatever you want to discuss with your brother, I leave it to you."

"I am going to do it today."

"Look, Nafisa, the tax guys walked out of my office this morning. If we don't account for the London money, they want to obtain a judgement to repossess your house in lieu of a fine. Look at this country. Increasingly, I say, make your money, and get out."

"No more lectures, Ismail. Tell me what I need to sign and return to you."

The conversation ended. Nafisa was left to think that, in a looking-glass world, a thing didn't make sense until you turned it over. Her husband would hardly have loaned the money to her brother. Her brother would hardly have murdered her husband. The idea was laughable.

It was not that Arif and Nawaz had been on bad terms with each other. They were on no terms at all. She had hardly seen them exchange a word in several years.

She called her brother on his cell.

"Where are you, Nawaz? I'll meet you."

"Not now."

"No, I have to talk to you," she said.

"You must be off your head, Nafisa. I am at Warwick market, on the side nearer to that tea room. When was the last time you drove through Warwick Junction? It's far too dangerous."

"I'll meet you."

She hung up the telephone, not wanting to hear her brother's complaints. She had the strength, with this warmth in her arms and face, to ignore his objections. For she was now sure that Arif hadn't intended to harm himself or her.

The knowledge made Nafisa see that she had the strength to do anything. She had done in Jadwat in one afternoon. She was triumphant.

She was bound to win. Nawaz shouldn't speak before he discovered what she was capable of. Her faculties, her hearing, her understanding, were suddenly as acute as a scientific instrument. She should have been able to hear it in her brother's voice all these years. Each one of his words was a lie.

One thing Nawaz said was true. Nafisa hadn't been to the market since it had moved to its present location. Ten years ago, when she had gone to buy fruit and vegetables on a Saturday morning, the owners of all the stalls had been Indian.

Warwick Triangle was now a small instance of Lagos. The market gardeners supplied Woolworths and Checkers rather than selling in the market. People who could afford to avoided the city altogether, confining their travels to Umhlanga, Ballito, Glen Ashley, Durban North.

In a normal frame of mind Nafisa would never have walked two kilometres from her surgery. Nobody thought it was safe. People were routinely knifed for their wallets, purses and watches.

Yet the walk made sense in her posthumous existence. Her supply of fears had vanished. It didn't matter if she was robbed, slapped, tormented.

Beatrice Street, outside her surgery, was already crowded with buses and taxis. Passengers got on holding their shopping which they were taking back to the township. Nafisa went past the Islamic high school and the Catholic hospital, wondering about their co-existence.

She saw that her brother was calling her on the cellphone and turned it off. She wanted to see what he had to say face to face. Then she could say better how much was a lie.

A little further down and the roads were exclusively African: motorcyclists standing on the kerb, truants in school uniform with their shirts untucked, a jockey from the Greyville track who strode stiffly in narrow white trousers into a café. She noticed that the jockey had the same stature as the schoolboys.

Somebody asked her for money, then another person. She heard their requests without looking around. It was vital not to meet anybody's gaze. Otherwise that person would gauge her vulnerability.

She was never going to make it to Warwick Avenue. It must be at least a kilometre from where she stood. At some point in this kilometre she would be seized, stabbed, and abandoned. She should sit down in the middle of the pavement to pre-empt her attackers.

This sensation passed. Nafisa made herself keep walking.

She worried about her handbag. It was conspicuous. She liked the precise tailoring. She associated the accuracy of each stitch with the sound of certain British accents. Yet she saw that the rectangle of green leather was unearthly against her arm. It didn't go with her outfit. She should have brought the red one to work.

She folded her arms around the bag. It wouldn't prevent a half-determined thief but the gesture was important. It was a spell of prevention. Her school in Gaborone abutted a convent. Nafisa had friends amongst the girls there and admired the Catholic habit of crossing oneself to protect against the future. She would almost do it herself.

Feeling more confident she walked quickly past the arcades on Commercial Road. Was somebody pronouncing her name? She hoped it was nobody.

The names on the signs were familiar while the roads were as strange as could be. They had become African since her previous life. She didn't recognise any of the shops or shopkeepers. She could as well be in Rio de Janeiro as in Durban, in Brazzaville, or at the bottom of the ocean.

It was impossible that she should return to her surgery. She was so deep in the city, far beneath its surface, that, to look up and see where she had come from, she couldn't reckon the depth between herself and the surface.

She realised that she was praying underneath her breath. Her mouth had been moving in the absence of consciousness. She was embarrassed. What had become of her?

She went past the Mobil filling station with her head down. She didn't want somebody she knew from her life to see her moving along. She was nothing which should be looked at.

A group of labourers in orange uniforms milled about on the tarmac. Their strong odour was reminiscent of the English liquorice she liked. They were arguing about something, perhaps a football match since one of the men mimed a kick. They pursued their disagreement in growling voices.

None of the labourers stopped her. It would have required only the touch of a hand to take away everything she carried. Yet nobody seemed to notice she was there, clutching the Harrods handbag. She still didn't relax. Something could still always happen on her way to the market.

The point was an important one. In their long ago conversations Shakeer quoted her a line out of his university setwork. Call no man happy, until he is dead.

Shakeer's reasoning or his professor's, as she remembered, was as follows. While alive, anything could happen to you. You could be in the best situation one minute and be struck down in the next. Afterwards, a person was protected from misfortune ... safe like the figure in the snowglobe Nawaz had kept on the window of the bedroom they once shared.

All the same you were dead. Could you be happy without thought, life, motion? It was moronic reasoning. Her son was a moron. So was she. Her brother, it seemed to some, had looted her London account, an act which led to the murder of her husband, while she worried about stolen perfume. She had been at the height of her stupidity!

She crossed the road into the market. It was the height of stupidity to imagine she could find her brother in Warwick Triangle. People moved in every direction, as if they were molecules in Brownian motion. She thought about calling Nawaz. But she preferred to wait.

The market floor was crowded. The displays of copper-eyed fish gave her the sense of being watched, pushed, slandered. They turned their flat faces to follow her. Their scales were orange, shimmering like one of the skirts Gujarati girls in Durban wore to their formal functions.

A mist rose over the fish and found its way into her eyes. There were vegetables strewn on the cement floor and clogging up the drains. At the same time there was an unexpected clean smell, air freshener, coming off the counters.

Nafisa hesitated. A man with a handtruck full of turnips shouldered her aside. She fell, sat for a minute. There was no pain.

As she got up she saw a man folding a shirt on his knees. He stretched out the arms of the shirt and crossed them over as if he were trussing a chicken. Then he packed it in a brown paper bag. Beside him was a stack of cotton shirts which he worked his way through. He must have been selling them from one of the empty counters.

After another moment it became clear that this man, who was thin and bearded, was her brother. She waited for him to notice her. His eyes widened and he put down the bag.

He came over to her and held her by the shoulder. "But why are you coming to see me, Nafisa? I desperately tried to reach you on the cell. Your secretary had no idea where you disappeared. It is just like you to leave us in the dark." He released her. Nawaz was softer than usual, especially away from his wife in front of whom he could be gruff. "Arif would never permit it. Someone could have put a knife in your side. Then what would we say?"

She didn't reply. Nafisa knew that she was considered delicate by her family. On the other hand she regarded her brother as the one who needed protecting. Whatever he had done did not affect this fact. Her heart turned to think where he spent his days. In factory shops and arcades he made in a month what she put away in a day.

It was unbearable. Behind the beard, behind the increase at his hips, behind the mosque-goer, he was a delicate creature ... still delicate. As a youth Nawaz had radiated the charm of Tony Curtis, her favourite character in the movies at the Gaborone drive-in. You still saw the skinny, energetic youth ... an after-image belonging to his present self. That was how the past attached to the present: an after-image.

She didn't acknowledge Nawaz's anxiety. She said, "I didn't know you worked here. I thought your business was buying clothes from the factory shops and selling to the retailers on Prince Street and Umbilo Road."

"I help out my friend Narendra who has a stall here. That is what it is like in business. You can lend a hand, then they can lend a hand. Today I have a consignment of Adidas shoes coming in, which is arriving at Victoria Wharf ... But why are we talking about this? I still cannot believe that my sister, at her age, is here in the market."

"The world is full of surprises."

They went to the Pale Moon tea room on the opposite side of the road. Nafisa smiled at the description. Somebody had an imagination.

The place was situated beside the depot where a hundred municipal buses were confined. Their green shells shuddered amidst lines of patient passengers. There were guards to stop any bus burnings.

A lot of unrest related to transportation. Under the new government the bus lines had been privatised. Old guerrillas were new bus lords. Many routes had doubled in price. Estella devoted a large part of her salary travelling back and forth to Chesterville.

Inside the café it was quiet. You went through a narrow entrance, past a cash register emplaced on a trestle table, and into the back. A minute passed before you noted that the enormous roar of the buses was gone.

Nawaz found a table on the side. They sat on rickety chairs. He studied the menu intently, as if there might be something on it he had never seen. It might be the case that he had never before read a menu. She had forgotten that Nawaz couldn't often go into a restaurant, even a halaal tea room. Religion had narrowed his experience. She would insist on paying.

"Do you know what you want?"

"Give me a minute, Nafisa."

While her brother was reading Nafisa looked at the wall behind him. A large picture was mounted there. It was a few centimetres thick. It resembled the dioramas installed in the Natural History wing of the Durban museum which the art department hadn't changed in a decade. The art department had ceased to function. There were other priorities.

She found the picture ridiculous. But it didn't offend her. In a corner was a crescent moon. It was made of thick paper. The desert dunes were folds in a length of satin while the Cheops pyramid was represented by a triangle of yellow cloth. There was a group of camels, slouching on red legs. She saw that the picture was plugged into the wall. Pipes of light rippled inside the frame. An electric picture?

Sharky dismissed such pictures, such houses, and all such Durban artefacts as preposterous – from the Peppermint Palace in La Lucia to the sailing ship décor of the old English hotels and the interiors of a thousand gilt households, and the Durban women with orange complexions which lifted off with a make-up brush.

Nawaz asked seriously, "Have you decided now?"

She shook her head. "I will just have the tea."

"Then I will have the same."

It didn't matter what Nawaz said. She wasn't going to try to catch him out in an answer. She could never lay a trap for anybody, including her brother. For this picture in the Pale Moon struck her as radiantly innocent.

There was some lesson it had to transmit to her. It had been waiting there patiently and implacably, stupidly, openheartedly, for her to discover it. If necessary it would hang on the wall until the end of time.

To place it on the café wall impressed Nafisa as the work of a saint. A saint was somebody who knew nothing of the sin of irony. Only a saint, Nafisa told herself, would have hung it there with his gentle hands ... only a saint ... and in the same moment she saw how ridiculous her deduction was.

She could feel tears waiting in her eyes. They wanted to come in. How ridiculous she was! How stupid were her thoughts!

The waiter brought a tray. He poured tea into two cups, and set spoons in front of them. He was a young black man who was proud of the apron tied on his shoulder. Underneath he wore a T-shirt and jeans.

The waiter placed the bill under the teapot. Instead of leaving, however, he leaned down to Nafisa.

"I can see that picture interests you."

She said, "I can't say I didn't notice it."

"If you like it we have one for sale. I can let Selwyn, behind the counter, know you're interested. He can make a price."

"I will let you know."

The waiter left them alone. Nafisa took stock. In his broken shoes, in his blue shirt with torn collar, her brother was a sad phenomenon. Her husband had been incapable of taking Nawaz seriously.

Without intending any insult Arif had once called her brother a clown. But Arif was dismissive where he should not have been. Didn't clowns murder and suffer?

She had the urge to check if her brother smelled of fish from the market. She was sure he wouldn't. Neither of them would. They would be miraculously unscathed. Circumstances did not entirely touch them.

As brother and sister, like their father who had been untouched by his stroke and all his misfortunes, they had this odd quality in common, some immunity to outside forces. It was the next best thing to good luck. Maybe it was even better than having the odds on your side.

Of course she had relied too much on this property. She had believed it extended from her to her son and also to her husband. Her immunity had disappeared in the single instant of an afternoon when Arif opened the security gate. She could see the gate opening as if she had been on the other side …

Nawaz checked his watch. "I go up to Asherville at four thirty to pick up my container. Narendra is supposed to bring it from the docks if he can talk his way through Customs. They are second-hand clothes from Hong Kong. They send a container across the oceans and it costs me less than to buy from the factory here in Isipingo."

Her brother's irrelevance irritated Nafisa. He didn't want her to get to the point. People conspired to obstruct her. But she had the upper hand. She had sorted out Jadwat.

"Nawaz, I cannot be bothered to make polite conversation with you. According to my accountant Kader, you are investing in a building along with Metzger, who, as you well know, forced Arif out of the university. What kind of friend is he to have? Now I find out you went through London last year without so much as notifying me."

"I must have told you, Nafisa. I did inform you of the fact. I had business in Dubai, in fact to set up these shipments of clothes. They organise it between Dubai and China. You do not remember because it was a traumatic time for all of us."

"Since when are you a foreign traveller? You hardly have enough money to put petrol in your car, Nawaz. You had better tell me what is cracking before the police find out first. For me Arif is gone. That is that. But if you are mixed up in any way, I want to know about it."

"You believe that Arif lent me this money for the building in Isipingo? Therefore I have some understanding of who shot Arif, if, indeed, there was someone. Are you sure you want me to answer the question, Nafisa? You don't know where questions can lead you."

"I would like to hear the truth from you for a change."

Nawaz shifted in his seat. He was glowing and, for all she could tell, it could have been anger or happiness in his face. It was different from her experience with Jadwat or with Shakeer. She was surrounded by incalculable men. But her brother, just because they should have so much in common, was the most distant and obscure.

For a moment Nafisa couldn't put a finger on the alteration in their relationship. When she did, the magnitude of the change between them stopped her breath. This change had taken place over years and years and was still incomplete. For their ways of life had driven them to opposite poles. Nawaz, her brother, had become her adversary ...

Nafisa had prior experience of such a change. After medical school she had been fired from her job at the Wentworth clinic because of Arif's political involvement. The order had come down from the Special Branch to the province, to the clinic from the province. None of her colleagues had uttered a word of protest, treating her instead like a creature it was somebody else's duty to finish off.

The Polish superintendent Jennifer Fleischner had delivered the news to Nafisa in her office with an unmistakable expression. It was a look of triumph. Fleischner took pleasure in her downfall.

If Fleischner was as enormous as a tree, if her face was misshapen, if her bum was the size of a sofa, then at least she had conquered Nafisa. She had political motives. Poles like Fleischner had been hired by the old government on account of their ferocious anti-communism. Now Nafisa compared the superintendent to her brother.

She wondered if the situation was symmetrical, if, to Nawaz across the table, she was a Fleischner of his own. For she was now his adversary also.

Indeed they were so far distant, this brother and sister, that she could barely distinguish the individual words coming out of his mouth. It was all sound. Out of his mouth flowed a continuous stream of deception ...

He was saying, "... not take a cent. In all these years I shouldn't complain to you about money, Nafisa, about not being well off. It has never been a point of contention between us. And, since you ask, I never even came out of Heathrow. I was sitting in the transit lounge. You can talk to Dr Mackey, whom you and Arif both love, if you want to know where the idea for the investment in the building came from. He was the one who suggested it."

"Don't blame Govin."

"Because Govin you should love. And Arif should love Govin above everyone. But this Govin is no better than me despite the fact he is a doctor. After everything Arif had to say about morality and medicine Govin put himself above God to save Arif's life. It is hardly a secret he took a kidney from the black market to save Arif. Govin talks about it." She could hardly say if her brother was still talking in English. "Between us, Nafisa, you and me and Arif, our disagreements have nothing to do with money. No amount of money could compensate me for a lifetime of condescension."

Nafisa got up from the table. She looked forward to the walk back to the surgery. If she was robbed, slapped or murdered she wouldn't resist. She would welcome the aggressor, like a lover, into her arms.

Nafisa was half sure that she had found her murderer ... although it wasn't Nawaz ... and although she couldn't put a name or a face to this identity. Everything was known in advance. This conversation with her brother, this morning's interlude with Rose and then Jadwat, had been fixed in each detail since the beginning of time. They merely waited to speak their parts.

She didn't leave any money on the table. Nawaz could pay for two cups of tea. She had paid for him often enough.

Blue Lagoon

~

IT WAS A TRICKY BUSINESS, TO PROBE HIS MOTHER'S MIND. IT was tricky with anybody and especially if, like Nafisa, that person didn't wish her thoughts to be shown.

Shakeer had ample reason to try. His mother wasn't well, something she wouldn't admit. She had been running a fever.

Nor could he pry a word from her regarding her conversation with Nawaz at the teashop. It was plain that she was concealing some datum or surmise about her brother's involvement.

You had to be roundabout to get anywhere with Nafisa. His mother was a monad, a nomad. She had a thousand confidants in Durban, in Lens and Laudium, in Pretoria and Johannesburg. She dispensed her opinions to all and sundry yet not one person could claim to know her private beliefs.

When Nafisa wished it, her solitude was inviolable. She would not allow Shakeer, or anybody else, to puncture it. Only his father would have known where to start.

There was an odd evening when no one else was around. They were between appointments with Nawaz, Govin, Estella, Leila, Jadwat, Zuleika Mayat, Ismail Kader.

Shakeer could see that his mother was restless in the house. She was perspiring and complained of a headache. At five o'clock, as if to conclude a working day, he proposed that they go out. His mother agreed.

Without discussing the matter they went to the beachfront. They hadn't been there together in a number of years.

There was parking on Marine Parade. Ten minutes of walking brought you to the old Natal Command. But it was too early, in life, in history, to be doing something for the pleasure of it. The walk, of course, had been a habit of his father's who often went by himself. The professor had enjoyed the liveliness of the beach ... and even its seediness.

Twenty years ago, when the professor had been a lecturer, this stretch had been reserved for whites. Africans were banished to the far side of the hotels. As an Indian you could go along the Esplanade and buy pink chemical ice-cream from the carts. The sand was restricted. The ocean belonged to everybody.

Twenty years ago people drove their vintage cars down from Kloof and Hillcrest for the sheer pleasure of the excursion. On Remembrance Day the same drivers wore poppies commemorating the losses of the British Empire in the Great War.

The poppies had disappeared. The holiday had lapsed. The drivers were no more. On New Year's Eve 1990, when the racial laws were suspended, the sand had been occupied by two hundred thousand township revellers.

Shakeer and his father had gone for a ride to North Beach. The two hundred thousand were concealed amongst the smoky headlights of the taxis and the many fires burning in barrels up and down the sand. In this huge mass of the poor and the black there was no threat to anybody else. It was a happy victory.

Now the lights were muted in the dilapidated bars. The piers, though not long, were truncated by fog.

Beyond them Sharky imagined the container ships. Their long decks were lit late in the evening. He considered taking a shot of the clouded ocean. The light was wrong. Besides it was an overdone subject. He was hoping his expedition to a medicine man with Estella was going to produce something more interesting.

"You can't see the ships."

Nafisa said, "Do you know, I was pleased, secretly, when it was overcast? Then your father wouldn't think about them."

The ships sat in the offing to avoid paying harbour charges. Even under the old government, during sanctions, the professor had been adamant. The country was being done down. On a clear evening he had been indignant at the mocking line of Panamanian and Taiwanese ships.

In this way his father studied the very thing which distressed him. Shakeer was different. By and large he didn't brood. He had taken after the other parent. Oddly the similarity didn't help him understand this other parent.

As they walked it struck Sharky that no photograph managed to capture his mother's particular expression. She was rapid, fierce, fluctuating. Taking a photo meant understanding the situation on the far side of the lens. This he had never been able to do with his mother.

In any event he couldn't take his camera out of the case in good conscience. Photographs were irrelevant, unserious. People were dying like flies.

When they got to the lifeguard tower Nafisa thought of something.

"That camera around your neck is only inviting trouble. If you want to have your camera tomorrow, if you insist on going with Estella, then you may want to put it away. I'll give you the keys and you can put it in the boot. If you think tomorrow is so important …"

"Don't bother. I'll take the risk. You brought your telephone."

"Well, as a doctor, people need to be able to reach me. If I am robbed so be it."

To underline this point the phone rang in her hand.

She spoke for a minute, then closed her hand over the receiver. "Let me talk to this fellow. He is the husband of my patient, Millicent. You remember he's called several times. Well, he seems to be changing his mind. He is keen for me to alter the cause of death. In exchange I want him to be tested. He wants me to write tuberculosis on the form."

"You can say no to him."

She waved him away. "Give me a chance. It's an opportunity to save the children as well. I will catch up."

Shakeer did not object to moving down the beach. The beach was relatively safe. He liked being alone. It was unbearable to harbour his increasing feeling for Leila around his mother. The contrast between their situations, and the unlawfulness of such a feeling, was too obvious.

He walked towards the Elangeni. You could see the glass elevator riding up the outside of the hotel.

He stopped to admire the handiwork of the Zimbabweans. They maintained complicated sandcastles. They charged tourists to be photographed beside their creations. They made something valuable of time and sand.

The men slept in blankets just above the tide line. They never moved from the shore even to bathe. They had taken over the territory, a claim which would not have been possible under the old government.

They were always young, often good-looking men, as dark as certain trees. Nor did they appear to have a complaint in the world.

One such man attracted his attention. He had a camera in his hands.

"Do you like your photograph taken?"

Sharky declined.

"Of course I see you have a camera of your own. Maybe you

would like to take a picture of me. Well, sir, do you have any illnesses?"

The man was skinny, of ordinary height. His coat and pants were so ill-sorted that they might be chosen from somebody's washing line ... and probably had been.

"Why should I trust you? Are you a doctor?"

The other man nodded. "You could trust me."

"But why should I?"

"No, I was in medical school for two full years in Congo, before the university burned down. I was planning to be a surgeon. Look at my hands."

The man put the camera in his jacket and proudly showed his hands.

"One professor, from Scotland, told me I had the talent to be one of the top surgeons, not just in Congo. We were rather good friends. Then the war started again. Most of Bunia disappeared in one week. The professor vanished back to Scotland. That is when I moved down here." He went back to his pitch. "Therefore I am familiar with a range of conditions. Tuberculosis ... Whooping cough ... Appendicitis ... Alcoholism ... Maybe depression? Maybe impotence?"

Sharky laughed at him. "I don't have any of those. Well, nothing treatable."

"I never met one person who has no need for a doctor."

Nafisa walked up. She didn't look well. Her face was pinched.

"Ask her. I'll pay you." He turned to her. "Do you want to show him your arm? We have a doctor on the beachfront."

Sharky was surprised when his mother did roll up her sleeve. She didn't usually play along. Yet she presented her arm gravely to the man.

"I didn't want to waste my time and see a doctor. But it has been troubling me. Can you say what it is?"

The medical student produced a magnifying glass. He supported

Nafisa's arm while turning on the light behind the lens. He moved the magnifier along her hand and arm. Then he shook his head.

"I can't say for sure."

"Put my son's mind at rest. He is a worrier."

While he put away his magnifier the young man assembled his thoughts. Despite his excitability he was a deliberate talker.

"The first thing I learned in medical school was not to promise the moon. I am not saying I don't have my suspicions. I saw similar distempers in Bunia. I am saying you must go to a doctor who has access to a laboratory." He was more earnest than one would have thought. "Then you can bring the results here and check it with me."

Nafisa gave the young man two rands. Yet she seemed to have forgotten him by the time they reached the open area where the rollercoaster had once cantered along the tracks. Not even the concrete pylons remained.

This, in turn, reminded Shakeer of his situation. In the past few days, without new evidence, Sharky's idea of the case nonetheless shifted. He was curious as to what had passed between his mother and uncle. But Nawaz, given his narrow style, was incapable of any action greater than a certain magnitude.

This incapacity was not, as his mother believed, because of the man's poor situation. In fact the limits of his imagination were narrow. Nawaz might have information, about Metzger and other parties, but murder was out of his reach.

On the way back to the car he asked, "So what did you make of our Congolese doctor?"

"I didn't think anything of him. I assumed you were amusing yourself. So I played along."

He said, "You haven't been well. Nor have you said a word about your conversation with Nawaz. Time is up now. You know that the police have never questioned him."

They arrived on Marine Parade. The Christmas decorations were going up.

Nafisa said, "Let me worry about my brother. I will call the coroner tomorrow and have a talk with him. If there's anything to tell, then you will be told. In the meantime worry about yourself. I can see you are restless. And after all, what keeps you here?" She spoke as if reading an indictment. "This country is too limited for you."

"That's not what I mean."

"Then I really don't know what you mean."

For his mother to be civil and unfriendly, at one and the same time, was a bad sign, worse than either of these attitudes on their own. It meant that she wouldn't give an inch in any direction. She would let Shakeer fly back to Papua New Guinea without saying a word to keep him nearby. They had never been able to communicate. He had to allow for what she might be thinking.

Their interests diverged. To work, take photographs, think, Shakeer needed to travel around the world. And his mother could hardly travel with him. But he could hardly leave her behind. His thoughts went back and forth between these impossible alternatives.

Estella was his mother's bugbear. Nafisa was sure that Estella stood ready to exploit any man in the vicinity. If, as usually happened, this source of distress had been superseded by a greater distress, Shakeer still didn't want to explain the terms of the arrangement he struck with Estella.

Nafisa was suspicious. She knew that he was going to collect Estella in Chesterville. They would go together to the healer in Eshowe where Shakeer could take photographs. The trip would take an hour and a half by car, four hours each way by bus.

Now, in the first place, Estella was used to travelling in these areas. Her son was not. What had Estella done to deserve a favour?

In the second place, Nafisa argued, it was inadvisable even to go into a township. The old locations of Chesterville, Umlazi, Clairmont, KwaMashu, the wrong side of Cato Manor, were off limits to someone in his right mind. Drivers had been stoned, pulled out of their cars.

Nafisa's suspicions about Estella, at any rate, were not altogether cockeyed. In exchange for taking him along Estella borrowed five hundred rand. Sharky had handed over the money with a sense of satisfaction.

Yet it was a self-interested gesture. The opportunity to take photographs of the ritual was a good one. Shakeer had never taken an interesting photograph at home. He could never quite understand what he was looking at in Durban, what he was supposed to make of it.

Shakeer was used to being elsewhere – in Guangzhou province in China, or Montevideo, or Caracas, or the back of a cement shop in Kathmandu where he had discovered the unending black keels of the clouds moving across the Himalayas and then a parade of battered trucks and vans on which the headlights, despite being switched on in the downpour, were the shade of the rainwater.

Shakeer was quiet opening and closing the gate. He didn't want to wake up his mother and have her come upstairs. It was early in the morning.

He felt some hope putting the equipment in the boot. He was going to see Leila later in the day. And to hold a camera, after so long, was like returning to humanity after a long absence. His new freedom meant something.

The middle class, he thought, was its own jailer. He had been everywhere in the world. It would be an irony if he could not go to Chesterville twenty miles from King Edward where he had been born. Many million people resided in the townships. Presumably most of them had no intention of committing suicide.

The drive to the entrance of Chesterville took twenty minutes. There was little traffic. An Engen garage was open. After that there were no landmarks, just rows of small houses and sandy streets.

There were no traffic lights at the intersections. The street signs had been taken down. Estella's directions, as his mother had predicted, were of no use.

After a minute he panicked. He had taken too many wrong turns already. He rolled down the window and watched the passers-by with a growing sense of alarm. They were already curious about his presence. To ask directions would be courting disaster.

He went back towards the highway. On the far end of the road was a station house. At the next turning he found the main road through the township. It was behind the station. From there he went back to following Estella's directions. When he found her house it was with a sense that he'd escaped a catastrophe.

"I didn't think I was going to make it."

Estella said, "It is not hard to find. There are only two turns from the highway to my house."

"Yes, but I've never been here before. I didn't know what was going to happen if I got lost."

"Nothing was going to happen," Estella returned. "We live here every day. Anywhere you go, somebody is living there every day."

"It's easier for you to see that than for me to see that," Shakeer said.

He hadn't won the argument. Estella looked annoyed. She was different in her own situation, away from her rocky relations with his mother. Estella was even prouder than he had guessed. But this was surely an advance, he thought; wasn't it less painful to find pride in a person than humiliation?

He had a minute to consider this fact. Estella left him in charge of her daughter while she fetched her neighbour Peter Dlamini. Estella had told him that her daughter Nomzuma was going to stay behind with Dlamini. Nomzuma's presence was not required at the ceremony in Eshowe. Indeed, in order to diagnose her condition, it was desirable that she not be present in the flesh. They had to take along a photograph instead.

There was a quality in the girl's face Sharky couldn't pin down. Nevertheless he made her stand against the side of the house and took a photograph. She had dots of black hair along the back of her neck which reminded him of the spots on a leopard. She didn't want to talk. He looked around the township street for anything interesting.

A window was cracked on the house next door. It was held together by ribs of thick black builder's tape. Through the window you could see the corner of the room and a bed in which the occupant was lodged under a blanket. Half a loaf of brown bread stood on the table in its ethereal wrapper.

Just to look inside Sharky could smell the brown bread. Closing his hands he could feel the lightness of the wrapper. Then there was a dish on the floor beneath a leaking roof, one shirt and a pair of pants on the shelf. So little!

But it was the natural state. People should have nothing. His mother was outnumbered by her objects. If it was ever necessary it would take years to dispose of her kingdom, from the open secret of her Bruno Magli shoeboxes to her perfumes, shoes, and all the unremembered accounts and insurances.

The man under the blanket rose, pushed off from the bed with a walking stick, and opened the door to admit Estella. It was Dlamini himself. He came out to where they stood, poling his way on the walking stick as if he were propelling a dugout. A milk pail swung from the other hand.

"Is it not a superlative morning? The birds are already at their offices in the trees. And who is this I spy?"

Dlamini set down the milk pail. It was full of flour, Sharky saw, not milk.

Dlamini went on. "Nomzuma will be safe in my hands. I don't blame you for going to the healer to ask about her fits. You can ask me about hospitals and doctors. I lost all five of my children and two wives in hospitals."

On the way to Eshowe Estella told Sharky something more about her neighbour. Dlamini was a retired headmaster. He was alone but his thoughts were full of his family.

Other people declined into their tragedies. Some put them out of their minds. Whereas Peter Dlamini was proud of his deceased wives and children. He seemed to live among the seven of them still, counting through his photographs each evening on his unsteady bed.

"There is another part of the story. Dlamini has proposed to me. He is very modern. He came to me, not to my family. He insisted on giving his speech to the bitter end."

"You turned him down?"

Estella said, "My impression is that everybody who comes into close contact with that man does not last long."

The diviner lived in a crumbling block of flats in the middle of the small town of Eshowe. The front door to the building was chained shut.

A boy came down to let them in. The boy wore tennis shoes and shorts. He didn't say anything, just gestured for them to follow him to the top.

By the time they had gone up six flights they had left the town far behind. There was no sound inside the building except for the noise of water sliding down an inside wall, probably, Sharky thought, through a broken drain. A child's tricycle stood outside one of the flats. It was missing its back wheel and covered in stickers.

"You can go in."

The boy unlocked the trellis door with a small key he produced from his pocket. He waited for them to enter. Then, standing outside, he locked it and pointed for them to go into the next room.

They emerged into a close chamber made closer by blankets nailed over the windows. Sharky was reminded of the servants' quarters in old Durban houses which had been so narrow it was startling that they should contain a human being. They all had a certain smell, a certain dull light, which was like a pang.

This room was decorated with bead necklaces, skulls of small animals, and a digital clock on the wardrobe which told the time in red numbers. Next to the clock stood a bottle of methylated spirits, radioactively purple in its evening surroundings, with a loaf of white bread beside it.

During Sharky's childhood blacks from the countryside drank methylated spirits after filtering the liquid through a slice of bread. He didn't know if it was still the common practice.

Then there were jugs of water on a small table and, reclining in a tatty chair where it took him a moment to discover her, was the nearly toothless diviner.

She had a very dark, very rugged face not unlike the Aborigines Sharky had encountered in a bar near Alice Springs and with whom he had spent a fortnight taking photos. The diviner was rocking back and forth, opening her mouth wide whenever she looked up to reveal black gums in which a few teeth were buried as sparsely as tombstones.

"Please will you sit down."

Estella was placed on her left while he was pointed to the opposite side of the circle. Estella gave the woman the snapshot of her daughter.

To Sharky's surprise the diviner continued to speak in English while studying the photograph.

"I threw the bones yesterday morning when I knew you were coming. I understand that your daughter suffers from fits. First you must understand how a person is requested to become isangoma. Do you know how I came to be what I am?"

The woman produced a pot of tea which was lying behind her chair. She poured the dark liquid into small glasses, and told them to drink. It was cold, sweet, but had a bitter aftertaste, as if you were drinking a solution of tamarind paste. Sharky gagged, then finished the drink in one go.

The woman continued talking. Her tone was flat and impersonal. Yet her voice was very far away, as far away as the town from the top of this dilapidated building.

Sharky had difficulty dividing word from word. The sentences in his ear had become an indivisible stream. But then the diviner's words became clearer than any he remembered hearing. They were the clearest words in his life ...

"I became ill after I had eaten a dish of beans. I dreamed constantly. I could hear voices calling me although I had no idea what they were saying. They talked in a foreign language but it was more foreign than Chinese. I would sneeze for an hour at a time and I started to take snuff. Like your daughter I suffered from severe convulsions. When people laughed I would weep. When others were asleep, even at midnight, I would wake them up by singing. I had pains throughout my body. I would often shed tears without knowing the reason. Later on I understood that the shadows were working on the spirit inside me so that they could surround me without driving me mad. They were the night which gathers around the lamp. I was the lamp." She looked at him. "You have finished drinking? Then take this and put it underneath your tongue."

She handed him and Estella the wafers, showing them how to place them under the tongue. Sharky found it an uncomfortable fit. While the diviner talked she opened a velvet pouch. She took ten bones out of it, counting them one by one in Zulu.

Sharky saw that Estella was restless, as she often was when she was being talked to, but he was transfixed. He had the certainty, again, that these two women were smiling at him ...

Somehow they knew that he had persuaded Leila to meet him later. Leila, in fact, had been reluctant to meet him. She had kept refusing. She had never agreed in so many words. Yet they had made an appointment at her place on Essenwood Road.

For the first time, with this diviner in whose magic he didn't believe, he had found somebody who could account for his situation. She had some quantity of knowledge. He wanted to ask her about his father.

Meanwhile the woman arranged a black cloth on the floor between them. It was weighed down by a white marble tied in each corner. She began to cast the bones, throwing them onto the cloth and studying their positions.

She muttered something over each bone, then recorded a stroke on a page, working from the top to the bottom. She placed the photograph underneath the cloth.

"When I was very sick, finally, a white beetle appeared in the doorway. It came closer and closer and said, 'Stand up! Follow me! Sukuma! Ngilande!' It rose into the air. I ran along with it. It went into a river where I followed and found that I no longer had the necessity of breathing. I saw many things at the bottom of the river – a python, snakes coiled on medicines. The snakes were my fathers and mothers. They looked at me with open eyes. The python had a lamp on its head. It asked me, 'What is the colour of the beetle?' When I answered correctly it told me to take the medicines. Those are the same medicines I have here. Afterwards

I followed the beetle out of the water, not looking backwards. There it said, 'I leave you here.' A mist rose around us."

The diviner packed up the bones and replaced them in the velvet pouch. She added up the strokes and crosses.

The diviner wrote the number on the photograph of Nomzuma, as if she was a Catholic marking her daughter with a cross on Ash Wednesday. She folded the black cloth, making sure the marbles remained on the outside.

"After that I went back to the village where I met many who were weeping. They told me they were mourning the death of a woman who had just drowned in the river. I told them I was that woman. They were amazed. I was accepted as isangoma from that moment. But to this day I still cannot eat a dish of beans."

She told them to get up. They took the wafers out of their mouths and stretched their legs for a few minutes while Sharky paid the fee. The diviner unlocked a drawer in the wardrobe and took out the change. She also gave Estella an empty tin of beans along with some instructions in Zulu.

It was time for the photographs. Sharky turned on the overhead light. It was nothing more than a bulb dangling on a cord but it would help the camera.

As he adjusted the Nikon Sharky thought that the future was as dark as the diviner's tea. So, now he came to think about it, was the present.

He took a few shots of the room with long exposures. He took one looking out of the back window. You could see the rigging of the washing lines on the lower floors of the opposite building.

The diviner stopped them in the other room. She had a greedy look which none of the photographs had captured. Sharky was sure that the woman was smiling at him out of her rugged countenance, although she addressed Estella.

"I explained the story of my education to you for a reason," she said. "I believe your daughter has been chosen by the spirits as a vessel. I can arrange it. She can come to me for lessons."

Estella said, "I can't afford it."

"When you are ready, you will be able to afford it. The money will arrive as an unexpected gift. Maybe this man will provide the sum." Shakeer didn't agree. The woman went on. "You will find that one of the nights, soon, Nomzuma will dream of a small brown snake. That is a spirit snake. The next day she will find the same snake in her way. Be careful not to injure it. It will bring a message from the *amakhosi*. Come back then. The shadows will not give up their property in this girl. She belongs to the ancestors." The diviner was suddenly talking in a matter-of-fact way. "And as for you, Shakeer, when you are also ready to look into the matters which concern you, you must also come."

"I wouldn't expect it. I am not much of a believer."

"We have a different view of sickness. You may find, if you lose your health, that someone is trying to harm you. It will not be returned until you have identified the guilty party. Or perhaps you are in love. I do not know for sure. The spirits are not always specific. They do not always choose to be clear."

As they were standing at the door, waiting for the boy, the diviner discovered something in her pocket and hung it around Shakeer's neck.

She said, "I have a gift for you. This is designed to steal the heart of a woman if you are interested in her. But be careful. It will only work once."

Shakeer was still wearing the amulet under his shirt when he went to see Leila. He had not seen her since she had left the vice chancellor's lecture.

For a while he had been conscious of a great feeling of tenderness whenever he repeated her name to himself. It had passed. But now he was convinced that Leila, like the diviner, more than the diviner, possessed the answer to some question he could not formulate.

Leila had been reluctant to see him but had agreed to meet him at her house while her children were at school. Her place was in Musgrave, one of the large houses which changed hands for a song in 1994.

Sharky felt that he was being borne through the city by a wave which would not put him down.

The wave carried him along Essenwood Road. The pastel-coloured mansions and apartment blocks along Essenwood defined the style of the old colonial city. Recently Nigerians and students from the former technikon had been travelling across the Berea into Musgrave.

The only person who wasn't smiling at him, who hadn't been smiling at him in weeks, was Leila herself. She looked like someone who had been slapped.

She let him into the house, saying nothing as she locked the door behind him. Not even his mother, Sharky thought, treated him with such brutality. He put his hand to the amulet around his neck.

"You can go through to the lounge."

She was wearing a brown skirt and blouse but it was impossible for Sharky to look directly. She was as tall as him. Leila looked you in the face just as the stars burned into your eyes. There was some fierce quality in her which he didn't possess for himself.

He wasn't her equal. As a teenager, he remembered, Leila had often been angry with him in particular. It was as if they had been in a relationship. Leila had expected him to understand her anger without explanation. Yet she had begun an affair with another student without notifying him.

Leila was closed. She had been capable of lying, being caught in a lie, and then blaming the other person for catching her. She had been furious with Shakeer, for instance, when he figured out that she had this boyfriend.

At the same time, as he recalled these impressions, he was struck by her figure in her skirt. Leila was utterly beautiful, Sharky thought, far more unearthly in her beauty than when she had been eighteen.

This unearthly beauty of Leila startled him. True, her face was slightly plumper than it had been at eighteen. The slight increase made her cattish, self-contained, the source of this secret he would never obtain elsewhere.

To get hold of this secret, which had nothing and everything to do with his father, he was planning to make several impossible demands. She should leave her husband and marry him.

Of course it was a selfish conviction. He was thinking only of himself. Leila was his compensation for everything which had become crooked. She marked the point on the line that he had to go back to, in order to discover his rightful path.

She led him into the kitchen. He saw that she was self-conscious.

"Why don't you sit down at the table? I'll make a pot of tea."

"I take skim milk if you have it."

"Of course I keep skim milk."

Leila turned her back to him and fiddled with the kettle. She opened a tin of tea leaves and placed three spoons in the pot.

Sharky imagined that for uncounted years the two of them had been sitting and standing in these positions, in this tiled kitchen with its saucepans, blocks of knives and ladles, and the sanded lozenge of the chopping board. In this imaginary kitchen they had become used to each other, had begun to fit into each other and become pieces in a single puzzle, which was the shortest definition of love.

But it was impossible to return to what should have been normal. What had happened had taken the place of what should have happened. Now it had a claim of its own.

For the jetsam of Leila's lives were everywhere around them.

They disapproved his presence … the child's bike helmet on the table, a half-used bottle of Nutella, a tall box of Captain Crunch cereal. They knew the reason he had come to the house.

He was a usurper. He had no right to ask them to move aside.

Sharky stood behind Leila.

Without looking she said, "Sometimes, Shakeer, it seems we are about to vanish. If it wasn't for my children, I think to myself, I would disappear into the ground. What is life for?"

Shakeer had been following his own thoughts. "People are so pleased to have a government of their own, that won't put them down, that they won't hear a word against it. Majorities always resist reality."

Sharky sensed, just as he replied, how dull he must seem. He was talking about politics and Leila was concerned with life itself … He couldn't come close to talking about life.

This dullness was a mask over his features. He was more alive, more alert to the world, than this mask would allow. He would have liked to lift it up and meet the world on his own terms.

"I wasn't asking about politics, Shakeer. I will tell you what I think. Life is intended for happiness. There cannot be any other answer."

"I can't imagine happiness has anything to do with it. It never helps me to figure out what I'm meant to do next. When I look back, I don't think there has been a single day on which I've been completely happy. So how can it be that I have been chasing happiness? Would I have so little to boast about?"

"Govin was here for dinner yesterday. You know that he is one of Omar's business partners along with your uncle? They are investing in some property. Anyway, he said almost the same thing, in almost the same words. It's uncanny."

It was clear that they were pursuing different threads of a conversation. Sharky reached around Leila and put his hand on her hip.

He was confirming that, however differently they talked, they were moving towards the same point. Everything which had happened had carried them along to this point. The wave which had brought him from the morning to her house and her hip continued to bear both of them along.

Leila didn't resist his hand. Sharky felt that the silk touch of her blouse was cooler than her body.

It had been a long while since Sharky had kissed somebody, even longer since the impulse had been a meaningful one. Ginger had prodded him with her tongue, as if she were trying to reach his brain. It had been unpleasant.

In the interim he had forgotten how unusual another person's lips, a woman's lips, could taste. They were as soft as a breath.

He found Leila examining him with open eyes. They were a shade of brown that was the same as her blouse.

"But why do you close your eyes when you kiss?"

After a while Sharky decided that he didn't want to push himself into Leila, or into anybody. Leila was open beneath him. Her mouth was open to him, and her arms which she held behind her as if she were afraid, her hips, her legs, her eyes which became as wide as pools, and even her smell which was dry and biscuity.

It was amazing how open to a man a woman in her thirties, a woman with a child, could be. She moved next to him without necessarily being synchronised to him, as if she were swimming alone.

For a moment he couldn't recall Leila's name. She was without a name, something different from a person.

Afterwards, in bed, Leila lay underneath him. She had her arms above her head. Her body was still cool next to him.

For a minute her eyes had stretched, changed in colour. She seemed to be praying. Then she was silent. She folded her arms across her chest. He was surprised by the large brown circles on her breasts. They were like strokes of a painter's brush.

Sharky rolled onto the other side of the mattress. He was overcome by tiredness. He wanted to go to sleep and wake up in the same position without having moved a hand.

Omar could join them. It would make no difference. He wanted to be open about everything. What had happened had been momentous, the conclusion of a process stretched out across the years. Omar, her husband, could hardly object to this logic.

For Omar was the usurper. Moreover they were lying, he thought, in her marriage bed. It should have been the very bed in which the two of them had been married.

Leila reached out for the amulet. It was a small black pouch with strong black thread along the top. There was nothing inside it.

"What's it for?"

"It's nothing. It's stupid. A sangoma gave it to me this morning. Estella, our worker, wanted to find out about her daughter. You know she has epilepsy. I went along to take photographs. Not sure I got anything good ..."

She opened it between her fingers. "No, what is it?"

"It's meant to help a man win the heart of his beloved."

Leila sat up. Her hair streamed over her shoulders. Her skin was lit from within and this light was streaming from inside of him. She brought the sheet over her shoulders. The light continued to radiate from beneath the sheet ...

She said, "I am not your beloved, Shakeer."

"Then what was this about?"

"Of course we had a feeling that there was something unfinished between us. It's not a secret, Shakeer. It was there on the day I came to your house, before the funeral, even though we didn't say a word to each other. Now it's over. You have never been interested in me, except as a way to connect yourself to something. But I don't want to be a means to an end. We can go on with our lives."

"I don't know if I want to go on with my life. But, you know,

I did feel, after Ginger, that, for the rest of my life, I didn't want to impose myself on another woman. Why would I add so much difficulty to an innocent person's life?"

There was no answer to this question. Leila, folded in the sheet, was already going on with her life. She was a thousand miles away.

He should never have tried to push himself into another person. It was a male imperative, Shakeer thought, with which he could no longer identify. Now the same desire turned his stomach.

The Lancet

~

NAFISA WAS HOT. HER FEVER HAD RETURNED. IT WAS AS STRONG in her head as the element of a light bulb.

In bed she was reluctant to move her arms because they were stiff and tired. Her temperature had not come down with two Panados. She didn't like to take drugs but the paracetamol in Panado was gentle. You could trust the syrup in children.

After ten minutes the bedroom began to turn. She was confused in the darkness and put on the bedside lamp. The house was silent. She was hot. When she sat up she found that she was dizzy.

She wouldn't go back to sleep. Her sleep was easily broken. The story about the princess and the pea had always made sense to Nafisa. Now the moisture under her arms made her feel soiled.

She would have liked to stand under the shower for five minutes but it was past midnight. The house would ring with the sound of the water. If she washed at the sink it might let her return to bed in better shape.

Out in the corridor it was silent. To keep her balance Nafisa held onto the cupboard at the foot of the stairs. She didn't want to wake Shakeer up in the next room. She disliked having her son around when she was unwell. He didn't know what to do with himself at such times. Estella, no doubt, would say he was an ear out of place.

Hand over hand she made it to the bathroom where she quickly locked the door. The ceiling light came on after a moment. She pulled down her trousers and urinated.

Her water was hot, almost steaming in the bright bathroom. She noticed the smell of lentils.

Where was it from? She hadn't gone near lentils in twenty years. Arif had noticed that whenever she ate something containing lentils she developed a headache by the following morning. Since then she advised patients who suffered from migraines to avoid common triggers like brown lentils, red wine and certain mushrooms.

Nafisa dried herself. Her temperature seemed to have gone down. She noticed that the coppery hair between her legs was stiff as a hairbrush. This red hair also ran along the bottom of her stomach, just as if it had been sewn by a sparing hand.

The red colour of it startled her. Underneath her clothes, where she didn't encounter them from day to day, were concealed any number of imperfections and absurdities. Their ranks increased with the years.

She turned off the lamp and went back to bed. In the dark her mind turned to the dog who would have to come back to the house from Jadwat's cousin. There was no need for the dog to move on. Everybody else was preparing to. Even Jadwat, pitiful Jadwat, had moved on. He had not been at the house since their conversation in the Botanical Gardens.

According to Zuleika Mayat, who laughed about it, Jadwat had found a new widow in Overport. Of course he had every right to make eyes at another woman. It wasn't his heart that interested her. How could it be? But Jadwat was a connection between her new and her previous life. To have him out of her hair disoriented her.

Still it was a looking-glass pain. It didn't hurt on inspection. Above her fever, which had risen again, it could scarcely be registered.

Nafisa sensed that her fears for the future had almost vanished.

She could close her eyes and visualise their circumference closing centimetre by centimetre. They would soon be a memory with no power to enchant her. Free of her fears, she could therefore surrender her contempt. She would be on the level, in the dust, with everyone and everything.

In the morning, she decided, she was going to call Jadwat in Richmond, or in Overport, and forgive him for everything, for himself. She would befriend his new widow. One had to ask, could a widow be described as new?

If, tomorrow morning, the accountant had not come to an arrangement with the tax department, she would clean out the house and sell off her possessions. They couldn't confiscate what she had burned, whatever she didn't sell or give away. If necessary she would live in the road. And, after her talk with Nawaz, she had some ideas about this.

Just as Nafisa arrived at this conclusion she was overcome by a feeling of astonishing tiredness. It rose up out of the heat inside her head and chest. Her final observation, as she lost track of what she was thinking, was that she would never remember any of this in the morning.

In the morning her temperature was down. The fire which had been burning in her body had consumed itself. Nafisa brushed her teeth to no avail. There were ashes in her mouth. She almost expected to find them in the basin when she spat out.

Not one of her resolutions was practicable. She didn't want to live in the street without a cent to her name. Nor did she want to lose the house, to part with Estella, to unload her burdens. She didn't want to travel the world with her son. There was no point exchanging one unhappiness for another. Her own unhappiness was deep, rich, the creation of almost a lifetime. It would be foolish to give it up.

She might have no choice about the house. Without some new information about the money in London, it seemed, the tax investigation would proceed to a finding. The government would level a substantial penalty. She was likely to lose the house in Westville, perhaps her rooms in town, and her insurances and annuities.

Ismail Kader had bad news to deliver on this score. Nafisa could tell because he didn't come to meet her. Instead he called her to Suncoast Casino on Friday morning before he flew out to Dubai. He wouldn't be back in the country until late in January. He was living in hotels and aeroplanes. That was his style of life.

Kader was on the Suncoast board. When he was in a hurry he met the occasional client in the steak restaurant. Yet Nafisa was sure that it meant bad news. He could have told her over the telephone.

Moreover she was late. To get through the line of cars at the checkpoint took ten minutes. People gambled from early in the morning until late at night.

Nafisa saw as she walked up to the entrance that a new wing was going up. Long neon tubes, pink and green, had been hoisted onto the edifice in sections which the builders were aligning with each other. When the construction was complete the casino and its grounds would occupy many hectares along the shoreline.

In the old days the same area had been covered in sawdust, once a year, by the Boswell Wilkie circus, used as a place to pitch its tents, park its trailers, and walk the elephants. From the main road you could just about see the nodding heads of the elephants above the fence. The pink showing in the collars of their trunks, which picked at the near side of the fence, was the most obscene colour in the universe.

The circus was gone. Meanwhile casinos, proscribed by the old government, carpeted the country. The same funds which owned private hospitals had taken a stake in the casino companies.

Today people chased fast money. To want to be a doctor, Nafisa thought, was old-fashioned. You could slave for twenty years in a Beatrice Street surgery and never attain the safe harbour of being a millionaire in dollars.

Kader, the accountant, was in the millionaire bracket. It did him no good. Kader had become as fussy as an old man over the past few years. Nafisa saw it as a protection against his freedom. The money made too many suggestions as to what he should do and where he should go.

As if to confirm her belief, when she sat down at the table, Kader was instructing the waiter about the preparation of his salad and vinaigrette. He wanted to live forever; he ate salads. Once Kader had spent ten minutes giving instructions to a waiter ... and further instructions when he solemnly sent the plate back to the kitchen.

If Nafisa hadn't been worried about the news Kader had to deliver she would have been irritated by his solemnity.

"You don't look well, my dear Nafisa."

"I didn't sleep well last night, Ismail. I am not at my best."

"Nobody expects you to be at your best," Kader replied. "Let me get you some tea. Then we can talk about where we stand with our friends from Pretoria."

Nafisa said, "They want to take the house from me? They are welcome to it."

"First let me get the documents out. Then we can go through the details in sequence from beginning to end. Everything has a time and a place."

As Kader unpacked his briefcase Nafisa watched the people pass back and forth inside the hall. At the end of the corridor, before you got to the slot machines, was a semi-circle of fast food outlets and then several jewellery and clothing shops.

There was no rhyme or reason to what was on display in the

shops. They sold leather, handbags, nougat, cigars, silk scarves, biltong, souvenirs. This jumble of anything and everything in the shop windows was bathed from above in steel-blue light which resembled a welding torch. The light was harsh. It reminded her again that she had not slept properly.

It wasn't a good environment. The people who walked off the casino floor looked as if they were working. They had determined expressions. Nafisa supposed they must have lost money already, were preparing to lose more through the morning, and were determined to hold on until a change in luck.

But the casino had all the luck. It hoovered up the good luck which was going. Ordinary people were left to the remainder and this was scarce.

Despite her wish for him to hurry Kader waited until the teapot arrived. The delay made Nafisa more impatient. Her headache was coming back. Kader was too careful when he had bad news to pay out.

Yet nobody could be truly prepared. Surely a recipient should be spared the length of these preparations …

Before committing himself to a word Kader looked around the restaurant as if there might be somebody listening to his advice free of charge.

"Nafisa, I cannot say it was a bad idea to keep a part of your assets outside the country. How is it your revolutionary friend Jadwat describes the slogan of those of us lucky enough to be in the middle class? Hope for the best to happen but keep your money in pounds! To him it is a joke. Whereas, to me, it is a serious proposition. What happens if the next president is a second Mugabe?"

"The current one is bad enough as it is."

"This one hasn't been bad for business as such."

The waiter arrived with Kader's salad. He inspected it, looked dissatisfied, but then changed his mind. He waved the waiter away and carefully salted the entire plate, seeming to count each grain of salt as he did so.

Nafisa's fever had come back. She was hotter than she could have imagined. She was going to swoon in the casino. She knew that Nawaz hadn't been involved in her husband's death. She was starting to suspect who it could have been ...

"From the Receiver's point of view the contents of that account in London belongs to them. They argue that it is income on which you have never paid taxes. And remember that, against my advice, you never filed for amnesty in 1998. That was where you went wrong."

Kader flexed those very dark eyebrows as if he were extending his arm. They looked like they had been darkened with a koki.

"If you can tell me where the money is, Nafisa, we can present an argument. We can negotiate. Can we tell them at least who emptied the account? It's not a simple thing, to have a letter giving power of attorney."

Nafisa drank her tea. "I have racked my brain on the matter, Ismail. Nawaz is not the one who did it. There is no one Arif would trust with a power of attorney, apart from myself and Shakeer. He would have come to you first of all, isn't it? You cannot say that he was distrustful of others but Arif was a reserved man. Look, he was a scientist. He had colleagues more than he had friends."

"No, that is true."

Kader picked at the salad. His cheeks, she noticed, were losing their definition, as if they had been filled out with putty. He was spoiling with age. Kader's would be an easy face to dislike, Nafisa thought, if you happened to be in the mood.

But she wasn't in any such mood. She had relinquished her capacity to hate. She was open to every type of spoiled existence.

Existence was there to spoil, to go bad, to go off, to go sour. Otherwise there would be no need for love and forgiveness.

Kader went on. "Then, if you don't come forward with the information, they have every intention of going after your house. It is your principal asset."

"Can they do that to us, Ismail?"

"I am very much afraid that they can. Everything else they are slack about – crime, poverty, the collapse of Zimbabwe. This is the one area, ironically, where the government has successfully tightened up. I can only do my best, Nafisa. I have always done my best for you and Arif."

Despite his words Kader didn't look afraid. It was so hot inside her, Nafisa felt, that she croaked instead of saying goodbye. She was going to go home and pack all her possessions. After twenty years she didn't want to spend another night in the house. After a minute the thought of leaving the house made her want to laugh out loud.

Nafisa restrained herself. Kader, if he overheard, wouldn't have understood her laughing. His limits, everybody's limits, were too obvious. It was her misfortune – the smallest of her misfortunes – that her appreciation of these limits of everybody was too keen.

On the other hand, for once in her life, her own spirit seemed to grow without any boundaries. Her scope was as large as the universe.

The temperature in Nafisa's head was about to make her fall down in the parking lot but it also made her senses far more acute.

In Westville, in front of the driveway gate, stood an African man. He had a small stature, not yet middle-aged, and wore a pockmarked brown leather jacket. He was smoking but put out his cigarette on the bottom of his shoe.

Nafisa had never seen him before. Yet she had the sense that, like Rose, like Estella, like her black swans, this man had been waiting in the wings, a nobody who became a somebody as he moved in her direction. Control of her life, the constant addition and subtraction of her sorrows, had been taken from her by these nobodies. These apparitions!

Nafisa sat in the car outside the gate for a few minutes, watching the man who was studying her in return. She took her cellphone out of her handbag, weighed it in her hand, opened it out so that the blue screen swam into her palm.

The contacts list scrolled into view. She found her son's number. He was still using a Vodacom telephone rented at the airport. She had warned him about it. It cost a fortune to receive a call.

She decided against calling Shakeer. Anything could happen if he confronted this man. They might come to blows. Blows might come to a knife, a spanner, a gun. Men were vulnerable. On the other hand she was capable of infinite resistance. Nothing could touch her.

Instead of driving through into the garage she got out of the car. She put the cellphone back into her handbag and made as if to give it over. It was the red bag. She had never really adjusted to the colour either.

To her surprise the man didn't take the bag. He seemed equally surprised that she was holding it out to him.

He said, "Doctor, I am Simon Dhlomo." He corrected himself. "Sipho Dhlomo. I am the husband of Millicent, who was your patient at King Edward."

Nafisa tried not to show that she was relaxing. She put the bag under her arm. "Right, of course. We talked on the phone. I recognise your voice, Sipho. You are the one who wanted me to take her off the treatment? You wanted to take her back to the village. You didn't believe she was truly ill?"

"I didn't know, doctor."

Her grievance was fresh. Something in his posture, tight underneath the leather jacket, refreshed it. "Afterwards, Sipho, you wanted me to change the cause of death. Where will you find a doctor, even in this country of ours, who is prepared to do such a thing and put his professional reputation at risk? One thing I cannot understand: Why is one cause of death better than another? On top of it all, then you refused to come in for a test, which is vitally necessary."

He didn't contest her charges. She went on. "Tell me one more thing, Sipho. Who are you really? Were you even Millicent's boyfriend? Were the two of you actually married in the first place? How do I know you are who you say you are?"

He made as if to brush the question away. Things, in the township, were perhaps too complicated for questions. He might not be Millicent's husband. People had been known to impersonate the relatives of a deceased person, if there was money to collect. But her heart was hard.

Nafisa continued. "If Millicent had come to me six months ago, she could be walking around today. By the time you are that sick our options are extremely limited. Now do you understand the necessity to seek treatment as early as possible?"

She had finally angered him. She was relieved to see it. The man's face was hard, handsome, she supposed, harder and more handsome when his expression contracted like this. Nafisa was puzzled at Millicent's choice. She herself could never enjoy being the companion of such a face, discovering it again in bed beside her each morning. Her husband, her son, her brother had softer features.

Sipho said, "You were right, doctor."

"Ah, now you admit that I was correct from the very beginning. Of course I was correct. I am a doctor."

She was too firm. She was too stern. She saw it at once in the face of the other. The seed of her desire to be firm with men had blossomed into a tree: each word she uttered grew up in its shade.

To Nafisa's astonishment Sipho burst into tears. He had given no warning. She could not recall seeing a man crying in public, and in front of a woman.

And who cried nowadays? Her family didn't express itself that way. Arif had cried only once during his illness, late at night in the hospital, when he had been unaware that she was awake on the couch. Hadn't Jadwat observed, incorrectly, and in another life, that she, Nafisa, was one part sunshine to another part rain?

She wouldn't allow herself to be affected.

"Will you come to my rooms where I can test you myself?" He nodded. She went on. "You can tell my secretary to give you an appointment. I am only thinking about your children. I remember your oldest son's name, Godfrey." She changed direction. "I believe Millicent had a watch and some other items of property. When you went to the hospital was everything there?"

Sipho shook his head. He had only cried for a moment. But he was already getting to be thin. He wouldn't last long if he didn't make an appointment.

He said, "They had nothing to give me. I could not even find her slippers. The nurse there blamed it on the patients."

King Edward never changed. It was a blade which cut into the people that came close to it. It was a microcosm of the continent.

Nafisa took a second look at her interlocutor. He didn't look old enough to be a widower. His age was probably the same as Shakeer's. Yet, she had learned, it was difficult to tell with Africans. They lived more, endured more, showed less.

"I am going inside now, Sipho. Is there something you want?"

The man's posture tightened. He was angry. Nafisa could not tell where she went wrong with African men. Things often went wrong with them. It wasn't necessarily her fault. Many of them made a point of their hostility towards women, and Indian women in particular.

Nafisa saw that she could hardly be expected to sympathise with the grudge even if she understood its source. For she was on the wrong side of history. History, numbers, in Durban flowed against her. They flowed against the Indians in Durban. Under the old government, paradoxically, history and numbers seemed to flow in the other direction.

Up to a certain point Indians had been on the right side of history and numbers. In February 1990, after Nelson Mandela walked out of Victor Verster, Arif had spoken to a hundred thousand in the square behind City Hall. Those hundred thousand, this army recruited across lines of race and class, had disappeared as completely as the builders of Great Zimbabwe.

"Doctor, you must pay to bury Millicent."

She saw that all this time, while she had been considering, he had been approaching his point. Their real conversation had only now begun.

"And why should I pay?"

"You were her doctor," Sipho explained. "Now she is sitting in the mortuary with nobody to bury her. Otherwise the municipality will put her in the public cemetery." He relaxed again. "I give you the estimate."

It was the kind of explanation that explained nothing. But she couldn't dismiss it out of hand. Like Gulliver she was tied to Sipho, to the memory of Millicent, to her black swans, to her memories. She could strain against them but never once loosen the connections. Why was this so? Perhaps she saw herself in Millicent. Perhaps, in Sipho, she could see something of her husband. But that was no coincidence. It was true of almost any man that he saw nothing except himself and the universe.

Sipho brought out a typed receipt from the Ephesians Funeral

Home in KwaMashu. The paper was thin. At the bottom the director had signed his name in a flourish.

Nafisa pretended to read it seriously. Her patients and others brought her photographs, certificates, and endless narratives of misfortune. It was hard to say what was accurate and what was made up.

She whistled. The funeral would be expensive. Prices had gone up. Then it struck her that this receipt from Ephesians Funeral Home was the limit of everything which could be written down about a human being.

On an impulse she said, "Sipho, why don't you come inside? I will give you a cup of tea. Let me think about the funeral costs. I am going to clear out the house in any event."

Estella was waiting at the gate. She was surprised that the man was coming into the house. She had made him wait outside the garage in the first place. But Nafisa was risking nothing. She asked Estella to make the visitor tea.

Nafisa went upstairs and unlocked the bathroom cupboard. She stacked the packets of old notes on the bed. It didn't matter if Estella knew about them. They were an open secret in any event. Some of them were recent enough to be usable. She counted out thirty-five hundred rands. It would cover the funeral expenses.

She wasn't giving it to her visitor for his sake. Her dislike for him had not evaporated. But it was in her own interest to clear out the house. She wanted to be free of this money, these envelopes, of having anything to protect.

If you had nothing to protect – no life, no house, no husband, no particular view of the universe, no quantity of health or happiness – then existence was without complication. Then she could live in her sleep if necessary.

She went downstairs and handed over the money. It was accepted without any evidence of gratitude.

Nonetheless the kitchen was the picture of peace. Sipho Dhlomo was beginning a cup of tea. He was subdued. She didn't have the energy to pursue their quarrel, whatever it had been. She watched as he counted the notes and folded them so they would fit in the inside pocket of his jacket.

It was odd for Nafisa to see how completely Estella had occupied the kitchen. It was Estella's room, her house, Estella's continent and cosmos. Little wonder that Estella had conquered Sipho Dhlomo as well.

Nafisa said, "Estella, you'll remind Sipho he promised to come to my surgery this week. I leave you to it. Meanwhile I am going to clear everything out. Do you know that I haven't even opened the mail in a month? By the time I am finished the house will be completely clean. I am going to come to that fridge last of all."

"It won't take long to defrost the fridge. I have done most of the work already, Nafisa. I have thrown away everything which needed to go."

While Nafisa took the pile of post from the top of the fridge Estella obligingly sat down next to the visitor. Maybe something would come of it. Maybe she had been wrong about the girl and Estella had no particular boyfriend. But her fever was not completely gone. And once the subject of her fever had been Estella.

Upstairs Nafisa placed the mail on the bed. She slit open the envelopes impatiently, feeling her head swim as she tried to read the contents of each one.

There were accounts from the telephone and electricity companies that she had to pay, some menus from the pizza and Chinese places around the corner. She never wanted to receive another piece of mail in her life. It would be a relief, if she lost the house, never to establish another address.

At the bottom of the pile were Arif's journals which he insisted on reading the day they arrived: *Nature*, *The New England Journal of Medicine* in its laminated orange cover, and *The Lancet*. They were covered in plastic.

Nafisa read the tables of contents. *The Lancet* reported on a conference held the previous year at the College of Surgeons in London. Chris Labuschagne, a name she recognised because he had collaborated with Arif, had written about the experience of South African surgeons during the epidemic. Even surgeons were dying.

She hadn't heard a word about the London conference. Usually someone would have mentioned it. She read through Labuschagne's article. She was suddenly hot again. This information had been hiding, on top of the refrigerator, for longer than seemed possible. Almost everything in the world, as Arif had often said, was hiding in plain view.

It was six in the evening. She might still find Govin Mackey in his surgery in Umhlanga. She knew that he often worked late because she had heard his wife complain about the fact.

From the entrance to Mackey's building Nafisa could see the lit corridors in the office blocks around her. In five years acres of construction had colonised hills covered with sugarcane.

She walked up instead of waiting for the lift. Right below Govin's floor was a radiologist's studio. Nafisa identified the tall machines bowed inside their hoods. They reminded her of monks but they were of Korean manufacture and had a parade of small Asian characters stencilled along the top. Everything was coming from Korea, and China.

As she went up the stairway the lights went off on the floor beneath her. It seemed that they were being switched off just behind her. She looked out at the landing and was rewarded with a view of the red-capped lighthouse on the left and, on the right, the small shopping centre with a Checkers.

New construction was going up from the beachfront to the ridge. The cranes were silent at six o'clock, paused over a lattice of girders and pillars which reminded Nafisa of the Meccano set she had bought for her son's tenth birthday.

The new rich, the corporations and holding companies at the top, altered Durban in one way. The new poor, the old poor at the bottom, perpetually altered the city according to their own methods.

Nafisa couldn't regret these alterations. She wasn't nostalgic. The place had never belonged to her. The city had once been the property of the whites, and in particular the English. When their power had ended, in 1994, it had passed into the hands of nobody. Nobody was the true emperor of Africa.

It came to Nafisa that Govin Mackey had once been the definition of a nobody. As a widow's son, a poor woman's son, Govin had been eager to please everybody from the first day of his first year of medical school.

Nafisa had cared for Govin even before they had become close. But she saw that in a way she had slighted the man. It was her sense of security that wronged him. She had not attended to his feelings. She had expected him to be grateful, polite, conversable. She hadn't expected him to be capable of anything. He wasn't enough of a man.

Indeed, up to today, it hadn't once occurred to her that Govin should have other feelings and that these concealed feelings might be her concern. How extraordinary she was! How numerous were the things she didn't see! She was so blind that somebody might have put out her eyes.

When she got up to the sixth floor Mackey's two secretaries were closing the office. Govin had hired two sisters. Nafisa found them likeable yet she had never been able to learn their names. In her head she called the one Tweedledee, the other Tweedledum.

Tweedledum and Tweedledee were thin and tall, unusually so for Indian girls. Their long bodies scarcely fitted underneath the reception table where she had noticed them kick off their shoes.

She wouldn't say anything to them about the case. Nafisa knew that, in the way of Durban secretaries, the two sisters worshipped their employer. They studied his moods and had befriended his wife. But their relations with Govin were entirely innocent. Nafisa was sure of her conclusion although she had promised never to be sure of anything.

Tweedledee said, "Govin is sitting alone in his office. Talk to him, doctor. If you don't mind my saying so he has not been the same this year."

"I don't mind," Nafisa replied. "Everybody knows that last year Govin saved my husband's life. If it hadn't been for this dreadful case he would be the leading surgeon in the country by now."

This brought their conversation to a halt. Despite the air of excitement, as many Durban boys must have discovered for themselves, there was only so far you could go with Tweedledum and Tweedledee ... and it wasn't so far.

Tweedledum said, "Go through, Nafisa. We will lock the door. You can't be too careful. People have been shot in their surgeries. Just last month they strangled that Pietermaritzburg lady in her own rooms. Afterwards, doctor can let you out."

The door closed behind her. Nafisa walked along the corridor, noting the cubicles used for examinations. On a table lay photographic plates, stained in black and white, piled up on patients' folders. They must have been left over from some previous epoch in history.

The new generation of radiologists could scarcely read an x-ray. People were spoiled by technology. For all their cleverness the ability of the new doctors to judge by eye and hand had, as Arif complained, diminished to zero.

So, generation after generation, doctors were in about the same place. Perhaps the same could be said of anybody. Generation after generation we stood in the same place with respect to the overall situation.

The secretaries hadn't warned Govin. He was working in one of the rooms, tapping at a laptop which was awkwardly positioned on an examining table. He was so young, so thin, that he could have been a boy swallowed up in the affectation of his white coat and sandpaper beard.

Govin, Nafisa thought after a moment, must have picked up Arif's way of typing on his computer in the most unnatural posture.

When he saw her he got up. His eyes almost focused on her. But they didn't quite come together. Then he sat down.

"Last you came here, if I remember, was before the operation. You remember we pushed Arif's wheelchair into the lift? We couldn't locate a kidney to save his life. I called Malawi, Botswana, Egypt, the UK, desperate to find a matching kidney. For me, Nafisa, that was one of the worst days of my life. It was like having my father take ill again."

Nafisa sat down also. She was still very hot.

She said, "It came to me this afternoon, Govin. Everything was connected to the court case. I should have connected the dots a long time ago. The first illegal kidney you transplanted was for Arif. You must have paid out of your own pocket."

He didn't hesitate. "I had one chance to save Arif's life. It meant working outside the ordinary channels. But working outside the ordinary channels is what I do each and every day. We are a different class in surgery."

"You went to see Arif when you thought the information would come out in court. To your surprise the province dropped the case. But by then something had happened to the money you brought back from London on Arif's request. I just saw in *The Lancet* that you were at the College of Surgeons in that very week the Barclays account was closed. Arif sent you to close it on our behalf."

He closed his computer. Nafisa saw for the first time that Govin had accumulated grey hairs, straw hairs, all over his head. They were quite distinct. Soon they would be white.

Every man she knew, it seemed, Jadwat, Govin, Ismail Kader, was suddenly a good deal older than she would ever be. She had no intention of getting another day older in her life.

"Mind if I close the door? My two secretaries, the ones you call Tweedledum and Tweedledee, already have put in a request for higher salaries because of the legal case. I don't want them to overhear this. They will ask for double. It's a sign of the times, I suppose. If, as a doctor, you cannot rely on your secretaries' loyalty, then what can you rely on? The moment you are caught in some difficulty, Nafisa, you see another side of people."

"Do I have anything to worry about?"

There was a flash in Govin's face, like a lamp being exposed from under a cloth and again concealed. He said, "Certainly not."

"Then, by all means, close the door."

Govin had some speech prepared. She didn't want to listen.

"In our community, as you know, we had no models in life. Indians were always chasing after a better house, and better car. Durban, even Pretoria and Johannesburg, can be narrow in that way. You and Arif were different. For one thing you had a different idea of what was important – science, history, the arts, a broader view."

Govin's words, which amounted to a confession, were the fulfilment of this premonition which had grown so slowly and methodically.

Somehow there was no pain in them because his words were already familiar. There was nothing in the world which had the power to distress her. She had triumphed over everything. In this there was a certain second-hand pleasure.

She said, "Therefore, because of your debt to us and to the world at large, you had to take away whatever we had. You had to create an equality between us. It had been our turn, in the past, you believed. Now it was your turn."

Nafisa had dreamed of revealing the person who had pointed a gun at her husband and imposed this new life on her. Yet her anger was unsteady. Just because Govin Mackey had a first name, unlike Jadwat, her anger was unable to concentrate.

"But it was never our turn. It was never our turn because there was always trouble in our lives, or else in the lives of people right next to us. It's nobody's turn." She went on. "I have talked to the coroner, Govin. Once they begin to investigate I don't think you can survive. You might as well be open about it with me."

"Arif wanted to write a letter to the Medicines Control Council about the kidney. For my career to end like that? What a career! You know the conditions we work under, as surgeons. Eighty percent of our patients are positive. I stand drenched in blood many hours of the day. I have been nicked on a dozen occasions. I don't even test myself anymore. Yet Arif wouldn't listen to a word I had to say. I have never seen him so furious. Then, I suppose, I was equally furious. He had no right to take away what he gave in the first place ..."

"And the money?"

"That was the least of it. I brought it from London through a complicated arrangement with Nawaz's contact Omar. It was sitting uselessly in the bank until Omar could figure out how to put it in your account. So I borrowed a part of it to pay the lawyer's fees. I didn't want the bank to take away our house in case something happened. I also have a family to protect. But I would have put the money back by the end of the year. You can understand?"

Nafisa ignored the question. Questions could deceive just as much as answers. They were merely a way of pointing.

"So what happened on that day I was at the airport?"

"The bloody gun was lying beside the bed. It was waiting for us, Nafisa, I swear. I had picked it up and Arif tried to take it away from me. He didn't want me to have it in my possession. You know what Arif's temper was, or what it had become. If the gun hadn't been there, if Arif was in a normal frame of mind, then nothing would have happened."

"I don't agree. You were the gun, Govin, we pointed at ourselves. Remember that you let us believe, for weeks, that Arif had harmed himself. You didn't say a word to enlighten us. All these weeks my mind has been filled with darkness."

As if he was about to become impatient Govin said, "As a surgeon I make daily decisions. I decided about Arif's transplant. Later I took the decision not to allow him to take away the gun. After the shooting I made the decision to avoid the complications. The one decision grew out of the other. But let's go out, Nafisa. It is late already."

He unlocked the door. Nafisa wasn't sure what footing they were on. But Govin wasn't violent. He had spoiled from the inside.

They went into the dark outer room, then through the building, and past the lit kiosk in which a security guard dozed.

They walked to the indoor parking where Nafisa recognised Govin's Audi. Last year she had considered buying an Audi but Jadwat had convinced her that a Mercedes was better on resale.

Last year! These fifteen months had hardened into a history as solid as permafrost. There was a mile of this permanent ice which surrounded the North Pole. It had begun to vanish as the planet heated up.

"Shall I drive you to where you're parked?"

"No, that won't be necessary, Govin. You know where you are going, I assume."

It was a paradox but she trusted Govin. He was a murderer, and he was a surgeon. Therefore his choice, this last choice in his hands, would be correct beyond considerations of right and wrong.

Right and wrong, she thought, were nursery school words. She wasn't doing what was right or wrong by Govin, Shakeer, Arif, or even by herself. Instead the situation had called something out of her.

The world was full of situations. Things were not intended to fit together. Each person was a puzzle piece drawn from a different set.

For this was a nursery tale in reverse: the story of a nobody who wished to rise in the world, wished never to fall, and who had therefore entangled herself and her husband in his story. The secret hidden from a nobody was that everybody was a shadow, and that never to fall, never to flicker, was not a reasonable desire for a shadow.

She walked towards the road where the streetlights had turned orange in the evening. Govin Mackey went past her at the boom gate.

She noticed that one of his headlights was out. Nafisa was superstitious about it. When a car with one headlight swung into her mirror she said the *shehada*, the profession of her beliefs. But now she didn't repeat the words. She could not see the bottom of her faith.

Her own car was parked beside the loading dock of Checkers. It was still standing there. None of the windows were broken, none of the mirrors had been subtracted, which is always a relief in Durban. The car guard accepted four rand from her with obvious appreciation.

The guard was so enthusiastic it hurt. Her heart pounded. Her temperature went up. Yet the inequality was on her side. She couldn't imagine getting a thousandth of the pleasure from a two-rand coin.

From the point of view of the universe she was below the guard, below Rose the nurse, below Estella and Jadwat and fat Zuleika Mayat. Yet she had never been more certain of herself in her life.

By coincidence Estella was in the garage. She stood against the wall while the car entered. She was finally packing the junk in the garage into boxes which she had stacked beside the outside door.

Nafisa's fever had gone. She had a sense of excitement, even urgency, about the conversation she was going to have with Estella.

This current reminded her of being in love. She was old-fashioned and hadn't expected the sensation to occur twice in a lifetime. She wasn't the sort of person who would fall in love, properly in love, more than once in an existence.

But here she was in love with Estella as if with the daughter she had never received. They had always been close without knowing it. They had been careless about being close but were nonetheless intimate. Estella was the one person in the world to whom her existence was not superfluous.

"See my arm in the light, Estella. You can see the rash." Nafisa rolled up her sleeve. She had been watching the discolouration spread across her skin like a pencil drawing. "I hurt myself in the hospital, Estella. I haven't told anybody a word about it. For God's sake don't mention it to Shakeer. But tomorrow, early in the morning, I am going to ask Jadwat to put me on treatment. Good old Jadwat. He will know the right course of action. An emergency pack, if it isn't too late already."

Nafisa was laughing and crying at the same time. She remembered that Arif had called the combination, which he observed only in her, her sunshine and rain. Or had it been Jadwat? She couldn't tell.

She put her hand on Estella's shoulder. She couldn't say what she expected to happen, or what Estella was supposed to do. But everything was coming to an end. At the same time everything in the universe was beginning again.

"Come with me to work tomorrow, Estella. We will test you as well. I should have done it five years ago. If it's necessary, and it almost certainly is given your sexual history, let me get you on the list for treatment. I do all this for a patient whom I don't know from a bar of soap. Why shouldn't I do it for you?"

Estella didn't reply to this remarkable speech. Instead she closed the box she was packing and folded its lapels. She sellotaped them together and deposited the box at the door. Then she disappeared down the staircase.

Nafisa hadn't anticipated Estella's reaction. After a minute she followed Estella down the steps. She didn't go to talk to Estella right away. She had always been happier arguing with her husband, and even with Shakeer, than confronting Estella.

Nafisa didn't switch on the lights. It was getting to be dusk in the garden, like a mist appearing around her as she watched. She could hear the summer flies rising from the ground, skimming along towards the house like helicopters. They bred in the tops of tin cans which people abandoned behind the bus shelter.

After a minute in the garden the flies were biting her and she had to slap them away. Nafisa walked over to the servant's room. The light had just come on inside it. Estella didn't pay for her own electricity. She would leave the light on all day and Nafisa would have to reprimand her. It was expensive.

The municipality was using their rates in Westville to pave and electrify Chesterville, Clairmont, Umlazi. No wonder the accounts for a large house were out of all proportion. It was impossible to keep up.

Nafisa looked through the glass without being seen. She could see Estella hunched over her cupboard, unpacking her clothes from the drawers and placing them in her small blue suitcase with a broken wheel. Jadwat had given it to Estella when he had inherited his second-hand corduroy luggage from an uncle.

In the suitcase were the pair of red shoes which Nafisa identified as the very soul of the woman she had employed for seven years. To prevent Estella leaving she was tempted to steal these shoes and lock them in her cupboard where they could never walk themselves away. She remembered her father telling her the story of the girl with red dancing shoes which had taken her dancing against her will, around the world, until she expired of exhaustion. But she was sure that Estella wouldn't leave. She would go in and talk to her in five minutes, or five hours.

Nafisa knew she would have cried if she were in a normal frame of mind, if the normal structures of her mind had been intact, but her tears had run dry. In this new life she was beginning, this new new life built on the foundations of another life, there would be no new tears.

How strange to live amongst strangers! These strangers had been deprived of their history, their culture, their gods, and above all their centrality! They had been removed from the centre of their own world and placed at the margins of a far greater and more fearful universe. Little wonder they resented having to live as strangers and maids.

Who was she to be forgiven? Who was she to run a business, to hire a maid, to follow her strange God, and to show no sign of requiring forgiveness? Who was she to exist?

After so great a quantity of experience it was marvellous to discover that she was alive, as fiercely alive as an atomic reactor. She had the certainty that this was the last day of her life, the last point at which the past could dominate, while tomorrow would mark the beginning of the future. Tomorrow she would have her first tomorrow ...

She had grown up so late in life. It had taken such a quantity of experience, more than was allotted to a lifetime, but she had blossomed into sympathy with every creature in the universe, even with Govin, with Ismail Kader, Estella, and Jadwat, with the gram-negative bacterium which Moonsamy's small lab cultivated on a petri dish, with herself and her son, with the pebble underneath her foot ...

The Taziya

~

IT WAS A REMARKABLE SERVICE. EVERYBODY WAS THERE. IT seemed that everybody in Durban had some attachment, however improbable, to Govin Mackey. In his brief career the young surgeon had touched many other lives. Many people, or their older relatives, needed a kidney.

Zuleika Mayat and Ismail Kader's wife and daughter attended the service. Several years before Govin had operated on Zuleika's knee and restored her mobility.

But this was an incomplete blessing. Every few paces Zuleika blanked her forehead with a cloth. The warmth of the day, and her bulk, meant that she couldn't move from place to place without raising a sweat. God had intended Zuleika Mayat to stay in one place.

The long table set in the yard of Govin's Morningside house had been borrowed from Mohammed and Karachi Delights. The workers had brought it roped to the open back of their van. They had carefully saved the sections of rope for the return trip.

Next to the table Mohammed and his assistants had settled two long benches. There should have been enough space for two dozen at the meal. Yet Shakeer couldn't find a place to sit.

Shakeer stood behind the table while Mohammed and his men went back and forth from the van. He was lost to pin down the mood of the occasion. What could it be? It floated out of his grasp like newsprint after ten minutes of reading.

While Shakeer was standing the workers arranged big sheets of paper to create a makeshift tablecloth. It startled the eye in the haze of the afternoon, white as enamel. On the table were bowls of condiments and many small trays. There were plastic jugs of water and orange juice.

A carton of serviettes stood in their midst. One serviette had been pulled half out as if it were the handkerchief of a suit. The dimpled copper pots were also from Karachi Delights. Govin Mackey was not a Muslim. There had been time to prepare the ceremony.

From the outside, where Shakeer was, one could not determine whether what was on the table was the remains of a wedding or funeral. Only the black hats of Govin's wife, his mother and aunts indicated that the occasion was a sombre one.

But the sobriety was odd, unenforced by the participants. Sharky almost expected to hear laughter when somebody forgot himself. There was a hum of conversation along the two long benches, as if people had been drinking.

Everybody was talking at once: Zuleika Mayat, Ismail Kader's daughter who had recently divorced, MacDonald Gumede the superintendent, Estella who was helping with the cool drinks, Jadwat.

The last named had set off at once from Richmond when he heard the news and had just now arrived in Morningside. Yet Jadwat had only left Durban to return to Richmond on the previous morning. He hadn't the chance to rest in the interim. The many hours on the road had done him no favours. He had never looked so tired.

Shakeer saw that the man's skin, under the inspection of the late sunshine, was as tatty as a piece of old leather. Once you saw something like that about somebody you didn't forget. Without intending it Nafisa had taught him to notice the complexions of people.

Shakeer was sorry for old Jadwat in his old pelt. His heart went out to the battered old doctor. There could be nothing new for the man from Richmond. He had reduced the universe to his own proportions. This had reduced him in turn, of course, and now his time was short.

After a minute Sharky changed his mind. He was relieved on Jadwat's behalf. Yes, his time was limited. But this was a piece of good luck. Soon Jadwat would be relieved of his burdens and cares. One day soon his unceasing manoeuvres with women would cease. Soon ...

Sitting on Jadwat's right were Leila and her husband. They were formally dressed, Omar in a suit and Leila in a long-sleeved brown dress.

Leila and Omar were hardly a couple. It wasn't jealousy on Sharky's part. You could see it at once. They didn't look at each other. They didn't turn to each other from minute to minute. One could hardly be jealous.

Leila and Omar might return to the same house on Essenwood Road, sleep in one another's arms, love the same children, yet never have a minute in one another's company. It was the most ordinary thing to live around people, in their presence, but never in their company. He knew as much from Ginger.

Shakeer saw that he and Leila, separated by the experience of almost twenty years since university, were more alike than ever before. This fact alone would, perhaps, keep them apart forever.

Throughout the afternoon Shakeer had tried to approach Leila. He had tried to talk to her for a few minutes after the service. In return, around her husband Omar, she had been pleasant, noncommittal, and insincere.

When they met she asked, "You are okay, Shakeer?"

"I am fine," he said. "Govin was your good friend. I hardly knew him."

"Oh, I hardly knew him myself."

She was lying. It was odd. Leila was the one person whose insincerity he didn't object to. In her it was not, as people assumed, a bad quality. If Leila was insincere, on occasion, then it was because she was self-contained. She didn't wish to give herself away.

Shakeer stood behind the bench and tried to engage her in conversation when she turned around. After all, Leila had some connection of her own with Govin. She could have some insight into what had happened.

Sharky sensed that the obscurity of Govin's fate had some implication for his own existence. Yet he couldn't work out this implication by himself. He needed other people to help. His mind never travelled far under its own steam ...

He started while somebody else was talking. "Leila, did you know that my mother went to see Govin that night? They had a long conversation."

Leila shook her head. Her eyeshadow was dark. It made her seem more attentive. She had changed her mind about talking to him.

"Nafisa didn't say a word to me about it. That's unusual, I grant you. Your mother generally confides in me. I don't know. What are you trying to say, Shakeer?"

"Nothing in particular. It's just that we've had so many misfortunes close on each other. My imagination needs time to recover. Without time to think I can hardly take a funeral seriously. I don't know how anybody can."

As he spoke Shakeer was conscious of Leila's hair, her chest, her hips by which he had once detained her. She had very dark hair at the roots, mahogany, like a piece of furniture. He wanted to touch her again at the hip. And he should do so. Her eyes, he imagined, communicated this instruction to him. But he never again wanted to push himself into a woman.

Her husband Omar, engaged in a discussion with Gumede the superintendent, might just as well have been in another part of the house. It didn't matter that Leila was sitting next to her husband and staring at him instead.

It startled Shakeer to see how much went on between human beings in public. The inside was on the outside.

"It wasn't true, that I hardly knew Govin, although there were things I didn't know," Leila admitted after a minute. "After your father, and now this with Govin, I have lost the only two people in Durban whose judgement I could rely on." Her eyes were saying something else. But this something else was as unclear to Leila as to Shakeer. This something depended on his reply. "Ultimately, it seems, life here is a long process of subtraction."

Sharky was silent for a minute while the caterers brought out another flight of dishes and Mohammed poured Indian tea into his cup. The tea smelled of cinnamon and made him think he could never touch it. Shakeer was reaching after a thought. It took him a while to get hold of it.

"After university, especially when I was in and out of the country and back and forth, it really seemed to me that everybody I knew here was going to live forever. I could leave everything as it was and it would be exactly the same when I came back. Do you know, Leila?"

He saw at once that this was the wrong statement to make. Leila bristled. She had been expecting something else of him. She had some other idea of what he should say, some other formula. But when people set tests for him he always failed.

His destiny with women was fixed. For Leila, like Ginger, was a maze. She needed mapping. Whereas he would take every last wrong turning and blind alley. He was dedicated to trial and error, and more to error ...

"Did you imagine, while you were away, Shakeer, that we were somehow kept in suspended animation?"

Leila turned quite away from the table. She didn't want her

husband to observe her anger. The conversation was over. Her face was burning with anger that he hadn't seen since their university days. It was frightening. Shakeer compared it to the candles burning in a Halloween pumpkin.

She said, "Since you're standing up, do you mind getting the cellphone out of my handbag? It's in the kitchen over by the oven. I want to check on the children."

"I'll get it. You stay here."

Sharky found the handbag in the kitchen. He opened it and considered going through Leila's property: her telephone book, cheque book, a pair of earrings. Instead he gave the cellphone to one of the children to deliver to Leila. His heart had started pounding again.

It was the end of any connection between them. Either nothing had happened between them or else, as Leila had told him with her eyes, things had been brought to the finish. In either case this feeling which had survived for twenty years had vanished in the course of a few hours.

Shakeer saw that he had no chance to make up for his mistake. It was like with Ginger. She had been looking for him to make a mistake in order to announce her decision. Leila wouldn't change once she had gone to the trouble of making her mind up. She saw it as a sign of weakness.

This was perhaps the reason he had never asked her to marry him. And perhaps there was a good reason Leila's marriage was what it was. There was a reason she had stayed with the man. This prison, with her narrow man, suited something in her nature.

Opposite Leila at the table was Zuleika Mayat, bigger than ever, her white hair tied in a pigtail. Her old woman's face was as solid as a hatchet. She made him think of a Red Indian.

She would make a wonderful portrait. Shakeer was again tempted to get his camera from the car. The opportunity was priceless. He imagined a series of portraits: Zuleika herself, Leila, Omar her husband, Jadwat while he still existed, Nafisa, and the others.

If he were to take a photograph who would he ask? The mood of the occasion was too strange, too fluctuating, and therefore too fragile to sustain such a request.

Nobody, and especially not Govin's wife and family, had absorbed the situation as it stood. Fate was too haphazard. It made no sense that the young surgeon, with a decade of medical training, should be so careless as to die on the scene of an accident. If anybody should be exempt it was a surgeon. Govin was careful about life.

There was no explanation. Govin had offered none of his own. He had been unable to say a word to the paramedics who took twenty minutes to arrive at the bottom of Argyle Road where his Audi had overturned. His ribs had been broken by the steering column.

There was something else at work. Shakeer began to feel as if he had usurped Govin's place. And would it be difficult to possess what had been Govin's? For had not Govin taken his own place, in some sense, in his father's affections?

In return Shakeer should slip directly into Govin's own place. He should accept the grief and affection of Govin's mother, and marry Govin's widow. He should sleep with Govin's widow and make her call out his name. With this odd suggestion in his ear he began to understand something about Jadwat's behaviour.

Just as Shakeer dismissed the possibility he found that the superintendent had come up to him. Gumede was standing beside him. They were almost the same height. He hadn't noticed. But Gumede, in his fifties, had the bearing of a potentate. He had inherited the city, or some part of it, and bore it on his shoulders.

"Shakeer, my friend, I am sorry we haven't continued our conversation. I have a note on my desk to call you in first thing next week. We have a lot to look at together."

"You leave us in limbo. Purgatory. But our only sin, in this instance, was wanting to know what happened."

Gumede wasn't taken aback. "I move my pieces slowly, my friend. You may remember as much from our game of chess. In fact I am going back to the station right now to review some evidence which has come in. You, Shakeer, are as impatient today as you were as a youngster. But rest assured. I have a clear view of the state of the game. I am only sorry about Dr Mackey."

He put his hand on his side. "I owe this kidney to him and David Gerson. If it hadn't come through in time I would truly have been in the ditch."

As Gumede was making his farewells Shakeer noticed that his mother was smiling. She sat beside Zuleika. Sharky almost fell over to see it. He saw at once that the oddness he had sensed throughout the afternoon was entirely his mother's doing.

It was from his mother that the disturbance in the mood radiated. Everybody else at Govin's house had followed her lead. Like Nafisa, it seemed, they were about to laugh, shout, and tell jokes. They were going to tell stories about Govin, and complain about their taxes and property rates. No wonder it didn't seem like a memorial service.

Given her attire Nafisa could have been at a wedding. She wore the pair of Indian sandals which she used for *nikaas* and housewarming prayers, *kuthums*. The strings on her sandals carried semi-precious stones. They glinted darkly underneath the bench, a line of dark green stones in the shadow. They seemed to be communicating a message to him in Morse code.

After a few more minutes the party began to break up. Nafisa helped Mackey's mother put the house dishes in the kitchen. Mohammed and his staff cleared the table of what belonged to the restaurant. Leila and her husband left. Jadwat lay down in the sitting room. His shoulder was hurting.

Nafisa started to wash the dishes in the kitchen. Sharky collected the cutlery and brought it over to her. He was curious. His mother didn't like to do housework. But she looked as if she was about to smile again. She had rolled up the sleeves of her blouse. The collar was lettered with roses.

They worked together easily. As she brought the knives and forks out of the water Shakeer dried them and placed them in the rack. The smell of the dishwashing liquid rose out of the hot water. He couldn't tell what the scent was supposed to be.

Behind them the men from Karachi Delights were breaking the table into sections. They had already put the benches in the van and roped them to the chassis.

Nafisa said, "I always told Govin this house was far too big for a small family like his. The gold taps alone cost a fortune, absolutely lavish. And with the interest rates as they are, think of the monthly bond. At least with the insurance settlement, if it comes as expected, his family can stay here so long as it makes sense. That's a relief to me."

"It's not your responsibility where they stay. You have problems of your own."

The irony, Sharky thought, was that their own Westville house might be lost long before Mackey's house. The position of his family was at once worse and better than anybody's. The universe seemed to have made some judgement about them. It wanted to impose experience, some education, upon his mother and himself ...

After finishing the dishes Nafisa turned to him.

"I knew that Arif wouldn't have trusted just anybody with the information about the Barclays account. I told you Nawaz wasn't to blame. You wouldn't believe me. But I can do detective work of my own. I had my suspicions already. Finally I saw in *The Lancet* that Govin was at a conference in London in that same week the account was closed. I can put two and two together."

"I don't believe ..."

She put her hand on his chest. "First you must understand why it was important for your father to bring that money back. For Arif it was a way of stating that we are now a normal country, that there's no need to keep money overseas. Whether he was right or wrong, I don't pretend to judge."

"I'm sorry ..."

Nafisa ignored him. Her eyes were shining. "Govin felt we owed him something because he saved your father's life. So he borrowed the money without notifying us. And that, in the end, led to the argument between him and Arif. According to Govin the shooting was an accident. Again, I don't pretend to be the judge, but think of what Govin put us through over these last weeks and months."

Nafisa stopped. She was the judge, Sharky thought.

She spoke more quietly. "Shakeer, don't feel sorry for a minute. He has escaped punishment. I gave him the opportunity."

His mother's voice was as full of teeth as a chainsaw blade. Yet she was full of love for him, for Govin's widow, for the memory of Govin, whom she had revealed. Shakeer looked around ... as if it would make a difference to have a witness to whatever truth had taken shape in front of him.

Mohammed the caterer was settling up with Jadwat who had taken off a money belt Shakeer had never seen before and was unlocking it in a corner of the yard. Mackey's wife was washing her face in the outside sink. But there was nobody who could have ever confirmed his sensation. His mother was the most astonishing person he knew in a galaxy full of astonishment.

Nafisa went on. "Nobody has to know. They collect on the insurance. It means that our name, your father's name, isn't dragged into this case. The disadvantage, of course, is that the tax people may take the Westville house. Let them take it. I have officially given up my shift at King Edward as of today. I haven't been altogether well, Shakeer, during these past few weeks. But I have made this choice. Frankly I have had experience enough for a lifetime."

Shakeer wasn't certain how to reply. He saw after a minute that the person his mother had triumphed over was him. In the larger scheme of things Govin was an irrelevancy. Govin had simply murdered his father.

Nafisa was still feverish. She drank a glass of water. "Is Leila not talking to you?"

"We exchanged a few words. In many ways she was far closer to Govin than to me. Her real interest in me, I think, was in completing whatever we had between us. Once upon a time she believed we were bound to be together."

Nafisa said, "So did I. So did you, I believe. Like two pieces of a jigsaw puzzle."

"That assumes we're two pieces from the same puzzle. Just because you knew somebody when you were growing up doesn't mean you're going to end up with them. Life is too big for that."

Nafisa was irritated by this thought. She said, "From far enough away everything is the same and, yes, it is useless. It is useless to get out of bed in the morning if you adopt the universe's point of view. But we don't live far away, Shakeer, like Govin. We're right here and the cosmic point of view, your cosmic point of view, is simply irrelevant."

But was it? Did the sky not have a point of view? Leila's absence, the end of any possibility of a relationship with her, was an enormous fact. It was as if a shape had been cut out of his sky. Within its boundaries there were no stars.

Leila, Govin, Gerson, were also irrelevant. Shakeer knew that his mother wanted to convey some other piece of information to him. He also knew that it would never be conveyed.

Moreover Jadwat had appeared in the yard. He was restless and wanted them to leave together.

It was impossible to breathe another word on the subject in front of Jadwat. For he would immediately bring it down to his own level. That was Jadwat's function.

Jadwat drove with Nafisa back to Westville. Shakeer stayed back for ten minutes to say his goodbyes to the stricken family and friends. They were his responsibility more than his mother's.

Shakeer wanted to see the bottom of this desire: to replace Govin in his own house and to win the affection of his wife and mother. Yet there was no way to inspect a desire.

The sight of Govin's wife stimulated a tremendous rush of tenderness in him. She wore slacks and revealed a large, unintelligent face when she looked around. She didn't seem especially upset. There was thick black hair on her substantial arms.

Govin's wife wasn't attractive to Sharky, from a purely physical point of view, and yet it seemed that he had never cared for anybody so much, even for Leila, even for Ginger when she had been young. He put the feeling out of his mind.

Shakeer was about to leave when Dr Gerson strode into the yard. He wore a rumpled brown coat and had been busy with an emergency at the hospital. Before he finished apologising to Mackey's mother the ward called him about another patient.

How remarkable that Gerson should exist! That he should be busy on his cellphone! David Gerson wrestled with all things, propositions and people the way he wrestled with his cellphone. It was as if he were trying to force it to the ground. Gerson in general, Shakeer decided, was trying to force the world to the ground.

Gerson stopped in front of Shakeer. His face fell. Gerson, Shakeer saw at this angle, had the face of a horse, a suede face, but horses were beautiful.

When Gerson closed his cellphone, he didn't seem to have Shakeer on his mind at all. Some inward scene possessed him.

"When a surgeon goes he is irreplaceable. How he sees things is irreplaceable. Above all, his hands are irreplaceable. Lay people don't understand. I have never known anyone to have such delicate fingers as Govin Mackey."

"I imagine, David."

"I don't believe you can imagine. As I see it, lay people are not the best judges of how professionals conduct themselves. Lay people don't understand the pressures and responsibilities. If we have to break certain rules to prevent a death, so be it. I am sure your father would agree with me if he were here today."

Shakeer was tempted to agree. But he didn't want to let stand the claim about his father.

"David, I don't know that he would. There's knowledge on the one side, yes, I don't deny it. We need experts, people with skills, especially in this country. But for questions of life, for the basic questions which are also the deepest ones, you don't need specialised knowledge. You need the same soul we all have. You need to take care of that soul and make sure that it is working just like a kidney has to be working. I believe my father would have put it differently. He would have said, everything we need we're born with."

Gerson looked impatient at the lecture. While he was listening he checked his watch, his cellphone, and both his pockets. It occurred to Shakeer that the surgeon must be tired from hours on his feet. He had come straight from theatre.

Since the dismissal of charges Gerson, as Nafisa said, had been working overtime to reduce the backlog of cases. People were dying without transplants.

"Is your mother here?"

"She's gone unfortunately, David, but you will find the family inside. They are expecting you. They are anxious to meet you. You know the role you played in their lives, and Govin's."

David Gerson's face fell again. Here was a man who had lost his beloved. He was bereft as a sufi singer in search of the absolute. Sharky's heart flew towards Gerson as if towards a father.

At the same time he knew that part of what happened was this particular man's responsibility. It was good, at some stage, to sort out praise and blame. David Gerson was just one cause in the net of causes that had entangled his father. Gerson had whitewashed himself in this matter as in the matter of the Brazilian transplants. But he wasn't blameless.

For this Gerson was a substitute father. He had failed an important test. He had adopted a younger man. If he had been properly equipped for his role he would have seen what was growing inside Mackey. He would have corrected it, scotched it.

But Gerson's argument was too much with the universe for him to stoop to individual persons. Not even for Govin did he stoop.

"David, do you mind if I ask a question before you go inside? If you forget the legal complications which ensued and you had to do everything from scratch, would you still do the transplants? Do you believe a patient should be able to pay for an organ if he or she needs it?"

"Ah, the money is irrelevant," Gerson replied, now genuinely angry. "The point is, we perform miracles. Someday, Shakeer, who knows what we will be able to do? The dead will rise."

The exchange had become an argument. Gerson was too angry with Shakeer to shake hands. He opened the door behind Sharky and went inside the house to greet Mackey's wife. You could hear his voice booming in the lounge.

Shakeer was overwhelmed. It was paradoxical. The news of Govin's accident and the funeral had touched him hardly so much as this encounter with Gerson. It had clarified certain facts.

The odds were unfavourable. There had been no real chance, in his own life, for Govin Mackey, who was up against himself. There was no chance for David Gerson, up against the universe.

There had been no chance for his father, against Govin, Gerson, their new universe, and this new government.

An action which had no single cause turned out to have as many causes as the Russian revolution. But, if you weren't a revolutionary, you couldn't arrest every cause.

The house was vanishing around Shakeer. The title deed had been mailed to the tax inspectorate in Pretoria. The broken window had been replaced but this seemed to diminish the house. Soon, it seemed, the very walls would be demolished around him.

Nafisa had cleared out the cupboards upstairs and downstairs. Leila was with her children in Cape Town. Jadwat was in Richmond. Meanwhile Estella had emptied the garage and discovered a supply of chemicals he had used to fix photographs.

The small tins of primer, fixer and extender gave him the idea to develop the shots he had taken. But it was difficult to focus while the house rang with sound. The house was the anvil and the workmen were the hammer.

Nafisa had made the decision to have the bed repaired. Part of the frame had broken after so many years. The unit would have to be taken as a whole to the factory shop in Pinetown.

The workmen were removing the bed from the master bedroom. They had set up a winch in the garden. The bed was being removed out the window rather than through the house because it couldn't be disassembled. The dog stood underneath the bed and barked as it descended. On the previous afternoon the dog had tried to return with Jadwat's cousin to Parlock.

Shakeer watched the bed tremble in the air. Somehow the width of a piece of furniture increased with each year it was undisturbed. The weight also increased. The bed was now a very heavy piece of furniture. The workmen shouted to each other as they tried to steady and lower the frame.

Shakeer couldn't bear the noise. He wanted to develop the photographs the old-fashioned way. He would need to recreate the makeshift darkroom of his university days. The activity distracted him from the disorder in the house.

The bedding was nearby in the downstairs closet. He tied a sheet on the corner of each window and hung a thick grey blanket over it. He fastened each blanket down with tacks. They wouldn't harm the wall.

From one of the tins came the cleansing, half-sour scent of varnish. He took out the baking tin in which he placed ice cubes. The ice dissolved. He settled the paper into the bottom.

Shakeer closed the door and lowered the light. He considered his mother who had scorched his mind. But where to begin? He and his mother hadn't exchanged another word about Govin. They hadn't discussed what to do about the house.

Nafisa seemed more intact than she had been a week and a month before but it was difficult to be sure. His mother was a creature of compartments. Neither of them wished to open these compartments.

After a few more minutes he turned his mind to the prints.

One photograph struck him. It was of his mother and Estella in the airport building before they spotted him. They managed to sit closely to one another, to be as close as mother and daughter, and yet to be as distant as if one was Saturn and the other Jupiter.

They might separate tomorrow and never see one another again, never think about one another. Equally they might die in each other's arms, forsaking all other lovers.

But that one was of purely personal interest. It was the photographs from Eshowe that would catch the attention of the galleries in California. They weren't bad. They weren't great. But they were predictable.

The best of them was of the herbalist and her chamber. You saw the room hung with leather ornaments, the curtains roped together, bottles and ointments spread on the floor, and plates covered with bone set out on the table, remnants of a ghostly meal.

He tore up the photograph. None of them should have been taken. People were dying like flies.

The other photographs, still soaking in the trays, hadn't fixed. Shakeer picked up one of them in his hands. There were only half-formed shapes of black and white. You couldn't make out what the scene was supposed to be. It was a looking-glass photograph. Light was different through the looking glass. It couldn't be fixed into a clear image.

Shakeer looked into the small mirror beside the bed and was struck by his own expression in the low light. He would have been moved if he had caught such a state of feeling in another person's countenance. This knowledge affected him in his own case.

The expression was not something he could define. It was entirely private. It was like having discovered some other colour, or a musical note which pierced to the centre of his being.

This private language, private music, private colour wasn't something to be put into a photograph, or even into language. All these particular vibrations flowed into him and out of him, into his father, mother, Govin, even Jadwat, even Leila and Omar, and would never be seen or heard twice.

He had just opened the windows when Estella came into the room. He judged that she was still beautiful. Her features were as sharp as a knife. This knife would never cut another person.

He asked, "Nomzuma is still well?"

Estella said, "She has not had a fit since we went."

"You think it's because of the ceremony? You don't think it could be the medicine?"

"I don't know, Shakeer."

There was no menace in Estella. His mother was wrong. It was simply that Estella understood the basic lesson: to endure. One had to be as sharp as a knife, or as blunt as a hammer.

"Can I bring you a cup of tea? I am going off."

He said, "Don't worry about it."

Sharky expected Estella to disappear. But she continued talking. Perhaps their experience at the diviner had altered their relationship.

Estella said, "I used to bring Nomzuma to the professor. He was expert with her, and not only her but all children. Just a few days before you arrived he examined her for the final time. I left her with the professor. So long I went to the tea room to buy vinegar. Nafisa needed the vinegar for a dish of prawns. Afterwards, I remember, the professor was unable to eat even a spoonful of the prawns. He was very ill. Still he was smiling at me, and at your mother, as if he was never going to stop smiling. A whole pot of prawns went to waste. Nomzuma wouldn't eat even one because they reminded her of insects. In fact that is what started your father smiling, I remember."

Shakeer wanted to take photographs of a religious ceremony in Riverside, near the old sufi mosque.

He had heard about the *taziya* from Nawaz. There was a good deal of excitement about it. The ritual of consolation had been common in the old days, when immigrants from the subcontinent preserved customs which had grown up over ten centuries.

Many years had passed since a *taziya* had been orchestrated in Durban. It was, strictly speaking, a festival of the vanishing minority of Shia in the city. Given the inclusive temperament of the planners, Sunnis, and indeed Jains and Hindus and Parsees, were more than welcome to join the procession. No one was sure whether there were sufficient Shia to make the ritual viable.

Instead of taking anything, he emptied his pockets, left his driver's licence and money on the drawer, hid the sheets of paper on which he had begun composing his novel, and switched off the cellphone he had hired at the Vodacom pavilion. He left his camera behind.

The procession had already assembled by the time Sharky got to Riverside. He didn't see anybody he recognised. It was a mixed crowd on the cricket ground. The women were surrounded by children, as if each mother or aunt was the centre of a naval convoy.

Some of the men were holding a large model of a coffin. Many of them held triangular banners on which Arabic lettering had been printed in silver type. Others were steering a replica of Hussein's tomb which had been mounted on two bicycles, one on either side.

The makeshift tomb was studded with green and white paper which gave it the colour of certain tiled buildings Shakeer had encountered in Shiraz, in Iran.

As Sharky stood on the margins of the crowd an old man began reciting a passage from memory. The man was dressed in flowing white robes which gave him the bulk of a much larger individual. His face was nut brown, unaffected by his age, and on his arm he held a leather satchel.

The crowd listened respectfully to his recital. Sharky wondered if he was speaking in Arabic or Persian. He didn't know enough to tell the languages apart.

He had never known enough to tell about anybody, about Jadwat, Leila, Estella, about Govin Mackey who came from nothing and made himself less than the smallest thing, and, most of all, about his mother and father. They were more opaque to him than when he'd started. This opacity was what made them the cause of such sorrow. And in every sorrow there was another sorrow waiting to reveal itself. And it was laughable, and they were laughable. Yet he had no desire to laugh.

Once the recital had finished, the tomb and the coffin began to move in the middle of the procession. Sharky found himself also moving, first closer to the centre of the crowd and then along with them towards the river. He was pressed on by the tomb which was moving behind him.

The excitement grew in those around him as they approached the water. Far away, long past the green entrance to the river mouth, he could see the superstructures of cargo ships. His father would have complained about the harbour fees.

After a while Sharky forgot himself and felt the heat rising at the back of his head. The men holding the tomb had set it alight before they could place it in the river. He felt the silent flames flicker on the back of his neck. The heat went into his head. So long as he didn't turn back to look the flames would never go out.

A NOTE ABOUT THE TYPE

This book is set in Sabon, a typeface designed by Jan Tschichold in 1964. It was originally a metal type for hand and machine composition. Sabon is based on the work of Claude Garamond, a sixteenth-century French typecutter, and on that of his pupil Jacques Sabon, who repaired and completed a set of Garamond's punches after his death.